THE FORTNIGHT IN SEPTEMBER

A Novel

R. C. SHERRIFF

SCRIBNER

New York   London   Toronto   Sydney   New Delhi

Scribner
An Imprint of Simon & Schuster, Inc.
1230 Avenue of the Americas
New York, NY 10020

First Scribner trade paperback edition September 2021

SCRIBNER and design are registered trademarks of The Gale Group, Inc., used under license by Simon & Schuster, Inc., the publisher of this work.

For information about special discounts for bulk purchases, please contact Simon & Schuster Special Sales at 1-866-506-1949 or business@simonandschuster.com.

The Simon & Schuster Speakers Bureau can bring authors to your live event. For more information or to book an event, contact the Simon & Schuster Speakers Bureau at 1-866-248-3049 or visit our website at www.simonspeakers.com.

Interior design by Wendy Blum

Manufactured in the United States of America

1   3   5   7   9   10   8   6   4   2

Library of Congress Cataloging-in-Publication Data is available.

ISBN 978-1-9821-8478-0
ISBN 978-1-9821-8524-4 (ebook)

THE
FORTNIGHT
IN
SEPTEMBER

CHAPTER ONE

O n rainy days, when the clouds drove across on a westerly wind, the signs of fine weather came from over the Railway Embankment at the bottom of the garden. Many a time, when Mrs. Stevens specially wanted it to clear up, she would look round the corner of the side door and search along the horizon of the Railway Embankment for a streak of lighter sky.

The Embankment—stretching without break to right and left— divided the world for Mrs. Stevens. On her side was Dulwich and her home: long friendly roads, dotted here and there with the houses of people she knew. On her side, too, half a mile across the housetops, loomed the Crystal Palace, which sometimes in the autumn flashed golden squares of sunset over to them. Away beyond lay the open country and the trees—green corners of heathland where they used to go for picnics when Dick and Mary were children.

On the far side of the Embankment lay the other half of Mrs. Stevens's world: the half she scarcely knew. Herne Hill, Camberwell, and the lights of London that shone in overcast skies like sulphur candles in a dark, dis-used sick-room—that washed away, on fine nights, a little of the deep blue of the starlit heavens.

At the end of Corunna Road an asphalt footpath dived under the Embankment and emerged on the other side, but Mrs. Stevens seldom penetrated far into this other part of the world. She shopped in Dulwich, and had her friends there. Fine Saturday afternoons called them south, to the open fields and trees, out Bromley way.

Although she had lived at 22 Corunna Road for all her twenty married years, Mrs. Stevens had little idea of what lay directly opposite the end of their garden—beyond the Embankment.

Sometimes, when they passed in a train, she had tried to find out. But the train was always full, and she could not run quickly from one window to the other to take in both sides as they passed their house. She had never, therefore, been able to solve the mystery of what lay exactly on the other side although one thing she always noticed because it made her proud. As the train rattled along the Embankment a strip of thirty gardens would pass in panorama before her eyes: the thirty which made up the even numbers of Corunna Road. None of them showed up to greater advantage than No. 22, with its close-clipped lawn, neat borders, and its lilac tree. No. 22 alone had no half bricks or disused slop pails on the tool house roof.

But the garden looked sad and sorry this dripping September afternoon. It had begun to rain quite early in the morning: it was spotting when she came out of the butcher's, soon after eleven; and now, at five o'clock, a silent, listless rain was filling the hollows of the paths. She was distressed and miserable. The night before they left home for their holidays was always one of family celebration. When Dick and Mary had been children it was a night that rose almost to the height of Christmas Eve: a night voted sometimes as the best of all the holiday, although it was spent at home and the sea was still sixty miles away.

But the sea would always be calling them that evening; and when Mr. Stevens took his after-supper stroll in the garden he could almost taste the saltiness in the air. It was a habit of Mr. Stevens to linger in the garden longer than usual on that night before they went away: the Office was behind him: he had slammed the lid of his desk for fifteen splendid days, and he liked to feel the holiday had begun that evening. On the little lawn outside—in the dusk—he would open his chest and breathe the air. Then he would go to his bedroom and lay out the clothes he would wear at the sea, his grey flannel trousers, tweed sports jacket, stout brown boots, and soft tweed cap. But he would seldom wear the cap. For a whole fortnight his thin brown hair would blow in the sunlight and the breeze.

Again Mrs. Stevens peered out. If only the rain would stop! The whole holiday would be damped if they were cheated out of this first evening—sweet because it was stolen: because it was not, officially, a part of the holiday at all.

A special supper always marked the evening, too. This year it was boiled beef, because it made good sandwiches for the train journey, and was easy to wash up, giving more leisure for the final packing afterwards. Then there were apple dumplings, Mr. Stevens's favourite sweet.

It was past five o'clock. In an hour the family would be coming home. Mr. Stevens first (he always left sharp on this particular evening), then Dick, and then Mary. By seven they would all be home. Supposing it rained like this for the whole fortnight? It had once: years ago. She had never forgotten the evening they trailed up Corunna Road from the station, in the twilight, through the endless rain—Dick with the bucket he had scarcely used, and his little sodden dripping spade.

But it wouldn't—couldn't happen this time: she prayed for it to clear up, and her prayer was answered. For now, as she peered round the corner of the kitchen door, she was conscious that it was lighter: the gravel path glistened: the drips in the puddle outside were fewer and farther between— and there—over the Embankment a tiny strip of blue sky was rolling up the heavy clouds.

She returned to the kitchen with a burden lifted. It would be all right now. If you had asked Mrs. Stevens why she was so happy, she would never have been able to explain: she would have shrunk from saying "Because the others will be happy"—it would have sounded noble, and silly. If you asked her "Do you enjoy your holiday?" she would have flinched at a question she had always feared, but which had never come. Nobody ever asked her. The family assumed she did: and her friends confined their question to "Have you had a nice time?" to which she had replied "Lovely" for twenty years. It had always been Bognor—ever since, on her honeymoon, her pale eyes had first glimpsed the sea. Her father had had a sister who lived on a farm, and scorning holidays himself, he had sent the children there—year in, year out—until this daughter had met her man and married him.

The sea had frightened Mrs. Stevens, and she had never conquered her fear. It frightened her most when it was dead calm. Something within her shuddered at the great smooth, slimy surface, stretching into a nothingness that made her giddy. For their honeymoon they had taken apartments with Mr. and Mrs. Huggett in St. Matthews Road—called "Seaview," because from the lavatory window you could see the top of a lamppost on the beachfront.

They had answered an advertisement, and discovered Mr. and Mrs. Huggett to be a strangely assorted couple. Mr. Huggett was stout and jovial. He had been a valet to a man who left him some money, and he had bought Seaview. He was easygoing, slightly patronising, and drank. Mrs. Huggett was thin, and anxious to please to the point of embarrassment. They had a small servant girl called Molly, who, being squat, bow-legged, and red-haired, had remained with them faithfully throughout the years.

But the house had been well done up and was scrupulously clean. The Stevenses had returned the following year, and they had returned ever since, for twenty Septembers, wet and fine, hot and cold.

They had often talked of a change—of Brighton, Bexhill—even Lowestoft—but Bognor always won in the end. If anything it held them stronger every year. There were associations: sentiments. The ink stain on the sitting-room tablecloth which Dick made as a little boy: the little ornament that Mary had made by glueing seashells on a card, which had been presented to Mrs. Huggett at the end of one holiday, and was always on the sitting-room mantelpiece when they arrived each year. There was the stuffed barbel on the landing which they called "Mr.

Richards" because it was like a milkman they once had in Dulwich—and many other little ties that would be sadly broken.

But Seaview, silently, relentlessly, had changed with the passing years. Mr. Huggett, originally blooming like a ripe plum—had begun to shrink. His crimson cheeks began to fade—leaving a network of tiny purple veins. One September the Stevenses had noticed how thin his hands had become, how the skin sagged round the knuckles, and how his hand had shaken as he signed the receipt.

Each year Mrs. Huggett had come one night into the Stevenses' sitting room, when the children had gone to bed, and told her lodgers in an anxious undertone, with frequent glances at the door, what a terrible winter Mr. Huggett had had—on his back on and off all the time, with bronchitis and other, more mysterious troubles which Mrs. Huggett could never properly explain.

Each year the recital had grown longer and more awesome, till at Easter one year the Stevenses had received a black-edged letter. It came from Mrs. Huggett to tell them that on the previous Tuesday night, at ten o'clock, her husband had passed away.

The following September they found Mrs. Huggett in black. She'd told them how wild it had been on the night that her husband died: how the sea had roared, how crumbs of snow had circled in the road; and although she described her husband's death as a happy release, she had worn mourning ever since.

Mr. Huggett had never been much use in the house towards the end. He had to give up his one definite job (the changing of the electric light bulbs) some years before, because looking up made him giddy. But that did not alter the fact that their landlady's partner had gone: that through the long winter she was alone.

The Stevenses had not definitely noticed anything amiss with Seaview in the years that followed. Mrs. Huggett remained as flustered, as tremblingly anxious to please as ever. Molly seemed on the go all day—and yet—there was just something different: some little thing each year. A few years back the bath plug had broken from its chain: it had never been recaptured, and lay each year in freedom at the bottom of the bath. Year by year the sheets grew more cottony and frail: and Mr. Stevens, happening one night to have a sharp toenail, slit his top sheet down the centre, and enlarged it accidentally with his foot each night as he got into bed.

The Stevenses never complained or pointed out these things. Their years of association with Seaview—their fear of harassing Mrs. Huggett—and perhaps a little pity for her—kept them silent. After all, they were out all day.

But to Mrs. Stevens, Seaview was only the background of a fortnight in each year which troubled and disturbed her. She hated herself for not enjoying it as the others did. It made her unhappy to pretend she was enjoying herself, because it was a sham: somehow dishonest. Dick, round about fourteen—digging in the sand—his sunburnt legs bare to his tucked-up shorts—would run to her suddenly with "Isn't it lovely, Mum!" and she would say "Lovely" and smile, and hate herself for the lie.

Only the honeymoon had been lovely: the coming of the children had made the fortnight a burden—sometimes a nightmare. At home the children were hers: they loved her: came to her in everything. At Bognor, somehow they drew away from her—became different. If she paddled, they laughed at her: saying she looked so funny. They never laughed at her at home.

When she was younger she had tried to play cricket with them on the sands, but she had no eye for a bouncing ball, and could not stoop quickly to stop it. They would laugh—and soon she would go and hide in a deck chair behind a magazine—while the hot sun brought on her headache.

But the journey was worst of all; for although the burden should have grown lighter as the children grew up—she had never conquered her dread of Clapham Junction, where they always had to change.

The rumble of porters' trucks: the wrong platforms: the shrieking trains: the losing of her husband once, when he came out of the wrong hole after getting the tickets—Hell, to Mrs. Stevens, would be a white-hot Clapham Junction with devils in peaked caps.

But if Clapham Junction marked the summit of her panic fears, the journey in the train reached the limits of patient endurance. The carriage was invariably crowded on the first Saturday in September when they always went away. On one occasion someone was taken faint and called in a hollow voice for the window to be let down. Once—some years back—a lady in a corner had had a kind of fit, and tapped her heels on the ground and moaned. It had turned Mrs. Stevens cold with terror. She still dreamed about it sometimes: and ever since, her first anxious duty on getting into the carriage was to scan the faces of her fellow passengers, hoping against hope that all would look robust and at ease. If anyone were pale and delicate she sought to hide them from view with another passenger between, despising her cowardliness for doing it.

One trouble at least had been removed by the growing up of the children, for Mary, as a child, was always sick in the train: sick with unerring regularity, just after the curve that took them out of Dorking. Mrs. Stevens had tried starving the child: she had tried strong peppermints—to no avail. Ultimately she learnt of a good plan from her neighbour Mrs. Jack, whose little Ada was just the same. Mrs. Jack always carried on railway journeys, in her purse, two or three small paper bags. They could be quickly opened—easily applied and conveniently dropped out of the window. So adept had Mrs. Jack become that she boasted sometimes of getting the whole incident over before her surprised fellow passengers knew what had happened.

But Mrs. Stevens hated that journey. She had never been a reader. She could not lose herself in a book or magazine. She came away with the luggage rack and the ominous red communication cord burnt upon her aching eyes.

Yet now, as she busied herself with the supper, as she lifted the saucepan lid and forked the boiling beef, she was happy—almost elated at the unexpected sunlight of the evening: happy because the holiday brought such joy to the others. She looked forward to their coming home this evening: bursting to be off next day, yet reluctant to leave home now that it had become for one night the anteroom to freedom.

There was another reason, too, why she looked forward to the holiday this year with less reluctance than in the past. Dick and Mary were growing up now. Dick was seventeen and Mary nearly twenty. Once or twice in the past year Dick had spoken vaguely of a camping holiday with some friends, and Mary had talked of the jolly time some girls in the shop had had together on a farm.

Dick and Mary went out a good deal in the evenings now. There was the Thursday Dance at St. John's Hall—and things like that. Home was not quite the same these days, and the holiday, instead of separating them, seemed likely to bind them together. Last year Dick had still been at school: now he had started work. He did not seem very happy in his work. The holiday would do him good, and settle him, perhaps. Only Ernie, the third and youngest child, was still at school: for Ernie was only ten, and although he did not know it, he had set the spirit of the holiday in the last two years as far as the gaiety and horseplay went.

Luckily the hints of separate holidays had come to nothing, for when the day came to book the rooms, no other plan was raised. Dick seemed in fact more anxious than ever for Bognor since he had started work: which seemed to Mrs. Stevens a little strange.

The rain had quite stopped now: the sun was shining. Mrs. Stevens took the tablecloth from the kitchen drawer and went into the dining-room.

Ernie, released from the house, was playing with a tennis ball against the wall.

"You'll get your feet sopping," called Mrs. Stevens.

"It's dry," shouted Ernie.

Six o'clock was striking from St. John's Church up the road. The others would soon be home now. It was lucky they had all managed to get their holidays together. It would be lovely if it kept fine, the whole fortnight, and everybody enjoyed it like they always had before.

CHAPTER TWO

"Now then," said Mr. Stevens, drawing up his chair—"Marching Orders."

Supper was over. Mrs. Stevens and Mary had finished clearing away. The washing up would have to wait for the time being.

"Marching Orders" was one of the family jokes. Or rather, the expression was a joke, for its meaning was an earnest one. There were many things to do before the house could be left for a fortnight, and only by doing these things methodically could they go away without a hopeless rush at the last minute.

Mr. Stevens produced a sheet of paper, closely written over in pencil. It was the result of many years of collected and sifted experience, built up and improved each holiday until now it was as perfect a thing of its kind as a man could wish for. It was even on occasions lent to friends.

He relit his pipe, brushed the fragments of burnt tobacco from the table, and cleared his throat. It was rarely, nowadays, that the family sat round like this, and Mr. Stevens clutched eagerly at the occasion.

Dick was at the table, opposite his father: his elbows forward, his chin cupped in his hands. Mrs. Stevens, with a last hasty glance round the room, popped the cruet into the sideboard cupboard, took her seat in the armchair by the fireplace, and gazed vacantly at the paper fan in the empty grate. Her hands fluttered to the opening of her blouse—

then quickly to her knees, as if they could not, at so short a command, take rest.

Supper had been a great success. At first, perhaps, they were all a little too consciously eager to make it an occasion, as if they half feared that the charm of the evening might have sped with the passing of another year—but gradually they had warmed up to it and the spirit of past going-away evenings was magically recaptured.

Questions had been thrown across the table only to be met by counter questions. Would Uncle Sam and his Minstrels be there again?—Uncle Sam must be getting frightfully old: for fifteen years at least he had looked the same. Would the same pierrots be there? Had they closed the footpath that led to the sea across the clover meadow where rumour said they were going to build? Would the real Military Band play again?—it was so much more exciting than the ordinary one.—If Mr. Stevens had lapsed into silence now and then it was because he was far away—trudging the downs with his stick and pipe—open-chested and bareheaded to the sun and breeze.

Outside, the evening had beautifully cleared: the Railway Embankment had begun to darken as the sun sank behind it: and through the windows of the little dining-room there came a pale golden glow, blotted out sometimes by the passing of a train, although even then a lightning gleam of sunlight would flash through the openings between the carriages as they passed.

But dinner was over now, and business lay ahead.

Ernie, who had eaten to repletion, lay on the sofa, trying to rub sparks out of Puss, watching the little specks of dust from his fur glitter lazily through the fading beams of sun.

Mary came in from the kitchen and stood by the mantelpiece. The family were ready for Marching Orders, each ready to note down the duties which by custom lay before them.

"All ready?" asked Mr. Stevens, glancing over his spectacles. He cleared his throat once more and began:

"*No. 1. Tool Shed.* Grease spade, fork, and trowel. Lock up. Put key on kitchen hook."

Mr. Stevens neatly ticked the entry.

"All right. I'll see to that myself this evening.

"*No. 2. Joe.* Take Joe round to Mrs. Haykin—also bath, seed, and two cuttlefish shells."

Mr. Stevens glanced uneasily over his glasses at his daughter— "Will you do that, Mary?"

The duty of taking Joe, the canary, to Mrs. Haykin next door was always disliked. There was a tinge of anxiety in Mr. Stevens's voice, for last year there had nearly been a quarrel over it.

For this duty meant thanking Mrs. Haykin and staying there a few minutes to talk: and Mrs. Haykin, though kind, was rather a silly, excitable little lady who told you a dozen times that she loved looking after Joe, because it really wasn't any trouble at all and Joe was such a little dear, and sang so beautifully in the morning that it made her feel half happy—and half sad.

It was hard to thank Mrs. Haykin and get away. It made you feel rather unhappy, too—and selfish, because Mrs. Haykin never had a holiday herself.

She lived alone.

Once, so neighbours said, she had had a husband, three sons, and a daughter there, and somebody was always going in and out. But that was long ago—before the Stevenses' time.

She only went out once a day. Sometimes you caught sight of a little fleeting figure—a few untidy wisps of hair, and she was gone. You never, somehow, saw her come in again. The Stevenses used to go and see her sometimes, but then she would get so excited and happy, and talk so fast—and sometimes laugh and cry—that the visits grew fewer and farther between, until now it was only on rare occasions, as when Mrs. Haykin looked after the canary, that any of the Stevenses went into her home, and the rareness of the visits made them more difficult still.

Mr. Stevens's pencil was hovering over the paper.

"Will you, Mary?"

Mary's face hardened. She was pale and tired, for she had had a long and tedious day. She had worked feverishly all the morning, so that she might have leisure for a careful clear-up in the afternoon. But then, after lunch an irritating, unexpected thing had happened. A customer had hurried in to demand some alterations to a gown which she desired to wear that evening, and Mary had spent two hours of the afternoon with eyes bent over the hateful dress, knowing full well that no alteration in the world would improve the appearance of its owner's shapeless form.

For although Mary was sometimes allowed to wait upon customers in Madam Lupont's little showroom in King's Road, most of her time was spent in the bare workroom behind, with its gaunt window looking on the corrugated iron wall of a garage. The sun never came into that room, though the sky sometimes gleamed very white and hurt her eyes. She was very tired tonight. Why should *she* take Joe, and have to listen to Mrs. Haykin? Why shouldn't—

She glanced down at her mother, sitting with her hands upon her knees—gazing into the grate. She noticed that one of her mother's fingers was bound with a little piece of rough linen. She must have cut it—getting dinner, and none of the family had noticed it. Mary glanced out of the window. The sun was almost lost below the Railway Embankment: there was a cloudless sky: in a week the sun would have burnt her arms a golden brown; and something suddenly leapt and tingled inside her. She looked across at her father with a smile.

"All right. I'll take Joe."

Mr. Stevens ticked the item with a sigh of relief.

"Thank you, Mary.

"*No. 3. Puss.* Leave scullery window ajar. Ask Mrs. Bullevant to put down milk every other day. Bloaters Monday and Thursday."

Mr. Stevens peered silently at his wife, and Mrs. Stevens looked up with a flutter.

"No. I—I—er—couldn't see Mrs. Bullevant today. She was out. I thought we could tell her when we leave the key in the morning."

Mr. Stevens's eyebrows rose a fraction.

"Isn't that risky?" he said, "supposing there's anything she wants to talk about. Details to discuss. We aren't going to have any too much time."

Mrs. Stevens's eyes travelled quickly to her husband and back to the grate.

"Well—I'll—I'll go now."

"It's too late *now*. We'll have to risk it."

Mrs. Bullevant lived directly opposite. Her husband was a retired policeman. An ideal couple to leave the key with. It was always arranged that Mr. or Mrs. Bullevant should run over each day, have a glance round, send on any letters with three halfpenny stamps, and see to Puss. In return the Bullevants took the runner beans and rhubarb that ripened while the Stevenses were away.

The Stevenses had felt infinitely happier since their arrangement with the Bullevants. The position of the house, directly opposite, combined with the retired policeman atmosphere, gave them a feeling of absolute security.

Before the Bullevants came, the duties of caretaking had been done by Mrs. Jack. But unpleasant stories had come to the Stevenses' ears— of Mrs. Jack eating the bloaters and giving Puss the skin. It might have been spiteful gossip—but the tale came from more sources than one, and the Stevenses were glad when the Bullevants took No. 23 opposite.

"Don't forget," warned Mr. Stevens as he reluctantly ticked the entry. "And remind her about the scullery window."

He turned to the paper again.

"*No. 4. Stop all tradesmen.* Except half-a-pint every day from milkman."

Mrs. Stevens looked up in relief.

"Yes. I did that this morning."

"Did you tell Johnson's to keep *Family Gardening*?"

"Yes."

The morning paper was of course stopped, but the weekly edition of *Family Gardening* was reserved—and the back numbers delivered on the Stevenses' return, because Mr. Stevens liked to keep them and bind them up.

"*No. 5. Gas.* Turn off at meter."

"Right," said Dick.

"First thing in the morning directly after breakfast."

"Right," repeated Dick.

Mr. Stevens ticked the entry.

"*No. 6. Lock up Silver.*" ("Silver" was the technical expression for the Princes Plate, the Inkstand which the Football Club gave Mr. Stevens as a wedding present, and a few plated cups that Dick had won for running at school.)

"All right," said Mr. Stevens. "Mine."

There followed a few minor duties which experience had taught them to undertake with care. The plug to be left out of the bath because the tap dripped: perishable food to be removed: the carpet to be turned up away from the French windows, where sometimes the rain drove in. Each item was taken by one of the family.

"Last of all," said Mr. Stevens, "*General Instructions.* Ruislip will call for luggage at 9:15. Do let's have it ready by 9. It saves so much rush and bother.

"Train leaves Dulwich at 9:35. That means we must leave here at least by 9:20—to give time to leave the key.

"Arrive Clapham Junction 10:02. Platform Two.

"Main line train leaves 10:16. Platform Eight."

Mrs. Stevens's heart gave a little flutter. Two to eight, read casually from a piece of paper: how easy it sounded!—but two to eight at Clapham Junction—measured by platforms!

"Don't you think," she murmured, "we might catch the earlier train from Dulwich. It will give us ten more minutes at the Junction."

Mr. Stevens looked surprised; a little pained that his carefully planned arrangements should be called into comment. He spoke slowly, as if his wife were a little dense.

"But there's fourteen minutes."

"Yes, but—"

"'Course there's time, Mum!" put in Dick.

Mrs. Stevens's eyes returned to the paper fan in the grate. "All right—never mind. If you think it's time enough."

She wondered why she had spoken at all. She knew it would be to no avail. She knew her husband and the children enjoyed the thrill of cutting it a little fine. . . .

The meeting was over. Mr. Stevens folded the paper and stood up.

"I think that's everything," he said.

There was a general move. Mrs. Stevens and Mary went into the kitchen to finish washing up. Dick went up to his bedroom to pack. Ernie lay half-asleep on the couch—his bucket and spade in a nearby corner, ready for the morning.

The room was growing dark now, but Mr. Stevens did not turn on the light. He stood with his back to the fireplace, his legs wide apart on the rug—his face towards the windows and the lingering glow of the sun.

Then, very deliberately, he went out of the room—up the passage to the front door—out, and round by the side walk into the garden.

He could have gone straight into the garden by the French windows—but he preferred this other way: Ernie, or Puss, would have followed him if he had gone through the windows, and he wanted to be alone to enjoy this final twilit hour of the happiest evening of the year.

CHAPTER THREE

The garden was at its best in the twilight. The harsh outlines of surrounding things were softened and more subdued. In this light the Railway Embankment beyond the lower fence might almost be the green border of a canal and the telegraph poles the slim poplars that would line its grassy towing-path.

The garden of 22 Corunna Road was not a large one. In common with its neighbours, it measured 60 feet across and 180 from the front gate to the fence that closed it from the railway. But in the dusk its fences seemed farther apart and vaguely like the wine-red, ivy-covered walls that Mr. Stevens loved to see round gardens.

He paused on the lawn: relit his pipe and pushed the match carefully, head-on, into the grass. There was a cool, fresh smell of moist turf. A vague glow still hung above the railway, but overhead the sky had darkened and the stars had come.

A faint sound came from the Embankment: a *rat-tat-a-tat*, *rat-tat-a-tat*, murmuring along the lines, heralding an approaching train.

The sound grew louder, swept madly upon him—flew by—and died away. A piece of newspaper whirled up behind the train and floated gently down—dark against the fading sunset.

A frown puckered Mr. Stevens's face as the din and rattle surrounded him, but it smoothed away as the quiet returned. For a moment there had been a fleeting vision of lit-up, crowded carriages.

The signal clattered up and everything was still again. It seemed to have grown suddenly a shade darker with the return of quiet.

Mr. Stevens removed his pipe and took a long breath of the night air. Cool, fresh air: the kind of air he was going to breathe all day long for a whole, splendid fortnight. Already he was feeling better: the musty air of the office was working out of his lungs: his legs seemed to be gathering strength for their work upon the downs.

Mr. Stevens was not an unduly sentimental man: no more so, probably, than the average. It was only that by instinct he had taught himself to relieve the drabness of his days by painting red letters to all that could possibly bear the title.

It was entirely by instinct that he did this: entirely subconsciously— for he would have been the last to regard his life as drab. It would be more just, perhaps, to say that he had the gift of establishing domestic "Occasions," which do so much to strengthen the links of a home.

Something almost in the nature of a ritual surrounded these special days: a ritual that bound the family together in thought and deed.

Christmas Eve: Whit Monday: August Bank Holiday: and family birthdays were painted with letters of carefree, flamboyant scarlet. New Year's Eve, and Going Away Eve had titles of a more delicate, meditative red: the former because of its wistful plea to strengthen fading hopes, the latter because it heralded the yearly release of emotions which Mr. Stevens neither wished nor sought to analyse and understand.

The man on his holidays becomes the man he might have been, the man he could have been, had things worked out a little differently. All men are equal on their holidays: all are free to dream their castles without thought of expense, or skill of architect. Dreams based upon such delicate fabric must be nursed with reverence and held away from the crude light of tomorrow week.

He wandered slowly down the gravel path, one hand supporting the pipe in his mouth, the other in his pocket. He passed the lilac tree that had grown beyond recognition since he set it, a waist-high stripling, ten years ago last spring. In the border by the right-hand fence the flowers of deep colour had merged with the fading light into clumps of dusky, indistinct shadow: only the paler blossoms shone wanly up at him through the dark: the evening primroses, and the tobacco plants with their delicate, elusive scent.

In the right lower corner were the Michaelmas daisies; very strong this year. Along the lower fence, nearest the Embankment, were the runner beans, with the rhubarb in front. Not quite so good as usual. Next came the perpetual spinach and the square of parsley.

He thought of the hours he had spent in the garden since Going Away evening last year: hurried autumn evenings, working against encroaching nights: bleak winter days, when tea would call from the fire-lit dining room at four o'clock: fresh spring Saturday afternoons, when heads bobbed about in almost every garden of Corunna Road: summer days when he lay in shirtsleeves, stirring only to move his chair round for the shade of the lilac tree. Other things, too, had happened since this evening last year. Dick had left school and started work: they had changed their milkman: Ernie had had chicken-pox. Strange how many things could happen without ruffling the surface of Corunna Road.

He relit his pipe and sauntered on till he came to the true landmark of the garden, the gnarled old apple tree that stood sentinel over the left-hand side.

One or two other gardens in Corunna Road had an old apple tree like this: twisted, dark, and dry—almost barren now. Most people had cut theirs down and set new, stripling trees—but Mr. Stevens had allowed his to remain.

There was in his nature a deep sense of the past: a reverence for things that had gathered strength and dignity from time. Long ago a great orchard must have spread round here, for Mrs. Blaney had a tree in her garden at No. 5 on the other side of the road. In Mr. Shepherd's garden at No. 18, only the stump of the tree remained, and the top had been hollowed out to take a geranium sunk with its pot into a little earth.

From the train he had noticed the same kind of old apple trees, here and there amongst the gardens on the other side of the Embankment, so the orchard must have been here even before the railway itself.

Scarcely one in a hundred of the old apple trees now remained: all bore traces of long-forgotten care in the faded band of whitewash round their trunks. The survivors, standing once in fine sweeping glades, now stood in solitude, in places made incongruous by the whim of the builder who'd laid the roads across the orchard thirty years ago.

Mr. Stevens looked up into its dry black branches. A breath of wind passed by: the lilac tree woke up and shook itself, but the apple tree seemed too old and tired, even to rustle its leaves.

He stretched out his hand and rubbed his palm against the horny trunk. He almost wished some power should ordain that the tree be cut down, so that he could say "Oh, woodman, spare that tree!" like the man in the picture in Mary's bedroom.

He felt somehow that he understood the tree, and the tree understood him: that it was grateful for his understanding of its solitude. He sometimes wandered back through the years and lingered with it in the orchard as it was before the railway and the houses came.

But tonight was no time for drifting into the past. This time tomorrow he would be strolling down the promenade listening to soft music: the tang of the sea in his nostrils and a fortnight of robust freedom in his hands.

He turned briskly away from the apple tree—leaving it to dream alone. A square of light flicked out from Mary's bedroom and her head bobbed about against the drawn blind. The washing up must be done—she had gone to finish packing.

How splendid it all was!—The whole family going away together again, after those dark, half-thrown hints from Dick and Mary about separate holidays with their friends. Thank God they had come to nothing!

What fun and bustle there would be in the morning! Mr. Stevens, throwing dignity to the winds, performed a circle of waltz steps on the lawn, then stopped, and looked with sudden foreboding at the French windows lest Ernie should have seen.

For a moment he had had an exulting, fleeting glimpse of sun and sand—of people shouting and splashing in the sea: of gleaming cliffs and rolling downs—of feeling gloriously hungry—

And the splendid part was that he was enjoying it before it had even started! His account books and inkwells lay behind him— he had done up his pens in an elastic band and slammed them in his desk—and everything that lay ahead was fresh and open and throbbing with fun.

Whistling quietly to himself he returned up the garden and went into the tool shed by the kitchen door. He should have done this before it got so dark. He struck a match, and by its light reviewed his garden tools, neatly arranged along the wall. He had cleaned and greased them the previous night to save time.

Everything was in order: he came out and locked the door. He always had an absurd pang of sorrow when he locked the tool shed door each year before going away: it seemed like discarding old friends for a passing acquaintance who had dazzled him by a flash of fickle brilliance—who would throw him over in a fortnight as surely as his old friends would staunchly wait for him. He nearly unlocked the door to glance in once again, to assure them that it was all right, and that he would come back. He stifled the ridiculous idea and went through the side gate, with its trellis panel, and so back the way he had come— through the front door, into the passage.

The lights were on now, all over the house, but it was a privileged occasion. Dick met him in the hall with the walking sticks and umbrellas strapped together in a bundle: one of his duties under Marching Orders.

Ernie was being pushed off to bed, hugging his spade and bucket which he would not allow out of his sight now that the holiday had begun.

"Dick!" shouted Mary over the banisters: "Come and help me with this bag!"

Mrs. Stevens was still busy in the kitchen. As Mr. Stevens looked in to hang the tool shed key on the hook he saw the boiled beef, a loaf of bread, the mustard, and a dish of butter laid out in readiness for the sandwiches in the morning; the thermos flask nearby.

He wandered into the dining-room and stood once more with his back to the fireplace. On the window ledge lay his haversack containing the telescope, the map of Bognor and District, and his diary. He smiled and put his thumbs into his waistcoat. He felt the satisfaction and leisure of the man who has organised so well that he is astride of time. What a splendid idea it was to have those Marching Orders. No breathless rush and feverish worry—no "Where's the camera?" or "Has anyone packed the clothes brush?" Instead, just a purposeful activity: everyone intent upon duties which never overlapped.

"Dad!" called Mary from the banisters.

"Hullo!"

"Come up here a minute!"

"What is it?"

"Never mind!—Come up here!"

Mr. Stevens went upstairs and followed Mary into Dick's room, which overlooked Corunna Road. She led her father to the window and held up the curtain.

"Look there!" she said.

A full, brilliant moon had risen. It hung above the distant Crystal Palace, almost midway in its length. The towers were dark, but the domed roof below the moon sparkled in a thousand cold grey splinters of light. A softer glow came from the wet slates of the roofs on the opposite side of the road, while the trees beyond were densely black against a steel-blue sky.

Mr. Stevens had not often seen this view so lovely.

"Isn't it fine!" said Mary, "having the moon like this for the holiday."

"Good omen," murmured Mr. Stevens.

Dick, who had seen it, was busy by his bed. He had changed into the grey flannels and blue blazer which he would wear in the morning, and was carefully folding his office clothes—the blue serge suit which was beginning to shine rather badly along the right sleeve, where it rubbed his desk.

CHAPTER FOUR

M r. Stevens lay for some time with his eyes upon the slit of light that shone between the curtains of his bedroom window.

It was bright enough to give him every hope, but he knew how deceptive that slit of light could be. He had known wet mornings when the sky had glistened and sent quite a bright shaft through the curtains, when he had been astonished, on drawing them, to see a pitiless drizzle of rain.

He listened, and the absence of dripping water strengthened his hopes. It would make such a tremendous difference if it were fine.

In some ways, of course, it would be preferable, if it must be wet, to have rain on the day they went than upon a day when they were there, because a greater part of the first day was spent under cover of stations and in the train. Yet there was something rather wonderful about starting off under a clear sky and looking out of the carriage windows at country bathed in sunlight.

A faint breeze eddied the curtains into the room, and his hope became a certainty, for there was no rustle of rain against the glass. He jumped out of bed, drew aside the curtains, and slowly smiled. He could not remember ever having seen such a perfect morning for the start. Last year there had been a gusty, uncertain wind and heavy, scudding clouds, but this morning it was beautifully calm; a thin layer of mist lay over the lawn and the sky was clear blue. The early morning sun, shining between the houses, lit up the leaves of the apple tree, and gave them a delicate sheen.

What a day for a start!

He slipped into bed again and folded his hands beneath his head so that he could better see the sky through the open window. It was a pity the sun didn't shine into his room in the morning—but he preferred the back of the house. The trains did not disturb him like the irregular, erratic sounds you got from the front windows, of people going home late at night, laughing and talking.

A train passed as he lay there. He could just see its roof as it slid by. Poor devils—going up to London!—at this time in the morning, too!

He stretched himself till his toes stuck out of the end of his bed, then drew up one leg and felt his calf. Pretty hard, considering how little real exercise he got, but it would be as hard as iron in a few days' time—after a spell on those downs!

It was just on a quarter to seven:—there would be ample time if he got up in half an hour. He turned over contentedly for another doze, but he was far too wide awake and excited to sleep again. He just lay there, thinking.

Suddenly a thought struck him. He jumped out of bed and put on his slippers and dressing gown. Quietly opening his door he crept downstairs into the kitchen and put the kettle on. He would take them all a cup of tea. A splendid idea!—A splendid beginning for the day! He listened fearfully lest anyone should stir before the kettle boiled, lest anyone else, by chance, should get the same idea. He wanted to go stealthily into each bedroom and wake them up, one by one. He wanted Going Away day to open for them all with a steaming cup of tea: he wanted to go to each window, and pull the blinds, and say "Look there" as the sun streamed in.

He rehearsed the business with the dining-room curtains as he was waiting for the kettle to boil, and remembered something else. He crept upstairs, as softly as a cat, and put in his teeth. He wanted to be able to smile at them all.

A few minutes later, tray in hand, he went quietly up again: he put the tray on the top of the stairs, gently opened his wife's door, and tip-toed in. The light was mellow and subdued. Luckily the curtains were drawn. His wife had the old double bed, with metal railings at each end and brass knobs at the corners. It had been one of their first purchases when they had married, but the springs had stretched, and Mrs. Stevens lay rather deep in it. At first Mr. Stevens could see nothing but the top of a little pink nightcap, but when he gently shook her, she pushed down the bedclothes and turned upon her back with a faint grunt. For a moment her eyes roved vaguely to and fro; then fixed themselves on Mr. Stevens and opened wide with consternation. She started up like a little frightened rabbit and began to scramble out of bed.

"Good gracious!—I didn't know the time!"

He smiled and held up his hand. "All right—don't worry—it's not seven yet—"

Intense relief and thankfulness came to her. How awful if she had overslept—on this day of all days—and got breakfast late—and made everybody impatient and cross. Then, as she lay supporting herself on her elbow, her eyes slowly took in the cup of tea.

Mr. Stevens impressively placed it on the small, round table by her bed.

"Thought you might like this," he said.

Mrs. Stevens could scarcely speak—she gave a little helpless giggle—"Oh, but Ernest—reely—!"

She could find no words to express what she felt. Ernest hadn't brought her a cup of tea like this for—oh—ever so long. Years and years.

He had crossed to the windows. He pulled back the curtains with a flourish and held out his hand as if he had performed a trick. The room was suddenly bathed in sunlight.

"How's that for a morning?" he said.

Mrs. Stevens fought to keep her eyes open in the blinding light. After a moment she gasped, "Isn't it lovely!" then slowly turned her head towards the cup of tea beside her, which was far more exciting than a sunlit day.

"It reely is good of you—Ernest—reely—"

He strolled to the door. "Don't you hurry. Another half an hour if you feel like it. Breakfast at eight will give us plenty of time if everybody's packed." He left the room. Mrs. Stevens sat up and wonderingly sipped the tea. It was very hot and rather weak, and some of it had slopped into the saucer, but well—just fancy Ernest thinking of a thing like that!

Dick was awake when his father took in his tea; he had drawn his curtains and was lying rather as his father had lain before he had got up, with his hands clasped behind his head, looking out of the window at the sky. Ernie, in the little bed in the corner, still lay fast asleep, but he was left as he was. Mr. Stevens's tea idea did not include Ernie.

Mary was still dozing. Her bedroom looked out to the side, onto the wall of No. 24. It made it rather a dark room in the mornings, and she had not been awakened by the sun.

"Why, Dad!" she exclaimed, as she sat up and saw the tea. "Whatever made you think of it!"

Mr. Stevens returned to his room—well satisfied with the result of his gesture. He went into the bathroom, lit the geyser, and proceeded to shave. He heard the paper-boy come up the front garden, flop the paper on the doorstep, and go away. He saw the postman pause at the gate, glance through a few letters, and go on. A pity he hadn't come in. It would have been rather nice to have had a letter this morning: an unexpected, cheery letter from some old, half-forgotten friend, which he could reopen and read in the train if there was anyone opposite him worth impressing. But still, what did it matter? Wasn't the day, and the sunlight good enough for anybody? Wasn't the fun and excitement enough?

He briskly washed the soap away and went back to his bedroom to dress. He pulled on his flannel trousers and his cricket shirt. Splendid, easy clothes—no stiff collar this morning. He would wear a tie of course, for the train journey, but at the sea he would leave the neck open.

Then he put on his tweed norfolk jacket and his stout brown walking boots and went whistling downstairs. Fine to hear those stout boots clumping along.

Mrs. Stevens was dressed and busy in the kitchen. She had the eggs boiling and was just putting Ernie's white sand shoes on the kitchen doorstep to dry. She had forgotten to pipe-clay them the night before, but they would dry in no time in this sun.

Breakfast was laid in the kitchen to save time. It was naturally rather a scrappy meal, because everyone was anxious to get finally packed up. They had boiled eggs and bread and butter because it was easy to clear away and easily digested.

"Hope Ruislip isn't late," muttered Mr. Stevens, as he cracked his egg. Ruislip, the elderly outside porter who annually called for their luggage and trolleyed it round to the station, had a deadly leisure about the way he collected it, wandered off with it, and labelled it on the platform that irritated the family beyond endurance. He would pause after wetting each label and look up the line to see if the train was coming, while the family stood by in a ferment of anxiety. Then by the time he had satisfied himself that the train was not in sight, the label would have curled up and stuck to his fingers and caused more feverish delay.

He always managed, somehow, to have the last label on as the train drew up, but Mr. Stevens never trusted him, and began to fidget and look down the road long before the man was due.

Supposing, for instance, Ruislip were taken ill and forgot to pass on the message about the luggage to someone else? What a fix they would be in! Still, it was no use meeting trouble halfway, he was not due for half an hour yet.

There was a good deal of fun and joking during breakfast, but it mostly came from suppressed excitement, for Mrs. Stevens's sudden little bursts of laughter were nervous and highly strung and Mr. Stevens constantly took furtive glances at his watch.

Mary was quiet, because of a duty that lay ahead: a duty she hated. She finished before the others and rose from the table.

"I'll take Joe round to Mrs. Haykin now," she said.

Mr. Stevens spoke with sympathy. He understood how hard it was.

"We'll get your bag down into the hall and have everything ready," he added.

Mary went into the dining-room. Joe, in his cage, was ready on the table, his bath, seed, and cuttlefish shell in a parcel beside him. Mr. Stevens had taken the cage down and got everything ready before breakfast.

It was not the parting with Joe that Mary hated. It was the visit to the little lady next door. She would not have minded if Mrs. Haykin had been a disagreeable, sour old woman. Mary almost wished she was, so that she could simply hand the canary in like a parcel and come straight away. Still, it had to be done. She covered the cage with a green baize cloth, took hold of the loop in the roof, and went down the passage to the front door.

CHAPTER FIVE

Mary hoped that none of the neighbours would see her carrying the cage. The Stevenses, as a family, were rather shy and retiring, and disliked having their business publicly known to Corunna Road.

But it was only a few yards to Mrs. Haykin's gate. As she walked along beside the short length of laurel hedge in front of the house she caught a fleeting glimpse of Mrs. Haykin, peeping between the curtains of the morning-room, but as Mary glanced that way, Mrs. Haykin's head disappeared with a little jerk.

She went in the gate and up to the front door, but even as she knocked she heard the quick little thudding steps of Mrs. Haykin coming down the passage.

The door opened briskly, but after a few inches stopped with a grating shudder. The chain was on; Mrs. Haykin had forgotten to take it off. There was a faint "Oh!" of consternation, and the door shut again while an agitated fumbling went on inside.

Mary's heart sank as she waited. She knew this untoward incident would excite and fluster Mrs. Haykin and take at least five minutes to explain away, but she steeled herself with a smile.

At last the door flew open and Mrs. Haykin stood revealed. She was flushed, and overflowing with apologies. She spoke rapidly, with little gusts of excited laughter. "I *am* so sorry, Miss Stevens! It was so stupid of me, too. I could have sworn I'd took the chain off. I always do, first thing when I come down in the morning. It must have been the hurry to get ready. It's not that I'm nervous—it's just my silly memory. Now, do come in. Isn't it a lovely *day*!" The last word rose to a little breathless falsetto. Mary followed Mrs. Haykin down the passage of a house built exactly like their own to the smallest detail, even to the frosted pattern on the glass above the front door. Yet how different, somehow, it was! The coatrack inside the Stevenses' front door was always a mass of jumbled clothes: overcoats, mackintoshes, and hats of all kinds, from Mr. Stevens's panama to Ernie's little blue-striped Grammar School cap.

There was a rack, just like theirs, in Mrs. Haykin's hall—but how different it looked! A solitary, curious little bonnet hung from one peg and a grey woolen scarf from another, but the rest were empty. Mary could never remember seeing an empty peg in their own hall at home: if you took a coat off one there was always something underneath.

When you went into the Stevenses' house there was always a warm, occupied smell to greet you: tobacco, cooking, Ernie's peppermints. Mrs. Haykin's house was far neater than theirs, but although it was scrupulously clean, there was a faint, elusive mustiness: a shut-up coldness about it that gave you a strange feeling of imprisonment when the door was closed.

Mrs. Haykin fussed her way into the morning-room, talking over her shoulder so excitedly to Mary that she bumped into a chair and nearly fell. She gave a high-pitched laugh and quickly pushed the chair back to the wall, automatically smoothing its leather seat with her hand. Then she almost ran round the table and pulled out the armchair for Mary.

"Do sit down, Miss Stevens!—Or would you rather sit away from the light?—It *is* rather a glare, isn't it. I tell you what!—If I just pull the curtain a little—so! Now it won't shine in your eyes!"

"I've got to simply rush away," said Mary.

Mrs. Haykin was suddenly silent. For the first time Mary was conscious of the hard, slow ticking of the marble clock on the mantelpiece. When the old lady spoke again her voice had quite changed. It was soft, and soothing, as if she were humouring an invalid.

"Oh, I *know*. You must be having *such* a time this morning—what with everything to do. But you *can* just stay—just a little while?"

She had not given so much as a glance at the covered cage containing the silent canary: her round glistening eyes never left Mary's face.

"I'll simply have to go in five minutes," said Mary, as she put the cage on the table.

Mrs. Haykin became eager and animated again: she pressed Mary into the armchair and drew up a little straight-backed chair for herself. She sat with one arm resting on the table, the other on her knee. She was close to Mary: directly facing her, looking down on her with a face wreathed in smiles.

"That's nice!—Just five minutes then. I do want to hear everything. Isn't it *lovely*—to be going away!" The last words cut Mary like a lash— for they were spoken without a trace of envy. They were spoken softly, and happily.

For six years now Mrs. Haykin had looked after the canary when the Stevenses went away. For six years, to the Stevenses' own knowledge Mrs. Haykin had not been away herself. The Stevenses' holiday had become Mrs. Haykin's holiday: she lived every moment of it from her little house in Corunna Road. Soon she would watch them pass on their way to the station. She would not settle to her morning's work until she had seen their train go by and satisfied herself that they had had ample time to catch it. She always hoped one of them might wave from the window.

She would follow the steps of their journey: "They'll be at Clapham Junction now."—"They'll be in the other train by this time."—"They'll just about have got there," she would think as she settled on the sofa for her afternoon rest.

To a girl of little understanding Mrs. Haykin's breathless flow of questions would be inquisitive—impertinent, but Mary did, vaguely, understand. She knew that in these fleeting moments Mrs. Haykin was gathering precious seeds that would bring a little fruit to her barren loneliness, so she answered the questions enthusiastically, filling them in with every detail that would add colour and interest.

Many years ago Mrs. Haykin had been for a Sunday excursion to Bognor and spent an enchanting day on the sands. A day or two after the Stevenses arrived they always sent her a coloured postcard, taking great pains to select a view that embraced as much as possible to revive Mrs. Haykin's memory. They were very careful what they said on the card: they never wrote *We're having a wonderful time*, for fear that it would make Mrs. Haykin sad and envious. They were almost glad when they could say it was cold, or it had rained, never for a moment realising that dull days at Bognor brought sadness to Mrs. Haykin, who loved nothing better than to sit in the reflected sunlight of her neighbours' holiday.

Mary was aching to be gone: to be out in the open sunlight again. Her eyes roved round the little room that corresponded to their sitting-room next door. The wallpaper was brighter than their own: pink roses climbing up pale-blue pergolas—and yet there was that strange feeling of everything in the room being cold and dead.

In one corner stood the piano: tightly against the wall, its lid closed, its top draped with a wide lace covering. Upon it stood a vase of dried fern and two photographs in silver frames; one of a young man with a vacant, moonlike face, the other a young woman sitting on a rustic seat with a fan, her hair dressed tightly up into a bun.

In a corner by the fireplace stood a walnut whatnot with a china cat, a few little shell-like cups and saucers, and six pieces of china with a coat of arms and *A present from Bognor* beneath: a collection added to yearly by the Stevenses as a small return for Mrs. Haykin's care of the canary. Incongruous with these little odds and ends lay a frosted ball that glittered in the sun. It had come from her married daughter's

Christmas Tree in Macclesfield, when Mrs. Haykin, a few years ago, had been invited to spend her Christmas there.

Over the fireplace hung an enormously enlarged photograph in an ebony frame. It revealed the head and shoulders of a middle-aged man with his hair trained over his forehead into a quiff, and a long heavy moustache that tapered away into the mists of photographic enlargement.

The shoulders and chest faded away so that the portrait was like a bust, hanging in space, although the neck was enclosed in a low, stiff, turn-down collar, and a small, compressed bow tie.

There was something uncanny about this photograph. It seemed to dominate the room. The heavy lids that drooped over the hopelessly dull eyes, and the smooth weak chin, haunted Mary for hours, after she left Mrs. Haykin's house. She could scarcely imagine that this face could ever have belonged to a living man: she could not picture it smiling, or frowning, or speaking, although once by some queer twist of imagination she had pictured it moving as it slowly ate a plum, its cheeks puffing out slightly to eject the stone.

She felt it was this trancelike face that brought the chill mustiness to the room: she felt that it held everything embalmed—that if it were taken away, the furniture and every object round it would crumble to dust.

She imagined, of course, that it was Mrs. Haykin's husband, and as she looked at the stout little woman in front of her, with her rosy cheeks and bright, glistening grey eyes, she felt that she, too, lay under the spell—that she would dissolve and become a restless little ghost if the picture were taken away.

In a dish on the sideboard lay some apples and a clump of three bananas: incongruous living things: things with life and juice in them. Mary could not bring herself to believe that they were real: she could not reconcile them to this little room, for if they were left they would turn colour and decay: they would be drawn along with time, while everything else remained rigidly fixed in a timeless vacancy from which even patience had faded away.

Suddenly Mary shivered, and wrenched herself free. She had been answering Mrs. Haykin with mechanical words and a mechanical smile: she must hold herself away from the vacant, brooding face over the fireplace.

Mrs. Haykin talked on—the words falling over themselves to get free. Were they taking sandwiches in the train? *That's* right! So much better than bits of chocolate, and oranges. Were they going to hire that little hut with a balcony in front? Of course it was a luxury, but why not? It was just those little extras that made all the difference. She remembered—

Mary had risen.

"I'll get left behind if I don't rush," she said with a laugh.

Mrs. Haykin almost jumped from her chair.

"And it'd be all my fault if you did! You must run along now, dearie, and get your things on. It *has* been nice to have a chat!"

Mary was by the table, unwinding the cover from the cage.

"It's awfully good of you to look after Joe. I don't know what we'd do if you didn't."

Mrs. Haykin ran round the table as Mary uncovered the cage, and stood close beside her. Joe, assuming that night had unexpectedly returned, was dozing on his perch. Upon the recurrence of daylight he blinked, stood up, and said, "Tweet."

Mrs. Haykin gave a little exclamation of delight.

"Isn't he just a darling!—It isn't any trouble at all. I love having him." She put a finger between the bars and wriggled it to and fro. She said, "Chuck-chuck," and Joe said, "Tweet," loudly and triumphantly. Mrs. Haykin would have remained beside the cage if Mary had not moved towards the door.

"Everything's in the parcel," she said; "I think there's plenty of seed." She was in the little quiet, cold passage again, back beside the curious bonnet, the woolen scarf, and the solitary line of pegs. She opened the door, and a gust of warm summer air took her into its keen masterful arms and hurried her to the gate.

She turned and waved to Mrs. Haykin, and Mrs. Haykin smiled and waved back.

"Have a good time," she called.

"Thanks awfully!" called back Mary as she hurried away.

A tradesman's boy passed whistling on a bicycle, peddling hard and swaying to and fro. There was life beneath his shabby clothes: he would be bigger next year—he was coursing along with the living flood around him. A cat shot out from some railings and raced across the road: a grocer's van came bouncing along and drew up. A man jumped out and slammed the door—went into a gate and slammed it—everywhere life was being sucked in and thrown recklessly out, and Mary plunged into it rejoicing.

There was a great scene of activity outside the Stevenses' gate: Ruislip had arrived with his trolley, but the piece of rope he had brought to tie the trunk on with was too short, and he was placidly knotting it to another piece. He was perspiring, and Mr. Stevens was perspiring in sympathy beside him. It was a quarter past nine.

Mrs. Stevens, in her hat and coat, was just pulling down and fastening the front room window. There were heads at almost every window in Corunna Road—glancing between lace curtains and over window plants—some brazenly, some shyly. There had been a sudden and violent upheaval while Mary had been gone, for Ernie, at the last moment, had had an overwhelming desire to take his yacht.

Mr. Stevens had said, "No! Leave it behind!" and Ernie had begun to cry. Mr. Stevens had lost his temper and shouted, "You're going to leave the damn thing *behind*—I say!"—and Ernie, who could be as cussed as a mule, had shouted, "I want my yacht!"

It had been maddening. Ernie had not raised a word of protest when a month ago the yacht had been crossed off Marching Orders.

Everyone knew and admitted it to be a failure at the sea. It had dignity and quiet power upon the boating lake of the Crystal Palace, but it simply was not made for rough water.

Hours of irritation had come from it last year. It could never be allowed free and had to have a long piece of string attached to its stern. It had to be pushed out with a stick, and after a moment would fall drearily onto its side—to be hauled in and laid on the sands for its sails to dry before the stupid farce was gone through again.

But Ernie wanted it. He would not go without it: he was preparing to hang on to the banisters and scream if force were used to drag him away.

Red in the face, Mr. Stevens had wrenched open the side gate—slammed it and gone to the tool shed: almost broken the lock—flung open the door—emerged with the beastly yacht and slammed the door and locked it.

And now, as Mary returned, Ernie stood sullenly by the gate—the yacht under one arm and his bucket and spade under the other.

The luggage was on. Heavens! It was twenty past!

"Better hurry," said Mr. Stevens to Ruislip.

Ruislip hurried to the extent of twisting the trolley round, but then his haste wore off and he trundled down Corunna Road at his usual speed.

Mr. Stevens took one last glance round the hall and slammed the front door.

They were off!

CHAPTER SIX

Mr. Stevens, Dick, and Ernie went on ahead to get the tickets while Mrs. Stevens and Mary took the key across to Mrs. Bullevant.

There was plenty of time, as there always is if you panic sufficiently early and get it over, but Mr. Stevens liked a good ten minutes in hand. There were so many little things that might happen: something forgotten, that must be gone back for—an unexpected queue at the booking-office window—a hitch in labelling the luggage. . . .

Ten minutes were sufficient—but not a lavish allowance, for one remote possibility always haunted Mr. Stevens with unreasoning and ridiculous fear. It was the possibility of a passing lady fainting, or accidentally falling down.

It would mean stopping and helping her up: brushing down her dress, picking up her umbrella and bag, possibly her spectacles. It was not that Mr. Stevens lacked humanity or courtesy—it was simply the agonising delay that might be caused. For under such circumstances you cannot leave a lady with the cold-blooded statement that you have a train to catch. Besides, there were many ladies unused to receiving attention, who, hurt or unhurt, might easily fall victims to the desire for publicity and hold the scene till they had collected a crowd. In the worst event, if it were a fainting fit, it might mean dragging the lady to the railings and making a cushion for her head with your coat. It might mean a policeman—an ambulance—five—ten—fifteen minutes of torturing delay.

It was an idiotic idea—a one in a thousand chance— yet it always lurked somewhere in Mr. Stevens's mind as he walked to the station.

There was no other main line train till nearly twelve, and his mind had often dwelt upon the awful hiatus—the awful anti-climax, if they missed the connection.

He supposed they would all go home again for an hour—and sit about with their hats on. There would be something horrible about getting the key back from Mrs. Bullevant, unlocking the back door again, and going in. It would be like breaking open and waiting in the tomb if you missed the train back from a funeral.

But whatever his feelings, Mr. Stevens let neither of his boys see it as they walked together—talking in excited and confidential voices of the things that lay ahead.

Meanwhile Mary and Mrs. Stevens had knocked twice at Mrs. Bullevant's and were growing anxious. When at last the door opened it was as if it were forcibly pulled back against the warm, overpowering cloud of fried bacon vapour that gushed out.

Mrs. Bullevant swallowed, presumably a mouthful of bacon, and smiled. Mr. Bullevant was standing in the shadows behind her, outside the morning-room door. He too smiled, but not having to say anything, continued his bacon.

The Bullevants were looked down upon by some of the people in Corunna Road because Mr. Bullevant always breakfasted without a collar, but the Stevenses knew their worth, and rather scoffed at stupid prejudices of that type.

There was a solidity about them: a complete absence of pettiness that can only come from the harmonious union of a police constable and the good old-fashioned type of cook.

"Well you *are* a lucky lot to get a day like this," cried Mrs. Bullevant.

"Isn't it lovely!" replied Mrs. Stevens (although, truth to tell, she had scarcely had time to notice if it were lovely or not)—"It *is* so good of you to go in and keep an eye on things. Such a comfort to us."

"No trouble at all," said Mrs. Bullevant with absolute sincerity—for there are few things more attractive than a leisurely nose round someone else's house—when you know you're absolutely within your rights in doing it.

"The milkman's leaving the half-pint every other day—just as usual—if you'd put down half of it each morning—"

"Why yes, of course. And the bloaters?"

"Every Monday and Thursday," said Mrs. Stevens, handing Mrs. Bullevant the key. "Puss wasn't in when we come away, but the scullery window's ajar, and 'e's certain to be around somewhere in the morning."

"I'm bound to have a few scraps I can take over," said Mrs. Bullevant.

"You'll go and spoil him," put in Mary with a smile.

"I'll see there isn't more than just enough—or we'll have the other cats in."

"—And you *will* see the window's just left on the jar?" urged Mrs. Stevens—(for one day, some years ago, Mrs. Jack, who was careless, had closed it for some reason, and Puss had been shut in the house the whole day, and done what he would never have done in ordinary circumstances).

"Of course I will!" said Mrs. Bullevant—"Well, have a good time and send us a card!"

"Good-bye," said Mrs. Stevens and Mary.

"Good-bye."—

They hurried out of the Bullevants' gate—followed by a broad friendly smile. Such a different affair to the one with Mrs. Haykin, thought Mary. They sensed a true guardianship over the house, too.

The lazy stir of a summer morning surrounded them: they were really off now. As they passed Mrs. Haykin's house, Mary saw the old lady watching them from her bedroom window, and waved to her—but Mrs. Haykin, thinking she was unseen, assumed the wave to be for someone else and continued to watch them without moving.

Mrs. Jennings next door was watching too—for Mary saw her

standing half-concealed behind her morning-room curtains. Old Mr. Burgin, morning paper in hand, was watching from behind his lattice side gate: at other windows she could see the knuckles that held back an inch or two of curtain.

Mrs. Stevens, trotting hurriedly along beside her daughter, seemed unconscious of the eyes upon her, but Mary, with her head stiffly erect, felt a sudden irritation. What was there to look at—just people going away for their holidays? *She* never looked—she never knew—nor cared—when other people went away.

Mr. Stevens and the boys were almost at the corner that turned into the straight road to the station—and Mary was surprised to see another figure walking with them.

An irritating incident had occurred, for as Mr. Stevens, with Dick and Ernie, was going down the road, Mr. Bennett, the commercial traveller who lived at No. 8, had come breezily out of his gate and fallen in beside them.

It was a stupid, tactless thing to do.

Didn't he know that people off for their holidays moved in a different world to those on their humdrum way to work? Didn't he know that their thoughts, their words—their very temperaments were linked to a chariot that moved through infinitely finer air?

Mr. Stevens, Dick, and Ernie were floating in blissful harmony towards a paradise that only they were entitled to talk about and dream of. What right had this commonplace man with his celluloid collar—and umbrella—and bowler hat, to butt in—how did he dare think he could join in their talk and blend with them, even for a few yards of the pilgrimage? He was going to London—to an office—and back to Corunna Road in the afternoon: a tiny satellite with a stupid little workaday orbit—while the Stevenses were moving away with the majestic sweep of a great planet.

"Lucky lot of chaps," he cried. "Off on a day like this!"

Mr. Stevens winced. Even in normal circumstances he would dislike being bracketed with Ernie as a chap.

"Bognor again?" went on the intruder.

"Yes," said Mr. Stevens.

"We were at Torquay this year. *You* ought to try Torquay one year. D'you still bathe?"

Mr. Stevens turned his head slowly towards Mr. Bennett. The last words had an offensive, impertinent ring about them.

"Of course I still bathe."

"Why not!" agreed Mr. Bennett. "I don't see why we old'uns shouldn't enjoy it like the rest. Got to be careful, though. There was an old chap at Torquay this year when I was there, went in too soon after breakfast—they worked on him for an hour, but—"

Mr. Stevens had stopped short on the pavement. He looked back, then turned to Mr. Bennett with a curt nod and smile.

"Going to wait for the wife," he said.

Mr. Bennett stopped too, and brightened up his smile for Mrs. Stevens; but Mr. Stevens's mouth set in a grim straight line. He turned on his heel, threw a "See you later" over his shoulder, and walked away, Dick and Ernie beside him. Heavens! What an idiotic, tactless fool!

Mr. Bennett, completely at a loss, lingered a moment, and then went on. Mr. Stevens's resentment cleared in a flash. The skillful throwing off of this unexpected nuisance seemed to clear away with it all the minor irritations of the morning. Suddenly he felt radiantly happy. He made artful signs to Mrs. Stevens and Mary: smiling and frowning to make them understand they must not hurry and that nothing serious was wrong. But Mrs. Stevens came panting up—

"Something left be'ind?" she murmured.

"No! It's only that fellow Bennett—wanted to come as far as Clapham Junction with us. Let him get ahead." Mr. Stevens winked at Dick and Ernie—and then they all went on together.

A Carter Paterson's van passed them at the corner of Corunna Road, and as they turned into the straight road for the station a postman paused and smiled indulgently at them.

It was going to be a real scorcher, for the sun was already quite hot, and they were all beginning to perspire as they passed into the cool booking-hall of the station with its high, gloomy ceiling and echoing floor.

Their station was a faded little place—very seldom busy, for most people, London bound, went from the other station that took them direct to Victoria.

And yet it was more exciting to start from this quiet, neglected little place, to work up to the crescendo of Clapham Junction and gradually down again, through sweeping meadows, to the sea.

Mr. Stevens went importantly to the pigeon-hole, peered in, and said, "Four and a half: Clapham Junction," in a crisp, businesslike voice.

The others waited in a little group, whispering to one another, because of the hollow sounds their voices made. Suddenly Ernie vibrated with excitement. "Look!" he cried. There upon the wall, above a gloomy, closely printed notice of traffic rates, shone three highly coloured posters: the centre one held Ernie's pointing finger, BOGNOR REGIS—FOR HEALTH AND SUNSHINE, with a smiling girl upon a brilliant yellow foreshore and behind her a stretch of deep-blue sea. Her hair was blowing in the wind and a little white dog was leaping at her feet.

They stood together, gazing at it. The picture would have mocked at them on any other day, but this morning they could look at it as part of their right.

"It ought to look like that this afternoon," said Dick.

"Come along!" called Mr. Stevens, flourishing the tickets. And they passed through the doorway onto the platform.

Ernie's eyes were riveted on the collector's hands as they slid the tickets together into a neat pack and punched a V-shaped nick in them with a sweep of the powerful clippers: then his eyes travelled to the collector's face to see if it registered the pleasure which he himself could never have concealed had he been allowed to do it. He resented the man's bored face, and placed him at once among the people who did not realise their luck. It was a mystery to him why so few people felt the fierce joy of clipping tickets.

In passing through the doorway onto the platform Ernie came into his own, for if Railway Stations had lost their thrill for the others, their tantalising mysteries still held him tightly in their grip.

It was not so much what you could see and do that mattered— but the things you could not see and could not do. Everything was arranged to whet the appetite but never to appease it. The Railway people seemed purposely to have arranged these things to mystify.

For years he had wondered how they got the man through that tiny opening from which he served the tickets. Was he pushed in as a baby—or built in at a later period of his life?

He had received a shock of disappointment when the romance he had built round this wistful prisoner was shattered by Dick, who one day pointed out the very ordinary side door. The Railway Company had dropped a little in Ernie's estimation.

Yet against this one discovered mystery stood a dozen that threatened to elude him all his life: mysteries hid behind doors marked PRIVATE, which made him shade his eyes and peer through the window into the darkened recesses beyond. The small, redbrick building on the side of the line a little beyond the platform, marked with the one word DANGER in large red letters. The bold notice on the far end of the station PASSENGERS MUST NOT PROCEED BEYOND THIS POINT. He often stood pondering upon that notice, fearfully wondering what dangers lay hidden in the asphalt path beyond, till one day—with trembling knees and thudding heart, he had taken a step beyond the board and stood there exultingly till his father had called him roughly back.

It was a moment he had often lived again in bed: a moment of triumph that revealed the Railway people in their true colours. They were frauds. Nothing had happened to him beyond the notice board. They had just put the notice board there because they were killjoys—grumpy people who begrudged the fun they had unwittingly provided.

The Railway people must be grumpy, for they never invited or smilingly encouraged you to do anything. They began with a notice on the approach gates, saying something about loiterers being prosecuted—which was a nice, enticing beginning: then your ticket said you travelled at your own risk, and the Railway people weren't responsible: that it was for one journey only—or that if you returned you must do so on the day of issue. You were not allowed to lean out of the window—or put heavy things on the rack. They told you that you must not throw anything out of the window that was likely to injure the men working on the line. They might at least, as a friendly gesture, have told you what kind of things were unlikely to hurt them.

It seemed to Ernie that when these people grumpily made their Railway they quite accidentally combined it with a gold mine of thrills and excitements and fun—which, being grumpy people, they tried to spoil with all the cold water they could find.

But they couldn't spoil it! They only made it better fun! The more they stuck up DANGER and DON'T DO THIS and DON'T DO THAT, the more they threatened to fine you and prosecute you—the more they made your feet tingle and your heart thump.

The train was already signalled as the Stevenses grouped round Ruislip to watch him label the luggage, and Mr. Stevens thought it wise that they should not wander too far down the platform. They could see Mr. Bennett, sitting on a seat near the booking-office, but fortunately he had found a friend, and threatened them no longer.

The trunk looked well with its new white label stuck crossways over the faded one of last year, for Mr. Stevens took great care to preserve the old travel stains of the past. One, which had flicked off by accident as he had dragged the trunk out for packing a day or two ago, had been carefully replaced with Stickphast.

They could always sense the train's approach a little before it came in sight round the bend. There was a kind of tightening anticipation in the atmosphere of the platform: a hush like that which heralded the invisible approach of the Lord Mayor's Show.

At last they heard the rumping of it as it came over the bridge just round the corner.

"Here it comes!" said Mr. Stevens, picking up his satchel.

Dick slung his raincoat over his shoulder and picked up the tennis rackets: Ernie hitched his yacht a little higher under his arm: Mrs. Stevens did nothing but clutch a little more tightly at her bag.

The train, half a mile distant, seemed to emerge silently from between two houses. Then it turned and faced them squarely, and appeared to stand quite still, except that sparks spluttered from its wheels and that it swelled a little in size. But very soon came the rattle of it, and directly afterwards they could make out the driver at his window.

Ernie held in contempt the drivers of electric trains. Glorified ticket collectors—that's all they looked like: smug, complacent men, just holding down a handle. Give him the blackened, overalled, sweating men who rocked to and fro on the footboard of the proper, full-blooded engine!

The train came crashing in. "There's an empty one!" cried Mrs. Stevens as the carriages began to flash by.

"All right—all right: there's plenty more," said Mr. Stevens in a voice that made his wife feel rather silly. Waiting for a carriage at the back of the train always gives a horrible feeling that the train is going to overshoot the station. The first carriages seem to whirl by with such terrific pace and weight that nothing can possibly stop them in time. Even Mr. Stevens, with all his carefully assumed calm, had to withstand a clutching desire to turn and run alongside an empty Third as at last the train began to slow down.

Finally a line of empty carriages in blue upholstery (Firsts) slid by— just far enough—and there before them was a row of stationary Thirds.

There was plenty of room, for Saturday morning after nine o'clock is an ideal time to travel towards London from its outskirts.

"'Ere you are!" cried Mrs. Stevens, running forward and clutching the handle of a compartment.

"Here's a smoker," said Mr. Stevens a few yards beyond her. He wished his wife would be more careful: it was only in excitement that she spoke like that. Her first word had been such a raw, bleeding stump: the aitch seemed to have been torn from it with a blunt hatchet.

"Here's an empty smoker," called Dick—for there was a man in the far corner of Mr. Stevens's carriage, and Mr. Stevens had stood irresolute for a second. But now the family, which had spread out and threatened to disintegrate, and had all opened separate doors, closed together again round the door that Dick wrenched open.

Ernie was pushed in first. He had to drop his yacht, bucket, and spade on the carriage floor and clamber over them: then Mary jumped in, then Dick—who stopped and pulled in Mrs. Stevens while Mr. Stevens cupped his fingers and pushed her gently from behind.

Splendid! All in safely. Mr. Stevens lingered with one foot on the platform and one on the running-board until the luggage was safely in the guard's van. Then Ruislip came up and touched his cap.

"All right, sir."

"Good. Five o'clock on Saturday fortnight," said Mr. Stevens.

"Very good, sir."

Mr. Stevens handed Ruislip his two-shilling piece with a smile. It was pleasant to be called "sir" in front of the family. The guard blew his whistle, and Mrs. Stevens made an appealing gesture towards her husband, as if to prevent him falling between the carriage and the platform—but he swung lightly in and slammed the door.

"That's that," he said—and ran his eye over the hand luggage and packets on the rack and seats.

CHAPTER SEVEN

The train gathered speed, and almost in no time thumped over the passage that led beneath the Embankment at the end of Corunna Road.

"Here we are!" said Mr. Stevens, and the family, who were still sorting out the hand luggage, grouped round the window for the last view.

There was Mr. Hughes in his garden: the end house, No. 2. He had his bicycle upside down and was busy cleaning it. Here was No. 4, with its rough, unkempt lawn and weed-grown flower beds—where the funny people lived, whom nobody knew anything about, and some thought to be film actors.

No. 6 and No. 8 slipped by: neat gardens, both of them, although Mr. Stevens never liked Mr. Bennett's grotto. You wanted a bigger garden for that sort of thing. . . .

There was No. 12 with its sundial, and No. 14, with Mr. Foster's untidy rabbit hutches. . . .

The train was moving too fast to see much now, and all eyes were turned ready for the fleeting glimpse of home. Ernie, Dick, and Mary enjoyed the panorama, for they rarely saw behind the scenes like this. They called out as each little detail travelled past, and laughed triumphantly when they caught Mrs. Fraser in her curlers, throwing something into her dustbin, for she was always dressed up to her eyes when she went out the other side, through her front door. There was a fleeting glimpse of Mr. Shepherd watering the geranium in the stump of his apple tree, and then a hush.

No one spoke as they passed the house. It looked strangely tiny and unreal from the train: very quiet and still with its blinds drawn, and the empty clothesline, and the deserted garden.

Looking down from the Embankment you could see the side of the roof where the new slates, put in after the storm last year, made a square patch of lighter grey.

The garden was mostly in the shadow of the house at this time in the morning, but a shaft of sunlight fell through the side passage and lit up the clump of white asters by the apple tree.

The brickwork on the side that took the sun seemed faded and a little tawdry, but the back of the house, in the shadow, looked cool, and rather dignified with the creeper and the lilac tree.

Mr. Stevens always felt a pang at this moment of the journey, and after one earnest gaze, he turned and sat down in the corner. But his mind was relieved upon one thing, for halfway to the station he'd suddenly wondered if he had closed the w.c. window, and could not for the life of him remember. He had dared not ask the others, for it was one of his own allotted duties and it would have sounded ridiculous to enquire. It was all right, though—it was shut, after all. Extraordinary how you could do things automatically.

Mrs. Stevens felt no special pang, although she of all the family was most firmly tied to the little house during all the other weeks of the year. Her only anxiety was to see that no smoke issued from the chimneys or windows—for she dreaded the possibility of having left a dishcloth near the hot stove or a few smouldering cinders in the kitchen range.

Ernie was the most deeply concerned. He had waited a month for this unusual view of the house, and as they flew by he desperately searched the roof gutter for his tennis ball.

It had disappeared uncannily in the dusk one evening when he had hit it up in the air higher than usual. The gutter round the roof was his last hope, but there was no ball there—not even a blob or hump that might be a ball. He too was looking away when Mary suddenly cried, "There's Puss!" and all heads were craned for a last attempt to see.

Yes! There was Puss—sitting on the tool house roof—gazing down the side passage into the road.

Poor old Puss: pity they couldn't take him with them. He would wonder why it was so quiet when he squeezed through the bars of the scullery window about teatime, when he always went in for a look round.

They forgot all about looking for Mrs. Haykin, and now the train was flying past the end house of the road. Mrs. Stevens put the sandwiches and thermos flask on the rack above her head, and settled down: Mary slipped the library tab from her book and began to read: Dick was examining the tennis rackets: and Mr. Stevens was jotting down in his notebook the two shillings he had given Ruislip and the price of the tickets. Ernie alone remained alive to the passing scene, completely at a loss to understand how the others could let it pass without concern.

For pure, concentrated entertainment the journey from their home to Clapham Junction knocked the rest of the journey sideways.

Ernie enjoyed the later part to a certain extent, but the open country, lying as it did, much farther away, passed too slowly—and there was a sameness about the open fields and downs, the cart-tracks and the gates, the woods and cottages. It was only now and then that a cow would go bucking away across a field—or a boy would wave to them—and the telegraph wires, falling in loops and rising to the posts, falling and rising, falling and rising, made him drowsy.

But this first part of the journey was different: superbly full of meat. Everything was so close that it passed in a flash before he had taken in half of what there was to see: a hundred fascinating things were enticingly offered—then snatched from him sideways. The Embankment ended before there was time to blink and they were running between giant walls of brick that sloped upwards and away. There were alcoves in it, like sentry boxes. Gradually the walls grew higher: it grew darker and darker till suddenly they boomed into a tunnel, and he realised for the first time that the carriage lights were on. Dark, sooty things flashed by: a green light, and something that was tapping like a clock without its pendulum, and just when Ernie was beginning to feel like a brooding, under-grown monster they shot out into the sunlight and he was looking down like a god at dusty streets of crowded people and gutters lined with market stalls. Then came the chimneys: hundreds of chimneys—fat and thin—red and black—tin chimneys, stone chimneys—brick chimneys: one with a helmet like a fireman—another revolving mournfully in the wind: another long, thin one with a little hat like a Chinaman.

Down again!—deeper—louder—darker. Stout brick walls again, leaning back, with fat cables writhing along the sides, and then, just as he was expecting to dive into another tunnel, it grew suddenly lighter, and a green bank of grass ran down and swallowed the wall in a gulp. Then the grass bank dived into the earth and there before him lay a yard full of gloriously old and rusty motor lorries, falling to bits: exactly what he didn't expect! That was the glory of it.

Into a station. A stop with a jerk. A whistle and out again, into the best part of all!

The part where a little belt of mysterious, untrodden no-man's-land ran between the railway and the fences beyond. Ernie's eyes revelled in that narrow, deserted strip of rank coarse grass because it had a romance of its own. No human foot seemed ever to have trodden there—no human being ever dared to move amongst those ghostly relics that struggled to bury their nakedness in the grass.

Here was a pile of bleached, decaying sleepers with a broken lantern lying on the top: here a pile of rusty bolts and a roll of wire—and then the rubbish!

The rubbish contained things that you could not guess if you had a thousand tries. The heaps of old crumpled newspapers you knew about of course—and the fruit tins—and the mildewed, decaying sacks. They were the flour, the suet, the raisins of the pudding, but what about that old, wide-open umbrella, with its bare ribs and tattered remnants of cloth? How, when, and why did *that* come here? No passenger would drop an open umbrella from the train—and surely no one would throw away an umbrella without first closing it?

How came that ghastly, rusty wound in that enamel slop pail? No one ever put anything into a slop pail that burst a jagged hole like that!—and look at that half a perambulator, upside down! What awful, forgotten tragedy could have dissected a perambulator, and left its remaining two wheels clutching at the air? Ernie looked fearfully about in the grass for half a baby.

There were no large heaps of rubbish, as if certain spots were permanently used and recognised: it was all in little patches, some old, and deeply sunk in the grass, some fairly new, with bits of newspaper still white. Enamel slop pails and buckets took first place amongst the casual things—and all were inexplicably battered and broken. Cats came next, although being alive were not, properly speaking, rubbish. But they mingled with it so naturally that they claimed some kind of kinship, they prowled amongst it or sat amongst it, and sometimes looked at each other across it. Nearly as many cats as slop pails.

Once they passed a rubber bicycle tyre—once a gramophone trumpet—and once a bowler hat, but now they were out upon a broader track with half a dozen sets of rails: trains flashed by or lines of trucks obscured him so that Ernie could not see so intimately as before. It was a pity, because the houses were so near that he might have seen people in their bedrooms in nightdresses. A row of scraggy poplars seemed to rise sheer from a blackened coal yard, and looking up a street he could see there had been some kind of accident for there was a crowd and a policeman. But it had gone in a flash, and the chief things now were the mystery signs of the railway. Baby signals beside the lines: tiny little things a foot high, that looked as if they had only just been set: posts with baffling numbers on them: one with a huge 8, another labelled 1 IN 1 which seemed to Ernie a stupid claim, for it looked exactly like the other posts.

His mother was worrying him on and off all the time—groping in front of him and trying the door, or holding on to the back of his coat. But this did not spoil it, really, it rather added to it, for it gave a sense of danger and daring.

They were over on the side track now—bang up against a row of very old and squashed-in houses with no gaps between like those at home. They had tiny backyards, and washing hung out, and sheds with their roofs piled high with pigeon boxes or rabbit hutches. The only flowers he could see were on the windowsills and the only birds in tiny wooden cages on the walls outside. A solitary tree grew straight out of an asphalt yard, but it looked tired and prematurely bald. They passed a dusty recreation ground where the earth was quite bare round the swings. A few boys were playing cricket, and a man nearby was lying flat on his back with a newspaper over his face and one knee raised. Ernie was sorry the cricket would be over by the time he got back, for he had good games with Ted and Sandy on their recreation ground: sometimes small, ragged boys came and watched on the outskirts, and eagerly gathered and threw back the ball if Ted or Sandy or Ernie called out "Thank you!" They formed rather an exclusive circle because they were all considering the idea of becoming professionals and very rarely allowed others to join them to bat and bowl.

Here was a long row of coloured posters and a splendid signal box on a bridge that spanned the line—but now the family were stirring—getting the luggage down and glancing out of the windows. For they had passed Wandsworth Common and were very near the Junction now.

He looked at his mother. She looked rather pale and ill, and he wondered why. She had taken the thermos flask and the packet of sandwiches from the rack and had them beside her, and she kept picking them up, putting them under her arm, then glancing out of the window and laying them down again.

His father was rather importantly fingering the tickets, and glancing at his watch.

"Clean up to time," he announced.

Two trains rattled by, one on either side, one electric, the other steam. A signal rattled up—an engine was whistling somewhere, and they shot into Clapham Junction.

CHAPTER EIGHT

C lapham Junction is perfectly all right if you keep your head.
No one knew this better than Mr. Stevens, and when their train began to draw up, his movements became slow, strong, and deliberate.

He reviewed the small luggage laid out on the seat, and turned to his wife with a smile.

"Plenty of time," he said. "They've got to get the trunk out."

Yes, thought Mrs. Stevens—but supposing they *don't* get it out!

Mr. Stevens could see that his wife was agitated, and although far from being a selfish man, he could not help a little secret satisfaction. His own coolness would have been thrown away and wasted if she also had been cool. He saw the unspoken question in her pale face: he saw her hands trembling, and he gave her a smile of encouragement and understanding.

The luggage van was only a few yards behind their carriage, and even as they alighted they saw the guard easing the trunk down to a porter, who helped it in a gentle somersault onto a trolley.

"Bognor?" enquired Mr. Stevens.

"Number Eight," replied the porter.

"You'll take it across?"

The porter nodded, and wheeled the truck away.

It had been absurdly easy, and Mrs. Stevens could scarcely believe that so much could happen consecutively at Clapham Junction without a single mishap.

Then suddenly she realised that it was not really easy—it was her husband who had made it seem easy. She admired him beyond words as she followed him down the platform. He was so quiet and purposeful. Clapham Junction seemed to draw from him a mysterious power.

Mr. Stevens was thinking about himself in the same way. He was conscious of it—this instinctive power—leadership, he supposed it was. His ordinary life gave little chance to draw upon it. It required a Clapham Junction or a burst pipe to bring it to the surface.

They came to the broad steps that led down into the subway, and Mrs. Stevens gripped a little more tightly at her luggage. It was here that she had dropped the thermos flask two years ago. It had broken, for when they had held it to their ears and twisted it round it had given out a faint sound of sliding bits of glass, like a kaleidoscope.

But it was all right this time, for Dick helped her down the steps, and they waited in the surging bustle while Mr. Stevens got the tickets. There was rather a long line of people at the booking-office, and Mr. Stevens looked a little grave at first. But he got to the window sooner than he expected, as you always do, and there was a good ten minutes in hand when he came away with the tickets.

There was a real sweetshop in the subway—exactly like a shop in an ordinary street—and there was time for Ernie, who had a shilling to spend on sundries, to go in and buy a chocolate whirl. It cost twopence for the single one, but it made a splendid travelling sweet.

Meanwhile the rest of the family went to the neighbouring bookstall. Mr. Stevens believed in reading matter for the train, and never stinted in this. He bought the *Red Magazine* for Mary, *The Captain* for Dick, *Chips* and *The Scout* for Ernie, and *The Times* for himself. For his wife he bought a little domestic journal. She rarely or never read at home and he knew she was far from likely to concentrate upon a magazine in the train, but he did not like to see her sitting opposite him all the while, looking at him, and this particular magazine looked more or less the same if held by mistake upside down.

For his own part he did not usually read *The Times* because it was difficult to open in the bus—but he liked its quiet dignity and the feeling of culture it gave out upon a more leisurely train journey, and he quite often found very interesting things to read in it. He liked the letters from Colonels, and the long, reasoned special articles about foreign affairs that left his mind excited and hungry to find out more about things one day, when he had the time.

Then Ernie returned, and they all went up the steps to Platform 8.

There was rather a big crowd waiting there, but that was to be expected on the first Saturday of September.

"Bognor?" asked Mr. Stevens as the collector snipped the tickets. The man nodded and jerked his thumb to Platform 8.

"Next train down?"

The man nodded.

They found the luggage all right with the porter beside it, but their trunk looked smaller at Clapham Junction, with the piles of other luggage, than it did when it stood by itself at their own station.

"Bognor train the next one down?" asked Mr. Stevens of the porter.

"Yes, sir," replied the porter.

Mr. Stevens did not like relying upon the word of one ticket collector and always preferred to take a consensus of opinion from as many officials as possible.

The crowd was certainly a big one: much bigger than last year, and Mr. Stevens could not help feeling a little worried. "Keep close together," he said in an undertone. "Whatever you do—don't scatter." With a smile to his wife he added, "Some are bound to be for another train"—but in his heart of hearts he was afraid they were all for theirs.

More people arrived every moment. They could not possibly all get into one train—even if it were empty—and he knew that it would already be fairly full from Victoria.

Ernie found himself in the fortunate position of having a large and imposing Automatic Machine behind him, and without moving away from the family he was able to examine it at leisure.

He had once seen a man reloading one of these machines from a collection of cardboard boxes round his feet. He had also seen the man unlock a secret drawer and empty a shower of pennies into a bag. From that day onwards Ernie had resolved to be one of these men one day, if he humanly could. It seemed to him the perfection of earthly employment.

He viewed the stacked-up packages—dimly visible through the narrow glass windows of the machine. You had the choice of Caramels: Chocolate: Almonds and Raisins: Marzipan: and Assorted Nuts. Underneath he read *Push drawer back. Press penny in slot opposite article required and pull drawer.* He read this twice. It was so crisp and businesslike. Underneath, upon an enamelled plate, was printed *Address any enquiries to: Victoria Automatic Machines Ltd., Broadway, Willesden.*

He was just wondering what kind of enquiry one could possibly make about Assorted Nuts when the crowd made way for a porter, who came along shouting "Sutton—Croydon—Dorking—Horsham—Arundel—Ford—Bognor!"

There was a general stir, and a picking up of luggage. The train was not in sight yet, and Ernie wondered how the porter found out it was coming. But here it was! Coming round the bend now!—running alongside a little electric train. The engine came in with long, wheezing, gasping sighs—slower than the electric train, so that you could see more clearly into the front carriages. Heavens! It was crowded already! The whole of one side taken in that carriage! at least ten in that!—It was going to be a bit of a fight! Mr. Stevens had the papers and his haversack under one arm—leaving the right one quite free. He was prepared to push if other people pushed.

It was a terribly long train—it went on and on, slowly passing them.

Once or twice they had a mad desire to rush along beside carriages that had empty seats. Some people, indeed, did do this and were swallowed up in the protesting crowd, but Mr. Stevens stood his ground with a gentle hand on his wife's arm, and at last the train stopped with a final vibrating groan. There had been one agonising moment when a line of Firsts threatened them, but they just crept past—and before them stopped a Third Smoker with only two people in it—a splendid bit of luck.

Mr. Stevens tried to manoeuvre the family solidly round the door so that they could all get in and sit together, but somehow two other people got mixed in with them—and after Dick and Mary had clambered up the step, the others had to wait, and so got separated. It was a pity, but it didn't really matter. The great thing was for them all to get seats in the same compartment.

They closed the door, but one or two people wrenched it open, looked wildly in, and ran off again. Mr. Stevens went to the window and watched the luggage in. There was a short wait—and then the whistle blew and they slowly moved away.

Dick and Mary had got corner seats at the far end, but two girls, sitting opposite one another, separated them from the others, who were seated in the middle of the carriage—Mrs. Stevens, with Ernie beside her, facing the engine, and Mr. Stevens directly opposite.

Mrs. Stevens reviewed the fellow passengers. She liked the look of the girls: they had haversacks and stout walking sticks and she was sure that neither of them would want to faint, or be sick.

There was a sort of naval man in one of the other corners. Not a sailor, but one of the kind with a bluejacket and brass buttons, and a peaked cap.

Then there was a stout, jolly-looking old man with gaiters: a farmer most likely, and next to him a young man whose mouth would not quite shut because of his teeth.

The only doubtful one was opposite her, next to her husband: a puffy woman with a baby. On the whole quite a lucky carriageful, if the baby was all right. The two girls with walking sticks and haversacks would probably get out at Dorking—then they could move up and be with Dick and Mary.

Dick and Mary leant forward and looked down the carriage at the others, and smiled. The others looked back at them and nodded and smiled to show that they were all right. Then they all settled down except the baby.

The woman was holding it in a clumsy, stupid way, so that it was forced to look straight at Mr. Stevens. It did this steadily for perhaps five minutes without blinking an eyelid. Then it reached forward and took hold of the brim of Mr. Stevens's hat.

Mr. Stevens pretended not to notice for a little while. He kept his head quite still with his eyes on the front page of *The Times*. Then the baby began to tug at the brim till it pulled Mr. Stevens's head a little sideways. This was exactly what the baby hoped would happen, for it began to chuckle: tugging, and letting go a little—then tugging again. It was maddening that the woman should sit there unconcerned.

At last Mr. Stevens pointedly removed the hat and placed it on the rack above his head. The baby's eyes followed it—then it let out a wail and began to cry. The woman gave it a mechanical slap and turned it away from Mr. Stevens, who opened *The Times* with a sigh.

They passed for a little while over the line they came by—past the dusty poplars and under the signal box on the bridge. Then they branched away and ran smoothly through several little suburban stations.

The two girls, who had talked vigorously at first, sat back and opened magazines: the naval man was placidly looking out of the window: the farmer and the baby went to sleep, and the carriage settled down to quiet.

Dick lowered his magazine to his knee and looked out of the window. At first it was all houses and factories and small bare gardens—

but gradually the gardens grew larger and greener, and sometimes the open country would shyly push itself forward, to be driven out again by another mass of houses. Sometimes there would come quite a wild field with countryfied bramble hedgerows, but generally a narrow strip of new, unfinished houses stuck into it like a dagger point, throwing before it a trench for drains—a rough temporary road and bare strips of earth where the turf had been rolled up for the dagger point to go still deeper.

But soon the open country began to surge in more strongly—and once, for a little while, Dick could see as far as the horizon in unbroken waves of grass. He sat with his chin in his hand, never moving his eyes to take in details. He liked the flowing country to form the background of his thoughts.

CHAPTER NINE

Mrs. Stevens opened her magazine and looked at the tall, willowy girls on the fashion page. She had grown a little tired of fashion pages, for they never offered suggestions to ladies of her own height. All the girls on this page were at least six feet high, or even more—just like they were in all the magazines. It was like offering daffodil vases to put violets in.

She turned over the page a little impatiently and the free pattern dropped out onto the floor. She had to stretch her foot down before she could reach it and push the soft pad of brown tissue paper under the seat.

She read "Today's Menu":

Œufs a la courtet
Petites cremes de Faisan
Tartelettes de Pommes
Fromage

It sounded lovely, but why didn't they sometimes give a new idea for cooking rice and jam—or a new flavour for cornflour shape?

Slowly the magazine dropped to her knee and she sat gazing at her husband. Only once a year they sat like this: close opposite one another. It never happened at any other time, for at meals they were farther apart and the crockery was between, and both of them had lots to do, so that they never really felt conscious of each other. In the train they were very close and could not miss each other's eyes if they glanced up from what they were reading. She could look at him now because his head was lowered over his paper. He swayed gently with the motion of the train. He still wore the steel-rimmed pince-nez that he got some years ago when his eyes began to ache in the evenings, but his eyes must have changed a bit since then, for he had to hold the paper farther away from him than he used to.

He had not altered much with the passing years. His hair, of course, had thinned, and he had tried several things for it lately. He parted it almost behind his left ear, much farther to the side than most men did, and brushed the long remaining wisps straight across his head. His moustache looked a little more ragged than it used to, but that was because waxing had gone out. It used to have beautifully glossy, sharp points.

But except for this he was very much as he used to be. His face was still smooth and quite rosy, and he had not grown fat like so many husbands did after fifty.

When he was close up like this, and yet unconscious of her because of his paper, he seemed strangely remote from her. It was hard, somehow, to think of him as the man she had lived so near to for so many years. She felt that if he were suddenly to look up it would be quite natural for him to peer over his glasses and say: "Let's see—you're my wife, aren't you?"—and for her to answer: "Yes!—and—and—aren't you my husband?"

She wondered about this as she gazed at him; ready to look quickly away if he glanced up. She wished she knew whether he were really happy. He seemed so restless sometimes. He would wander about the house and look out of the window—then go for a little stroll, and come back, and roam in the garden.

He did not speak to her very much when he was in those moods, and she wished she could go to him and slip her hand through his arm and talk to him.

She often wondered whether it was the Football Club that still worried him. The trouble had happened so long ago that he really ought to have forgotten it by now, and yet, somehow, she was afraid he would never quite be able to forget—even when he was a very old man it would still nag like an old, deep-seated wound. He had been such a good footballer once. She remembered, when they were courting, how she used to go and watch him play, up on the old ground behind the piano factory that was covered in houses now.

He had been the goalkeeper and had looked fine standing there on the alert with his grey woolen sweater up to his chin and his cap pulled down well over his eyes.

He had been one of the keen young men who had founded the Sydenham Grasshoppers a year or two before their marriage, and looking back upon those distant days Mrs. Stevens found it hard to separate her early wedded life from the bustle and excitement of the Football Club.

The boys had given them a wonderful send-off for their honeymoon and had tied an old football on the back of the cab. They had given them the inkstand in the name of the Club, and one or two of them had quietly given little presents on their own. It had been a lovely time.

Mr. Stevens had gone on playing for a year or two after their marriage and then he had given it up and become Secretary. What happy, busy, bustling years those were in her husband's life—and her life, too! The Club had grown a lot since it was started and they had two teams, and sometimes three by then. Every evening Mr. Stevens was hard at work: quite late into the night sometimes—sending out reminder cards to the teams, writing up minutes, arranging fixtures—and a hundred other things. He would often get three or four letters in the morning post and open them at breakfast. Sometimes shy boys would call and ask to see him, wanting to join the Club—and he would be so jovial and nice to them, clapping them on the shoulder, asking if they had played before and whether they'd got plenty of grit and were ready to work hard. Then sometimes Members of Committee would call for a confidential chat and he would take them into the drawing room and close the door and talk quietly and secretly for a long time, and she would make some coffee, and when he called, take it in with the tin of ginger nuts. She would never take it in until he called, because what they were saying was so secret and important.

Every Saturday they would walk down to the Ground to watch the team that was playing at home. There was a special place midway down one side of the field where the important people stood: the Committee, and the Officers, with their wives, and on wet days, boards were put down for them to stand on. This group would not shout so loudly as the ordinary crowd: they would sometimes call out a few words of encouragement but would never hoot, or give catcalls. At halftime the men of the group would gather together and talk in undertones, and perhaps call the Captain over to them, while the wives stood chatting together a little way off.

Sometimes a young man, passing the group with his girl, would say in an undertone, "You see that chap there?—that's Stevens the Secretary," and Mr. Stevens would pretend not to hear, but would stand a little differently so that the girl would be able to see him to better advantage, and Mrs. Stevens would throb with pride. After the game they would walk back down the roads, and home to tea, and sometimes one of the Committee with his wife would come back, too. Dick was a little chap of about five then—and Mr. Stevens would show him to his friends and lift him up and say, "He'll make a stocky young player one day!" and the Member of the Committee would laugh and say, "Make 'im another goalie, like his dad!" They were lovely days. Full, busy days—and they went on a long time.

But time can lay its hand quite firmly on a football club. The older men—Mr. Stevens's special friends—gradually dropped away. Some got married, and others left the neighbourhood—some lost their keenness and found other, newer things to do; and gradually their places were taken by the younger men—the timid boys of a year or two before, now grown to important young Members of Committee with quite a lot to say.

But although many of his old cronies went, Mr. Stevens still remained Secretary: he was still the big man of the Club—although instead of being the centre of that old, earnest band of pioneers, he began to become a little isolated—rather the heavy father instead of the cheery, benevolent old goalkeeper turned Secretary with a joke for even the youngest boys of the team. Instead of laughing with him, the younger men seemed to respect him: he couldn't get so near to them as he used to do.

Then began those sullen, restless moods that worried Mrs. Stevens. He still worked long and late upon the business of the Club: he still kept his finger firmly on its pulse, but he seemed to do it with a heavy heart.

It was after the monthly Committee Meetings that he appeared most worried and depressed—and then at last the evening came that still remained deeply cut upon her memory.

He had finished supper, and although he had sat down to address the weekly team cards, he had suddenly risen, leaving them half-finished, and crossed and stood before the fire.

"The General Meeting's next Thursday," he said; "I'm going to resign."

And then, before Mrs. Stevens could think of anything to say—he had begun that terrible pent-up flow of words—all the bitterness that had been fighting for release throughout his long moods of silence.

"Just because I've worked for the Club, year in and year out—ever since it started—just because I do the donkey work cheerfully, without asking for thanks—they take me for granted!—They think I'm an automatic dummy that goes on forever! They think I *like* doing it! They think I'm clinging to it because I've nothing else to do. They think I like the importance of it! They think they're damned good to let me go on doing it! The fools don't realise there isn't another man in the Club who's got its business at his finger ends like me!"

"But—but—you aren't *reely* going to resign?" she had murmured.

At that a gleam of amusement had come into his eyes, and she had felt reassured.

"We'll wait and see," he said. "D'you suppose they'd *let* me resign—d'you suppose they *can* let me go? They know perfectly well the Club would fall to bits if I chucked it.

"No," he went on more quietly, "perhaps I won't resign—but I'm going to give them the shock of their lives—I'm going to make them crawl to me with a thumping big vote of thanks before I do anything else."

She knew that he slept very little in the nights that followed. In the evenings he worked with greater care than ever on the minutes for the General Meeting, and twice went down to the Unicorn to see that the longroom was ready for the Thursday. He wrote a number of jocular postcards to some of the older Members and told them not to be lazy—and to turn up for the meeting.

She still held the vivid memory of that Thursday night, ten years ago. The children were quite small then, and did not notice how little supper their father ate.

"I'll take the key," he said. "Don't you wait up. You know how these meetings drag on."

Then he had buttoned up his coat, lit his pipe, and gone out into the drizzling rain down Corunna Road and round the corner to the Unicorn.

It was many days before she heard the full story of that meeting—she pieced together the fragments, day by day, as they came with a deadly, uncanny calm from her husband's lips.

The formal business, it seemed, had dragged its placid, uneventful way before the election of Officers for the coming year.

There had been a little subdued talking when Mr. Stevens rose, but people said, "Ssh!" and he spoke in silence.

He touched briefly and lightly upon his own career with the Club: the inspiring days when he helped to found it—their early battles for existence. Then his years as goalkeeper—and finally his ten years as Secretary.

"But there comes a time," he said, "when a man feels past the days of his usefulness: when it is time for him to stand aside and hand the torch to younger, more vigorous men."

There were one or two murmurs of "No!"—but he went sternly on—

"I have other things to consider, too: this Club, although I love it—is far from being my only interest in life. I have many—secret hobbies"—he smiled—"hobbies which I have long promised to give my time to—and they are calling me more strongly every year. My business, too—demands greater concentration as my position in it has gradually become more responsible. I have given great reflection to the matter—if I felt there was no one fit to take my place I would sacrifice everything for the old Club—but I am proud to feel there are many energetic young men who can honourably step into my shoes."

You could have heard a pin drop as he sat down. It had been a good speech—and quickly thinking through it he was glad to feel he had not forgotten any of it. He sat with a grim serious face—artfully hiding the tongue in his cheek and the chuckle in his throat. It was just what they wanted. Something to make them sit up and pull themselves together.

Then at last—after what seemed an endless stillness, old Mr. Harrison, J.P., had risen—the quiet white-headed old gentleman who was President and always took the Chair once a year at General Meetings. He did not know much about the Club, although he always subscribed two guineas, and Mr. Stevens was sorry to have put this crisis on his shoulders. Still, it would not hurt him. He began to speak.

He said what a sad blow this was for the Club, and spoke eloquently of Mr. Stevens's ability—and loyalty—then suddenly Mr. Stevens stiffened in his chair. What was the old man saying?

"But it would be grossly ungenerous of us, after all his sacrifices for the Club, if we were to exert unfair pressure upon him to stand again. We know him to be a man who would not take this step unless he felt it vitally necessary. We must remember that a man's duty towards his profession must come before his recreations. I feel you will all join with me in a hearty vote of thanks for his past services and a deep expression of regret at his resignation. . . ."

A cold feeling of sickness had gripped Mr. Stevens: his hair was creeping and prickling at the nape of his neck—his mouth was suddenly dry. With a strange sense of unreality he heard someone else speaking—a young man at the back—the Vice-Captain of the First Eleven was proposing Joe Bullock as Secretary—Joe Bullock, the young Committee-man who always had so much to say at meetings. . . .

He heard a ripple of applause—and one or two "Hear! hears!" . . .

Someone else was speaking, seconding Joe Bullock . . . he saw through the mist of tobacco smoke a show of upraised hands. . . .

He was conscious of rising stiffly to his feet, of handing over his beloved minute book to a grinning young man, flushed with excitement and embarrassment. His beloved minute book, with its worn leather back—his friend through ten long happy years of quiet evenings at the table by his fire . . . a part of his very home. . . .

Oh, well. Things don't last forever. . . .

A dull droning suddenly changed its tone and a bright light seemed to eddy round. Mrs. Stevens sat up with a jerk. She had dropped into a doze, and the train, running out of a tunnel, had brought her back to consciousness.

They were passing through a little village station now—over a level crossing where an old horse and cart stood waiting.

Her husband still read with slightly lowered face, his pince-nez a little crooked, as they had been since Ernie sat on them. It was ten years now since he had come home from that meeting—a long time. Yet somehow he was strangely the same as when he came into the bed-room that night, where she lay awake, waiting for him.

To her unspoken question he had said, "I'm tired now, Flossie. I'll tell you all about it tomorrow." And she had heard him restlessly turning beside her, turning and tossing till she had fallen asleep as the dawn was creeping through the curtains.

But it was days before he began to tell her. It was an evening when quite suddenly, after supper, he had asked her to come for a stroll.

She didn't usually go out so late, and her legs were aching, but she put on her shoes and they strolled round the roads, quite a long way.

He was glad, really, he said. He'd really wanted to resign. It was only the wrench of doing it that hurt. It would give him a lot more time for the garden and—and other things. He'd take up his bicycling again. There were lots of nice lanes and quiet roads down Beckenham way that he hadn't been round since he was a boy. And his work, too—he'd got to give more time to it now that he was getting quite senior in the firm.

He had said it cheerfully—with flashes of defiance, and she had talked cheerfully, too—of all the things he could do now that he had more time . . . but in her heart she longed to comfort him, for she knew that nothing would ever come to take the place of the happy days on the touch line—the busy evenings with the minute book and his little team cards. . . .

She knew, too, that he still sat in the corner of the Office behind the glass screen—where he'd always sat. If only his freedom from the Football Club was *really* necessary for more important work!

He joined the Bowls Club, but only went there twice. He said they were a "sticky lot"—too old for him—and she knew he was thinking of the shy boys who used to come and call him "sir" and ask to join the Football Club. . . .

Still, there were the children—and the garden—and the holidays. . . .

The jolly-looking farmer, dozing in the corner, helped to support Mrs. Stevens on one side, and Ernie, wedged on the other side, held her in place so that she did not loll over. Her head nodded once or twice and then remained still. Once she gave a little grunting snore, and Mr. Stevens looked up with a shadow of a frown.

CHAPTER TEN

M r. Stevens knew that his wife would snore if she got into a certain position with her head bent too far down, and he watched her anxiously for a little while. He had looked up in time to see the two girls exchange a smile when his wife had given that solitary little grunt, and he got ready to raise his foot and tap the sole of one of her shoes if she started in earnest.

But luckily her head began to loll a little to one side, and he knew she would be all right like that. He laid his paper down to rest his eyes and looked thoughtfully across at her.

She was wearing the blue serge coat and skirt that she had bought for the holiday two years ago, and the bright sunlight made him notice the part across the shoulders that had faded. It had worried her, and he had said it didn't show, but he could see now that it did. He saw, too, some little fallen grey hairs upon her collar, and upon the faded part.

It had been a rush to get off, and no doubt she didn't have time for a good brush down. He liked to see well-dressed ladies, and wished sometimes that his wife were a little neater. She was small, of course, but he had often seen small ladies looking very smart. His eyes travelled slowly from her little fawn hat to the grey silk scarf around her neck, from the woolen jumper to the coat, which he had always thought to be rather too long in the sleeves. From the skirt, with the magazine upon its lap, to the slender little legs that did not quite reach the ground. It worried him that she always seemed to get her stockings a trifle too large, for he noticed now a ripple round each ankle—not enough to really show, but just enough to make you think it might get worse. He looked at her shoes and was glad they were the soft black ones with the straps and buttons. He knew they didn't hurt her, although he wondered what on earth he would do at the seaside if he came away in patent leather dancing pumps—for that was all hers really looked like.

Still, she never came on the rough, sturdy walks across the shingle and the stubble fields, so it didn't matter much.

He pondered, as he sat there, upon the tiny things—the trivial little chances—that order the lives of men. He would never have met this little dozing lady but for Tom Harris working overtime beside him one winter night—if Tom's sister had not been keen on acting, and made Tom take tickets for the musical show she was in at the Camberwell Church Hall.

Tom had spoken to him quite casually as they had put on their coats to leave the office.

"Ever go to musical shows?" he said.

Mr. Stevens said that he sometimes did.

"I've got a couple of tickets for a show my sister's in. Expect it'll be pretty bad—but I had to take 'em. It's on Friday. Like to come?"

"I'd like to," he had replied.

Who, he wondered, would be sitting opposite him now—what kind of children would be sitting round him if he had said, "No—I don't think I'll come"?

They had had high tea that Friday evening at a little place where they always went for lunch. They were good friends, Tom and he—and after they had had a game of dominoes Tom looked up and said, "Oh, well—I s'pose we'd better go."

Supposing instead, they had said, "Let's cut the show—let's have a quiet evening playing dominoes?"

But fate had Mr. Stevens firmly in its hands that night, and they had buttoned up their coats and gone out, down Peckham High Street to the hall at Camberwell.

St. Mark's Hall was a large, gaunt place. It looked as if its architect had started halfheartedly upon a church, and then lost courage, and played for safety. The tall iron railings outside displayed a row of notices and posters in descending order of decay; some new, some half torn down, according to whether the event they advertised lay in the future or the past. Whist drives, dances, lectures—it seemed a popular place.

They had had difficulty in finding their seats, for the hard little chairs were numbered on the backs, and many had been twisted round and left by disappointed searchers. People coming before them had knocked some of the chairs out of place, so that row G, at one end, had apparently become row F. Twice they sat down, and were chivied away by anxious, flustered officials.

But the show was unexpectedly well done. There was a big orchestra of amateurs with two or three professionals (so Tom told him) for the brass instruments, and when at last the curtain rose, the two young men settled down to enjoy themselves in a condescending way— nudging each other now and then in the dark.

It was five or ten minutes after the show had begun before the thing happened that altered the life of young Mr. Stevens. Fate let him sit there for a while—gloating over him before letting its hand down upon his shoulder.

The first part of the show was mostly about a funny man and a lady. The funny man wasn't very funny, so when a chorus of milkmaids entered, Mr. Stevens stirred himself for a diversion from the funny man rather than anything else.

The strange part was that he did not see her at first. There were about a dozen milkmaids, half of them carrying little three-legged stools. First they all danced, and then the ones with the stools sat down and daintily crossed their legs while the others ranged themselves behind. A comic fat man dressed as a shepherd with a three-cornered black hat and pink knee breeches came dancing in and walked up and down before the girls singing a song which the girls took up now and then in chorus. The audience had clapped the comic man when he had come in, and young Mr. Stevens watched him for a little while to try to find out why. Failing, he turned his attention to the girls once more.

For some time past he had taken to looking for nice girls more than he used to: he had never had one of his own, because his ideals were rather high, and also because he was a little diffident, but when he was walking to work and walking home he searched the passing crowd more keenly than he used to, often with something of irritation. There were so few pretty ones: *really* pretty ones. But now and then a girl would pass who nearly came up to the standard he had set, and sometimes, if he could do it without attracting attention, he would turn round casually, walk quickly back, and wait, as if for a bus, so that she would pass again to give him another sight of her.

Sometimes the second view was disappointing, but sometimes it sent him home aching because of the thousand-to-one chance of ever seeing her again—wondering what would have happened if he had fearlessly stopped her and made an excuse to speak.

For Mr. Stevens, at thirty, was growing rather lonely in his rooms at Penge.

He had his football friends, of course, but most of them had girls, and hurried away with them after the Saturday games, leaving him lonely evenings to build up the picture of his own ideal. She would be slender, dainty—very lively and full of fun: her face must change quickly from laughs to little frowns: she must not be too dark, nor too fair. Nice golden-brown hair would be the best. . . . She would have eyes that lit up quickly to his flashes of wit—she would see the funny side of things but would not try too much to say funny things herself.

It was for her that he searched in the passing crowds. Sometimes his heart would bound at the sight of an approaching girl, but only once or twice in the past twelve months had his dream blazed to life for a passing second—leaving him a lovely vision and a few restless, empty days.

His eye ran along the seated milkmaids: nice girls, some of them, but not quite . . .

Tom's voice whispered in the dark.

"That's my sister—the second from the end, standing up."

"Oh, yes?" murmured Mr. Stevens. She was a tallish fair girl, rather like Tom in a way.

"And that's Flossie Perkins, her chum—the little one next to her at the end."

The hall was dark, and Tom did not notice that his friend's hand was quivering when he passed him a caramel a minute later—he didn't notice that his friend held the caramel uneaten in his hand—that he clenched it till it lost all shape.

For Mr. Stevens had suddenly felt his body quiver like a gigantic hair standing on end.

Was there anything wrong with his eyes? Had that entrancing little vision been there all the time, ever since the milkmaids had first come in?

She was singing now with the others. They all had to swing their hands up and down and sway their heads. She was a thousand times the best of all of them. My goodness!—Look at that wonderful little face!—All lit up with excitement—laughing up at her friends, then smiling down at the audience! The fat comic man was standing in front of her now—goggling his eyes and twisting his face. Mr. Stevens had to clench his chair lest he should leap up and yell, "Get out of the way, you fool!" For a moment he had a terrible fear lest the vision should have faded when the fat man moved away.

But no! There she was again! Not singing now—just standing there smiling—with glistening eyes. . . .

"What d'you think of it?" said Tom. The lights were up now—a few people were going out for a breath of air, and some were standing up to stretch their legs. Mr. Stevens was conscious of not being able to open his hand—and he had to bend up his fingers and scrape the caramel off with his nails.

"I think it's quite good," he said, and was proud that his voice was calm.

"Some of it's all right," said Tom, in a noncommittal way.

A terrible thought surged in Mr. Stevens's brain—and he felt suddenly cold. He looked up at his friend. She was his sister's chum—supposing she were his girl! For a wild second he had to battle and crush the awful feeling that he would kill Tom if this terrible thought were true.

Then he knew that he would never bear the rest of the play in doubt: he must grip hold and settle it now.

"Your sister's good," he said.

Tom looked pleased. "She isn't bad, is she?"

Damn it! Why not say it! He swallowed, and spoke casually—as if what he said were an everyday thing for him to say.

"I like her chum, too."

It was amazing how Tom took this. He did not even turn his head. "Yes, she's a nice little bit."

A nice little bit! Was Tom blind—were his eyes and senses dead?—Or was he, too, concealing his true thoughts behind a suppressed, off-hand voice?

"D'you know her well?"

"Just a bit. She comes to the house now and then. My sister got her into the play."

"I'd like to meet your sister—and—and the other girl. Can we—afterwards?"

"Rather! We'll go round when it's over."

People were coming back from their breath of fresh air, stumbling along to their seats as the house lights faded. The hall was dark again now, but even in his trancelike happiness, young Mr. Stevens found it hard to sit through the second half.

She only came in once again. By some mad oversight they had not put her in the chorus of maypole dancers—but for a fleeting second he saw her in the crowd of villagers at the wedding—beautiful in a simple cotton frock and bonnet.

"Come along," said Tom, "we've got to get out and go round the back way."

One or two fusty people muttered and scowled as Tom and he pressed past them. Then they were in the open air, hurrying down a dim-lit street to the back way in. Mr. Stevens had never been behind the scenes before. This alone, on any other day, would have excited him, but the big slats of scenery, the sweating men in shirtsleeves, and the baskets of jumbled costumes passed him in a misty dream.

They were in a narrow passage now. "D'you know where Miss Harris is?" Tom was asking.

A fatuous idiot put up his arm to block the way. "You can't go down there. They're changing."

Mr. Stevens would gladly have felled the man, but people pressing behind—calling loudly for Millie, and Susie, and Kate—did all that was necessary, and soon they surged by in a crowd. There were lots of half-open doors, and Mr. Stevens could see the girls inside. There were little squeals, and bursts of laughter as people went pushing boisterously in. After peering into several rooms Tom turned to his friend with a triumphant smile. "Here she is!" he said.

There was a crowd of girls in the room—mostly in the costumes they had worn on the stage, but one or two in dressing gowns. Mr. Stevens's head swirled: he had never tasted a scene like this before. Convention had blown away on the wings of laughter, everybody was pouring words straight into each other's souls—nobody was weighing what they said. One or two other young men had got there before them and were holding the hands of girls or playfully pulling the ribbons of their maypole costumes, and over the whole scene lay the heavy seductive scent of greasepaint and powder.

"This is my chum, Ernie Stevens," he heard Tom say—and then, "My sister!" was bawled into Mr. Stevens's ear, and he found himself shaking hands with a tall, fair, laughing girl.

Someone bumped into him at the back and another young man had Tom's sister by the hand before Mr. Stevens could say a single word. It was a good thing in a way because he could turn his eyes to search the room. There was a strange dryness in his throat, and in his lungs there seemed a lot of air which would not come out when he breathed. He had a terrible uneasiness lest . . . No! There she was! Over in the corner . . . He had been terribly afraid lest some fond parent had spirited her away . . . but it was all right! Splendidly all right! Yet now that the moment had come—now that he could see that she could never escape the room without passing him and facing him— his heart began to hammer till he thought it must burst his ribs. She stood alone, in a corner that seemed a little backwater from the surging stream that eddied round the centre of the room. It was strange that no crowd surrounded her. A jolly good job though! He almost crossed to her—for in this mad, excited atmosphere it would be quite a natural thing to do—but then he checked himself, and pulled Tom by the sleeve.

"Here!" he cried, in a reckless, careless tone that blended with the room. "Introduce me to—to Flossie!"

For a moment Tom looked at him in surprise—then he cried out, "Sorry!" and led his friend across the room.

She was still in her simple cotton frock—exquisitely more beautiful than the tawdry maypole clothes around her—but she had removed her bonnet, and her lovely brown hair fell round in tumbled, excited waves.

Thank God for the turmoil and laughter around them! Quietly, and alone, he could never have done it, he knew. He had never spoken like this before—in all his life—the words seemed scarcely to be his own—

they seemed to sweep into him from the fevered atmosphere and pour out of his lips.

"... I thought you were wonderful!—miles and miles the best of any of them!—I—I never *saw* the others! ..."

Her lovely little rosebud lips were quivering, and he thought for a moment there were tears in her dancing eyes—but it was the excitement, he knew, that made them glisten so—

"I've never done it before," she whispered.

"Never done it—before! Oh, but—but you must have!"

"No—reely I haven't!"

"Then it was just simply marvellous!"

He looked out of the window with a sigh. They were passing a chalk pit, shining in the sun beside a dark, cool wood of firs.

Twenty years now—since he had seen her home to the little house in Anerley. He wished she had gone on with her acting, but she never seemed keen again. It would have kept them in touch with all those lively people if she had. Tom's sister seemed to have been her only friend, really, but she had dropped her directly they had married. He rather thought Tom's sister had taken her as her chum because she was so trusting, and admiring, and keen to do what Tom's sister did.

It was a pity she never had the knack of finding friends. He had tried so often by asking men of the Football Club to tea, with their wives. She would get excited, and talk and laugh so gaily that he felt sure that bonds were being forged. But somehow it never came to anything. The friends would go, and nothing seemed to happen to bring his wife in touch with them again.

Yet what did he want? A domineering woman who bossed him? A woman who filled the house with her own friends and drove him to his bedroom—or one who was always out, neglecting the children and the house? Or one who whimpered and grumbled for more money?

He knew that the household management of their small home strained her fragile little body and mind to breaking point, but would he have had a masterful woman to run it contemptuously with her little finger?

A train passed them with a roar, and his wife woke up with a little jerk. For a moment she looked around her in bewilderment—then for a second she met her husband's eyes, and he smiled at her.

CHAPTER ELEVEN

Long experience of the journey to Bognor had taught Mr. Stevens that you very seldom got any further passengers in your compartment when once you were safely clear of Clapham Junction.

Generally a mere handful of people were waiting at Sutton and Croydon, and your luck was right out if any of them chose your particular carriage. But the chance was always there, and Mr. Stevens usually found it a wise precaution to go to the window as they came into these stations, and look out with his elbows resting on the frame, and a tired, miserable expression on his face—as if he were standing in a very crowded compartment.

This always served its purpose, and once past Croydon the danger had gone, for at Dorking more people generally got out than in.

He had rather expected the girls with haversacks to leave them at Dorking for a walk on Box Hill, but they made no move as the train drew up. Unexpectedly, however, and very fortunately, the lady with the baby had got out. Mr. Stevens had decided that she was a sailor's wife, going to Portsmouth—and he was very surprised to see her go. But he had scarcely spread himself when a Salvation Army man had jumped in with a small black bag, and Mr. Stevens had to close up again.

Still, it was quite a satisfactory exchange, and the Salvation Army man was a natural thing to happen, for passengers waiting at Dorking would know the train to be full, and would obviously make for the carriages where people got out.

But now, at Horsham, a really remarkable thing occurred. Mr. Stevens was almost certain the walking girls would get out here, and he was correct. But as the train drew up, not only the two girls, but the Salvation Army man, the young man with the teeth, and the man with the gaiters all trooped out together, and no one got in to take their places.

It was a splendid stroke of luck. Horsham was just halfway and there were no more stops till quiet little Arundel, where no one in Mr. Stevens's memory had ever got out or in. It meant that for the rest of the journey they were practically certain to have the carriage to themselves, with the one exception of the naval man. But he was a pleasant, seasonable passenger on a day like this.

Some years they had been crowded and uncomfortable all the way to Bognor, and this sudden turn of fortune seemed to add a full hour of unexpected pleasure to the holiday.

For Mr. Stevens always put down the train journey as a doubtful quantity in the sum of happiness. Even under the worst conditions you might conjure up a faint sense of exhilaration in racing through the country towards the sea, but when anything happened like this: when suddenly your limbs are freed from the aching pressure of other people's hips and elbows: when luxurious spaces of empty seat lie around you for the spreading of your magazines and papers, and arms and legs—only then can you triumphantly sweep the doubt aside.

There was almost a touch of smugness in the way that Mr. Stevens threw his paper into the dent left by the woman with the baby, which had been loosely filled by the little Salvation Army man since Dorking. He stretched himself and smiled. He knew that he would often think of this moment in the months to come, for this was the precise moment— the turning point when the last of his anxieties lay behind, and every moment of the holiday lay full and unbroken ahead.

The early morning and yesterday evening, exciting though they had been, were shaded by those ominous little clouds that inevitably hang over the beginning of a holiday. The anxiety of leaving home: the burden of the luggage: the bogeys of Clapham Junction and the worries about seats—they were things of the past now: things to joke about—and ahead lay the holiday—basking under a clear, untroubled sky—stretching away to the far distant horizon of Sunday fortnight—so far away that you could scarcely measure its distance in terms of tightly packed minutes of sunlit days and starlit nights.

The solitary remaining duty of finding a porter to trundle the luggage from Bognor Station to Seaview would be child's play compared with the difficulties they had surmounted, and as they steamed out of Horsham Station and Mr. Stevens slid along the seat to Mary's side, he was thinking to himself, "The holiday really begins *now*—at this precise moment."

Mrs. Stevens and Ernie moved along until they were beside Dick, and the family, together once more, greeted each other as if they had been separated for a month.

They exchanged experiences and impressions of the journey, gained from their respective positions in the carriage.

"You didn't see that haystack on fire?"

"No—where?"

"Just after Leatherhead."

"Why didn't you say!"

"How *could* I—in all that crowd!"

"Weren't you awfully uncomfortable, Mum?"

"No! We were quite all right—weren't we, Ernie?"

No mention was made of the baby—and Mr. Stevens's hat. Even Ernie knew instinctively that it was something that one pretended not to have seen—he merely referred to the strong smell of camphor balls that came from the baby whenever it was moved.

"Now then!" exclaimed Mr. Stevens, clapping his hands together. "What about those sandwiches!"

"Yes," agreed Ernie.

Dick jumped up and took the little packet off the rack while Mary handed down the thermos flask.

They were passing the smooth playing fields of Christ's Hospital—heading for the broad South Downs, and a silence fell as Mrs. Stevens untied the parcel and laid bare the sandwiches. There was a touch of solemnity in the way that each took their tiny relic of home. A long time would pass; and who knew what might have happened before food from home would pass their lips again?

It seemed quite natural for bags and trunks to come away from Corunna Road, for bags and trunks are restless lodgers, only alive and happy upon porters' trolleys and train racks. But there is something different about sandwiches, cut upon a kitchen table that now lies deserted and alone: each little mouthful seems to contain a whisper of familiar sounds: the same kind of whisper that comes from the little stream of sand that falls from your shoe as you undress on the night you return once more to your bedroom at home.

As Dick ate his sandwich he thought how strange it was that no one, in all the life of the world, would ever know the feeling of an empty, curtained house, for the very entry of a human foot dispersed it.

The cork came out of the thermos flask with a *pop!* and a coil of steam floated up through the sunlight.

"Wonderful things!" murmured Mr. Stevens, and when Ernie turned from the window to ask how it kept hot, Mr. Stevens replied, "Ah, that's just it." He had never believed in misleading his children with a false pretence of knowledge, and to save further questions he got down his haversack and took out his collapsible aluminium cup.

They no longer talked in the subdued voices necessary to a crowded carriage: they talked now just as if they were in the dining-room at home. With the clear-out of passengers at Horsham a crisp, cool breeze had swept through the carriage and blown the stagnant air away. Mr. Stevens liked to feel it blowing on his face and through his hair. At home it would have been considered a draught, and the window hastily pulled up—but this was quite a different thing.

The country outside was growing lovelier than ever now. Here and there a late harvest was being gathered in, and people waved to them from lazy, mellow fields. They passed a garden riotous with great clumps of Michaelmas daisies, and a clover field splashed with the last red poppies. Now and then, through glades of trees they would glimpse the gables and turrets of a stately house, with spreading cedars and arches of velvet evergreen. Sometimes they saw men scything the lank autumn grass. There was no sadness hidden for the Stevenses in the faint streaks of gold that gleamed in the sunlit beech woods, for the first timid finger of autumn had always been the herald of the holiday.

They had come to the marshy flats of Pulborough when Mrs. Stevens rolled the sandwich paper in a little ball and threw it from the window, and it was here that they always had their first hint of the sea. The little Arun River wound through the flat meadows on its way to the distant coast: it looked as if it were tidal, for upon its muddy sides there clung a few flecks of foam. They came to the river several times in its winding course: each time it was broader, and bolder, and once they saw a seagull sitting on a white post by its bank.

They were all upon the alert now. The nearer they came to Bognor the more exciting were the familiar landmarks, and suddenly, almost together, Dick and Ernie cried, "There's the Castle!"

Mr. Stevens bent forward, gazed for a moment, and then said, "Yes. There it is!" Arundel Castle rose in the distance like a huge grey rock from a rippling sea of grass. The train curved a little, and gradually the Castle seemed to swell and rise. Then, as they drew nearer, the old red-roofed town began to cluster round it and a bank of misty trees gathered behind. They only lost sight of the Castle when the train slid quietly under the bridge into the station.

The stop at Arundel was another landmark of the journey. It marked the passing of restlessness and the coming of peace. There was no clatter of people and anxious cries: just the placid stillness of a country station that lies a little from the town, and the soft Sussex burr of passing voices. Everybody moved slower, and even the guard was conscious of the subtle change. At the other stations he had stood rigidly upon the platform—gazing along the train with eyes of strained anxiety, but now he was a different man. He leisurely crossed to a porter who was standing beside a crate of chickens and, after a word or two, playfully poked the handle of his flag through the bars of the crate. He laughed at the flutter that followed, and when Ernie, from the carriage window, joined in the laughter, the guard looked across at him and smiled. Imagine the guard smiling at you at Clapham Junction!

They lingered for a few moments in the cool shelter of Arundel. It was so quiet that they could hear people talking in nearby carriages, and the lowing of cattle from some trucks in a siding. Then, almost reluctantly the guard pulled out his watch, consulted it, and briskly waved his flag, as if to say, "Now then, back to work!"

The country was flatter now: to the casual eye not so fine as the country they had passed, and yet to the Stevenses every yard of it was pregnant with memories. They passed a white house in a winding lane which had scarcely got its roof on when they passed last year, but now there were curtains up, a dog in the porch, and a garden laid out with stripling trees. They saw with sorrow a place where last year a dense wood had been—where now there was a bare clearing spattered with stumps that shone yellow in the bracken, and a pile of logs beside a new-churned, muddy cart track.

"I suppose one day," said Dick, "there'll be houses—all the way from Clapham Junction to Bognor."

"Never!" said Mr. Stevens—"they'll do something about it before it gets as bad as that."

Ernie asked what they'd do, and Mr. Stevens, winking at the others, said they'd stop any more little boys like Ernie from coming into the world and crowding the grown-ups, and Mrs. Stevens, joining in the laughter, found herself laughing easily and happily for the first time in this weary day.

It was close upon one o'clock when they drew up at Ford Junction. The train had to be broken here, for one piece was going on to Portsmouth, and as they came to a standstill the naval man looked restlessly out of the window. After a moment he leant forward and spoke to the Stevenses for the first time.

"All right for Portsmouth?" he enquired—to which the Stevenses eagerly, and almost triumphantly, replied in chorus, "No!—Bognor!"

The naval man quickly snatched up his small black bag and dived for the door. Outside he turned and smiled.

"Thanks. Lucky I asked."

The Stevenses were silent for a moment or two after he had gone, all having risen slightly in their own estimations, but feeling at the same time the shy embarrassment that follows the doing of a good turn. It was Mr. Stevens who broke the silence.

"Lucky he asked when he did."

"Fancy 'im not finding out before!" cried Mrs. Stevens in dismay.

Ernie enquired what would have happened if the naval man hadn't asked them—and had gone on to Bognor.

"Found himself in the wrong place, of course!" replied Mr. Stevens.

"Would he be fined?" asked Ernie.

"Not if it was an accident. They'd let him catch the next train back."

Ernie's opinion of the Railway rose a little at this, although he could scarcely believe that they would show any such compassion: he could more readily imagine the naval man being clapped into prison.

Dick had noticed one or two people getting down to stretch their legs, and he and Mr. Stevens cautiously climbed out to do the same.

Ford Junction was a bleak, windswept place, although the air was fresh and bracing, almost like the sea. They were through the Downs now, which lay behind them like hazy banks of cloud. Ahead the country was flat; a windmill or two dotted the distant meadows and you could follow the course of the railway a long way by the curving sweep of the telegraph poles.

Mrs. Stevens watched anxiously as Dick and her husband strolled to and fro. Suddenly the train gave a slight jolt and she cried out, "Quick!"

"All right," said Mr. Stevens—"only the engine coming on," but he clambered in quite quickly, and looked a little pale. It certainly had seemed for a moment as if the train were off.

It was time to get things together when they left Ford Junction. They would be at Bognor now in a quarter of an hour. The flush of excitement that had swept the family when they gathered together after Horsham had spent itself now, and in place had come a quiet expectancy. They no longer pointed out to one another the landmarks as they passed: they sat in the corners with faces to the windows, waiting.

As they came to the crossing gates at Barnham, Mr. Stevens buttoned his haversack and got his hat down, while Mrs. Stevens tucked the thermos flask beneath her arm. There was a little trouble with Ernie's spade, which had got entangled in the rigging of his yacht, and by the time it was straightened out, Dick was leaning from the window, waiting to give the sign.

"Here we are!" he said—and turned to pick up his mackintosh and the tennis rackets.

The train began to slow down: houses closed round them, and they passed the gasometers that announced the end of their journey. They gently ran between the platforms. They were there.

A porter fatuously called out, "Bognor!"

CHAPTER TWELVE

If you were taken blindfold to Bognor Station, you would know directly your eyes were unbound that you were by the seaside.

For although, in common with all good seaside stations, the sea is carefully hidden from your view, you would notice that bleached, dry appearance about everything, and the freshness of the broad platforms, that look as if they are swept each day by a surging wave.

In London things grow dark with time: at the seaside things grow pale—(except of course the people). In London dirt and rubbish creeps into the corners and lies sluggishly there till someone comes and sweeps it away. At the seaside it runs into the corners, circles gaily round, and chases off again.

It would be poor showmanship on the part of Bognor to reveal the sea to you, in all its glory, directly you stepped from the train: it would be like raising the curtain at a theatre before you had finished the pleasure of wondering what was hidden behind. Bognor knows the tricks of the trade, and keeps the sea up its sleeve as long as it can. It teases you with winding streets and tantalising cul-de-sacs: it plays with you—leads you on and disappoints you again and again—till when at last you see something glittering between the houses, you feel absurdly surprised and quite grateful.

The train can go no farther than Bognor: if the brakes failed the engine would burst through the buffers and run down the main road into the sea. It is a perfect seaside station: the engine comes boldly into the town and stops with its heaving chest square to the coast. Later on another engine takes the train by its tail, and drags it, protesting, back to London.

There is consequently no great hurry for passengers to get out: there is time to linger a moment, and look under the seats. All that Mr. Stevens found was the pattern from his wife's magazine, but after poking it reflectively with his stick he decided that its value was negligible and left it where it lay. The family took up their hand luggage and went along quite leisurely to join the crowd round the luggage van.

They were just in time to see a trunk come out that made their mouths water: it was covered all over with romantic, highly coloured labels from hotels in every corner of the world—Venice, Cannes, Rome: Majestic Hotels, and Grand, and Metropole—some were partly torn off, just as if they did not matter, and across the trunk's weather-beaten chest was painted a broad blue line, in both directions—making it look like a huge registered letter. It was a pity that their own little trunk was made to follow immediately afterwards; it made a valiant attempt to look travel-stained, but nothing could disguise its tinny sound as it was pushed along the platform, and its little collection of uncoloured identical labels seemed to blink up at them with tears of apology. Why didn't Mrs. Huggett have a bright, imposing label with *Seaview* on it? It would cost very little, and bring a flutter down Corunna Road on their arrival home.

But it was neither the time nor place for jealousy. What did it matter after all? Bright labels smelt of vanity and conceit, and the fat, pale man who claimed the magnificent trunk hobbled on a stick, with a gouty leg. Mr. Stevens pondered on the curse of riches and turned to get a porter.

There were plenty standing by and Mr. Stevens, after inspecting them, selected one who looked like a lobster. The family put their hand baggage on his trolley beside the trunk and followed him down the platform to the barrier.

A group of people were waiting outside the gate, and one man specially caught the Stevenses' eyes. He was bareheaded, clad in khaki shorts, open shirt, and sweater rolled up to his elbows. His face, arms, and bare knees were burnt to the colour of oak, and the very sight of him made the Stevenses anxiously hurry their steps and push gently through the crowd. A moment later they saw another man, exactly the same, and they almost broke into a run.

A lanky youth with a hand barrow took charge of the luggage, and flattered the Stevenses considerably by knowing where Seaview was without having to be told. As the family stepped out into the broad station yard a boisterous breeze bit their faces and bent their heads.

"The sea'll be rough," said Mr. Stevens in as calm a voice as he could muster.

It was lunchtime, and the streets were fairly clear as they turned from Station Road into the main street that leads to the Arcade. On every side were things to welcome them, and things to urge them on: things that stirred the memory so vividly that it was hard to believe they'd last walked up this street a year ago. They passed the shop with the sand shoes hanging outside like clusters of bananas; and the shop with the fat rods of Bognor Rock candy—(with the name stamped right through, so that however much you sucked or broke it you still read *Bognor Rock* in its centre). Here was the shop with the glistening wet fish, sleeping amongst soft beds of freshly gathered seaweed—and the toy shop filled with spades and buckets, shrimping nets and yachts—with sheets of transfers, and indoor games to play in twilit evenings when your legs are too tired to move, and your mind is peaceful and drowsy from its drenching with fresh air; and your face burns, although your eyes are cool.

They passed the shop with the postcards in the revolving stand that would never push round—where you bought the little folding cards that let down a zigzag strip of pictures. The grocer, with his dull packets of sago and bottled gooseberries, cut a sorry figure amongst these glittering competitors.

Tin signs swung and rattled, and awnings flapped in gusts of intoxicating air. A few people passed, hurrying back to lunch: bronzed, laughing people with shockheads and wet bathing-dresses in their hands. More than once Mr. Stevens turned to his wife and said, "Come along, hurry up!"

Mary caught sight of her pale face in a mirror, and happily thought of the days when her skin would gradually blend with the sun-browned people round her, till she could stand beside them without shame.

At the corner where they turned into the High Street a gust of wind caught Mr. Stevens's hat and took it bounding along on its brim towards the Arcade. He shouted, "Hi!" dodged round a bicycle, and chased the hat to the opposite pavement. "No place for hats!" he called out as he returned to the laughing family. "It won't see Bognor again— till the day we go!"

There was a big grocer-shop a little farther on, and Mrs. Stevens lingered by its window.

"What about a nice bag of crisps!" she exclaimed—"to go with lunch!"

"Oh—come on!" shouted Mr. Stevens. "Can't hang about!—Mrs. Huggett's bound to have some boiled. Get them another time," he added more softly—and they hurried on again. Quite apart from anything else, Mr. Stevens was anxious to get to their rooms so that they could dress themselves properly for the seaside. They were horribly out of place amongst this bareheaded, open-necked, bare-legged crowd. Mr. Stevens wanted to get rid of his hat, take off his tie, open the collar of his cricket shirt, and get his white canvas shoes on.

It spoke well for the artful designers of Bognor that the Stevenses could never remember which turning it was that gave them their first sight of the sea.

"It's this one, I'm certain," said Dick, as they approached one of the many roads that led off from the High Street. But it wasn't. A square house smugly blocked their sight at the far end. Mr. Stevens laughed, and Dick said:

"It must be the next, then."

"I tell you it's the *third* turning," persisted Mr. Stevens.

"But Clarence Road twists halfway down!"

"It doesn't!"

"What'll you bet!"

But before any odds were laid, Dick and Ernie broke into a run and raced each other to the next corner. Mr. Stevens saw them stop, and stand quite still, side by side, looking down the road, shading their eyes from the sun. Then Dick turned and called out, "Guess!"

But the others had reached the corner now. For a moment they all stood together, gazing down a road that ended as no roads end—except at the sea. Between the last houses just a square blue space—a low line of railings and a narrow strip of silver light.

"What did I say!" cried Dick, "I knew—" but his words were blown away by a boisterous gust of wind that came racing up from the sea to greet them.

They stayed no longer than to allow the view to softly penetrate their thoughts, for the crisp air was sharpening their appetites, and they had all seen the letter Mrs. Stevens had written, asking Mrs. Huggett to get five thick mutton chops for lunch. They turned back into the High Street—three more turnings, then St. Matthews Road!

St. Matthews Road grew up in Bognor fifty years ago—at a time when people still had a lingering weakness for ornamental stone knobs and porticos. Tall, narrow houses tightly lined each side, their backs of brownish-yellow brick, their fronts faced with pale-grey plaster. A few stone steps led from the iron railings to the front doors, and half-buried basement windows looked appealingly up as if the weight of the houses above had been too much for them.

Seaview was halfway down on the right-hand side—very like the other houses, except that it was Seaview. Tall and very narrow in comparison with its height, with a few cracks in its plaster front and a few bare places where fragments of plaster had broken away. The lower windows were long, but the top floor ones were shorter, as if the builder had allowed too much room below and had had to crowd the upper ones as best he could. A pot of geraniums in a wire basket hung from the portico, and SEAVIEW was painted in bold black letters on the right-hand pillar.

Mrs. Huggett kept rigidly to the etiquette of the seaside landlady, for although she always came to see them off at the end of the holiday, and waved to them from the gate till they had turned the corner, she was very careful to be out of view when the family arrived. They never saw her, like lesser landladies, watching from the front sitting-room between the curtains, and there was always a decent, dignified pause before she answered the door.

Mr. Stevens knocked: Mrs. Stevens beside him. Ernie crowded onto the top step beside his parents, but Dick stood on the lower step, and Mary just inside the gate. Mr. Stevens watched through the frosted glass, with its old, familiar pattern of stars. He could see the red-white-and-blue window at the far end of the passage, which looked out onto the garden, and after a pause a figure came from the kitchen and approached the door.

Then the door opened, and Mrs. Huggett stood smiling before them.

There was no false convention in her greeting. "Well—this *is* nice to see you all again—and *such* a day!"

"Isn't it grand!" said Mr. Stevens—"Just the sort we want!"

"It is indeed!—and Mrs. Stevens!—and Ernie—what a big boy!"

There was a shade of diffidence in her greeting of Dick and Mary: no loss of warmth, but just a touch of shyness. She had known this trim young girl since the day she had come in her mother's arms—and this shy, rather good-looking boy had first come in a little one-piece woolly, when he was six months old—and touched her cheek with a podgy hand, and laughed.

They were grown up now—and Mrs. Huggett instinctively felt that shade of finer colour that comes only to children of good parents. She knew that if ever she lost the Stevenses it would be because Dick and Mary would like a bigger place, with more fun, and other young people in it. Her fear of this brought neither suspicion nor hostility: only a little greater effort to make things nice for them—a little extra care to give them all the comfort she could manage.

"I expect you're all famished!" she exclaimed.

"We *are* a bit peckish," laughed Mr. Stevens—"but I can smell something good!"

"It's all ready! Now, do come in!—Is the luggage coming along?— Why, here it comes now!"

The lanky youth had just turned the corner and was trundling the baggage down the road.

"Don't you worry!" she said—"I'll see to it. You just go along in and have a nice rest."

They passed into the narrow, high-ceilinged passage, with its old familiar picture of Kitchener's return from the Boer War. They hung their coats on their rickety old friend the hall stand and went into the sitting-room.

The table was spread for lunch: a loaf on a wooden platter, a dish of butter, and the cruet. A vase of fresh but rather hungry-looking roses stood in the centre of the cloth, with knives and forks and neatly folded serviettes before each place.

They stood together and silently looked round.

All just the same: the old gilt clock under its glass cover on the mantelpiece—the two china figures—the two old shrunken leather armchairs—the picture of Grace Darling rowing to the lighthouse, and the dark oil painting of the heap of fruit. A strange feeling, touched with sadness, comes over you as you enter a room that whispers the memories of a chain of years. On the mantelpiece, a little out of place, and looking as if it had recently been put there, stood the little card, glued with a design of seashells, that Mary had made when eight years old, and given to Mrs. Huggett, with many blushes and downcast glances, on the morning they went away. As Mrs. Stevens glanced round the room she could almost see Dick as a little boy, standing on the old leather sofa, trying to see if anyone were looking out of the windows of the distant lighthouse that Grace Darling was struggling to reach. She remembered the great thunderstorm, years ago, when the room had grown so dark that they had had to light the gas.

It was quite a long time before any of them spoke. Through the slightly open window they could hear the tinkle of a gramophone in a house on the other side of the road. It was cool and dark; a little musty in this sitting-room after the dazzling freshness of the open air. Mary sat down stiffly upon a chair by the table, Mrs. Stevens blew her nose with a hard little sound, and Mr. Stevens wandered to the window, thrust his hands into his pockets, then drew them out and clasped them behind his back.

Finally he turned, and said rather lamely—"Well, here we are."

They had reached the strange, disturbing little moment that comes in every holiday: the moment when suddenly the tense excitement of the journey collapses and fizzles out, and you are left, vaguely wondering what you are going to do, and how you are going to start. With a touch of panic you wonder whether the holiday, after all, is only a dull anti-climax to the journey.

You are, in fact, groping to change gear: you are running for a moment in neutral emptiness between the whizzing low gear of the journey and the soft, slowly turning high gear of the holiday—and in this moment of aimless uncontrol you are liable to fidget with your hands, shift about, and say, like Mr. Stevens, rather lamely—"Well—here we are."

It was Ernie who unconsciously set the holiday moving forward again—by suddenly turning and making for the door.

"Just time to run down to the sea—before lunch!"

Mr. Stevens leapt at the chance to disperse this stagnant moment of inaction. He turned briskly from the window and good-humouredly clapped Ernie on the shoulder.

"No you don't! After lunch—it's just coming in! Then we'll all go down together."

They were off again now! A bumping on the steps and heavy breathing in the hall took Mr. Stevens and Dick to help the porter with the luggage. The trunk was dragged upstairs and left on the landing, while the family claimed their hand luggage and piled it on the floor beside the hall stand, ready to take up to their bedrooms after lunch.

Into this general bustle a new figure came: a squat, thickset little woman nearing middle age; red-haired and rather shabby. She came up the kitchen stairs and edged her way along the wall of the passage with a steaming dish of chops and a tureen of gravy. She waited, unobserved, in the dark corner by the stairs while the trunk was pulled down the passage, and it was only when at last she had room to emerge that Mr. Stevens saw her, and jovially shouted out:

"Why, here's Molly!—How are you, Molly?"

It was an awkward meeting for Molly—pent in against the wall, with a heavy dish in each hand. She flushed, lowered her head, then looked up with a little laugh.

"I'm very well, thank you, Mr. Stevens."

"*That's* all right!"

Molly had been a young girl when the Stevenses first came to Seaview, and Mr. Stevens still treated her rather as a child. Her plainness was almost an affliction: her large flat face, her podgy nose and pale, freckled skin would have been repulsive without the unfailing good nature and patience that turned physical ugliness into a trivial thing. A stout little dynamo of energy worked her squat, stunted body and drove it unceasingly from dawn till night. She never seemed to tire and she never lost her cheerful smile.

In normal times she shared the work of Seaview with her mistress; in busy times she seemed to do it all. For when the work outran Mrs.

Huggett's frail capacity, she dulled the acuteness of her responsibility by running about, smoothing down curled carpet edges with her foot and standing irresolutely in the passages, wondering what to do first, while Molly moved from bedroom to bedroom with no sound but her laboured breathing and the swish of her grubby house cloth.

She only seemed to leave the house once a week: every Sunday afternoon at two. The Stevenses wondered where she went as she bustled out of the gate and up St. Matthews Road with a set, purposeful face and quick, springy steps—always in the long green coat that nearly reached her heels, with the pale strip of fur round its collar. The house seemed suddenly empty when she had gone, it drifted stagnantly until she returned promptly at nine.

The chops looked magnificent, lying round the slopes of a mound of mashed potatoes, and the family eagerly followed them into the sitting-room and took their places at the table.

With a sweep of her arms Molly had the dish before Mrs. Stevens and the tureen of gravy by her elbow. In a moment she was gone, and the family were alone for their first meal at the seaside.

CHAPTER THIRTEEN

"It was a terrible cold spell we 'ad in June—just after Whitsun. People out in overcoats. Did you 'ave it like that in London?"

"Yes," said Mr. Stevens, "we did have a cold spell in June."

"Well, I thought you must have," exclaimed Mrs. Huggett, as if she had waited weeks to know. "It seemed general. My July people said they had it, too, at Sidcup."

"Did they?"

"Yes. And of course they were very glad it was June, and not July."

"Yes, it was a lucky thing, that."

There was a slight pause. Lunch was over, except for the cheese that Mrs. Huggett had just brought in. Mr. Stevens was thinking what a very happy place the world would be if people could lead each other quietly aside, and gently but firmly tell each other the little things they unconsciously do that irritate and annoy their fellows.

If only he could have taken Mrs. Huggett aside! If only he could quietly say to her: "Mrs. Huggett. You have an annoying habit of lingering at the door and talking as we are finishing our lunch. I know you do it because you feel it is right, the friendly thing to do—but we hate it: it makes us all terribly uncomfortable: we like to eat alone. Just one word and a smile is enough. We'll have plenty of friendly chats at other times—but don't—*don't* linger at the door!"

And Mrs. Huggett would have said, "Thank God for telling me,

Mr. Stevens! You don't know how I dread trying to think of friendly things to say—with all you sitting round, looking at me. I've just got to do it because it's the right thing to do—but I think for hours of things to say—and then it all goes when the time comes, and I can't get away. The door seems to grip my hand and hold me—I struggle to find a pleasant word that'll let me easily out of the room—but it never seems to come. . . ."

"Yes," said Mr. Stevens. "It must have been general—if they had it at Sidcup, too."

"Yes."

Mr. Stevens watched Mrs. Huggett's hand sliding slowly up and down the side of the door.

"We 'ad a fête down 'ere last month. Pity it wasn't now, so that you could 'ave seen it."

"Why, yes, that was a pity."

"For the 'ospital. There was little boys and girls dressed up as animals. A scream, it was."

"Pity we missed it."

The silence that followed was broken by a muffled sound; half pop, half thud. Ernie had hoped to release the top button of his knickers in the midst of someone's words, but his timing was bad. Rice pudding always gave a blown-out feeling.

"Yes," said Mrs. Huggett—in answer to Mr. Stevens rather than to Ernie's button—"you *would* have enjoyed it."

There was only one way to help her to escape—and Mr. Stevens resorted to it. He rose briskly from the table, clapped his hands together, and breezily said, "Ah well—there's bound to be plenty of other fun. Now I'm going to get these stuffy London clothes off!"

Mrs. Huggett's face lit up: her hand fell from the door to her side— the ordeal was over. It was only necessary to linger and talk like this on the first day when her people came.

"Oh, you'll find plenty of fun, you bet!—and what's more you know how to enjoy it!" She realised with a glow of pleasure that she had found the ideal words to help her from the room—she gripped the door firmly, smiled round it, and disappeared. The door closed, and Mr. Stevens sat down with a sigh to finish his cheese.

The family was not annoyed with Mrs. Huggett: they sympathised with her, and when she had escaped they rejoiced rather at the relief she had secured than at their own pleasure in being alone again.

"What I think is this," said Mr. Stevens—"A walk down to the sea and a saunter along the front right away now. Then straight back here to unpack the trunk and get everything in its place before tea. Then we shan't have anything more to worry us, and the trunk'll be right off our minds once and for all."

The family agreed. They nearly always respected the sound sense that lay behind their father's plans—and the idea of going for a short stroll by the sea before unpacking was an excellent one.

Unpacking is an irritating business at the best of times—but to wander about with rolled socks and underclothes, to hang coats in stuffy cupboards and lay things out in drawers before you have even smelt the sea is a stupid punishment to inflict upon yourself.

Yet there is a devilish temptation to leave the job undone: to dive into the trunk as and when you want things, day by day: to allow it to become a bogey that haunts and disturbs your rest. The longer you leave it the untidier it becomes, and the harder it gets to find what you want.

The best plan of all was to go down to the sea—stay there just long enough to roll it round the tongue—then come back and dive into the trunk with the tingle of salt in the nostrils, and the promise of a long unhurried stroll in the evening. Unpacking can be made a pleasure, done in Mr. Stevens's way.

They trooped out of the sitting-room, gathered their baggage by the hall stand, and ran upstairs. It was only necessary to raise the lid of the trunk to get the rubber shoes out, for they had purposely been packed on top.

A few minutes in their rooms, and they gathered once more by the gate—a very different party to the one that came in an hour before. But for their pale faces you would never have known they had only just arrived. Mr. Stevens had pulled off his tie and triumphantly thrown it into the cupboard, he had opened his collar and slipped the stud into his waistcoat pocket; he had tossed his hat contemptuously onto the top of the wardrobe and slipped on his white rubber-soled shoes. All in a couple of minutes—but what a difference it made!—how light, and young he felt! He could quite easily have leapt into the air and cracked his heels together.

Dick and Mary had thrown aside their hats and got their canvas shoes on, while Ernie, after some opposition from his mother, had peeled off his stockings, and now sat waiting on the steps, bare-legged and bright-eyed.

Only Mrs. Stevens remained dressed as she had come: she had tried without success to think of something she could do to make herself look different—but neither she nor the family could think of anything for her to put on or take off: one year she had tried white sand shoes but they made her insteps ache, and she was never comfortable without her hat. Mr. Stevens had suggested a yellow jumper, and although she had thought it a good idea, she never seemed to think of getting it. As the family set off down St. Matthews Road, she still carried her right arm close to her side: it was hard to forget at once that she no longer had the thermos flask to carry.

There must have been a distant strain of sailor blood in the Stevenses' veins: a strain from some old merchant adventurer who knew the sea meant freedom and power—who loved it for its giant freshness, its gentleness, and strength: a tough old strain that tightened the throats of his distant children and held them silent as they gripped the rails of the promenade.

For Mr. Stevens and his children loved the sea in all its moods: they loved it when it lay quietly at its ebb, murmuring in its sleep—

and when it awoke, and came rippling over the sands: at its full on a peaceful evening, lazily slapping at the shingle. But best of all they loved it as it was today—roaring wildly round the groins, booming and sighing in the cavernous places beneath the pier, crashing against the seawall and showering them with spray. Every one of its thousand calls had a different note—every sound was wild with freedom.

Wave after wave lashed the concrete wall, to sink back with a moan of pain as though clutched and drawn down by a great sea monster. The countless little pebbles lay motionless, petrified as each wave came crashing on them—then they would leap to life and go madly chasing it with a sound like the far distant cheering of a mighty crowd.

Now and then the Stevenses turned their faces from the gale and gulped in great lungsful as it passed them: it rushed right through them and made their skins feel smooth and cool against their clothes.

They stood a long time without speaking, each dying wave drawing the aching little shadows of ledger figures from Mr. Stevens's eyes. Once or twice he closed the lids so that his eyes could float in the cool spaces that were forming round them. His nostrils were cool—his throat was cool, yet strangely his body glowed with warmth.

At last they turned. One by one they let go of the promenade rail, and walked on in straggling single file, their eyes still out towards the sea.

It was Dick who broke the silence. They had gone a few yards when he paused, and looked round.

"Where's Mum?" he said—and suddenly they became aware that Mrs. Stevens was no longer with them.

She had certainly crossed the road with them to the promenade, and they remembered her lingering with them as they first gripped the rails to watch the sea, but now she was gone, and they looked about them in anxiety.

People were passing to and fro, a steady, streaming crowd, bending to the wind—but Mrs. Stevens had vanished as though from the face of the earth.

"Where's she gone?" said Mr. Stevens, hiding his anxiety under a note of irritation. He could not possibly remember how long they had stood there, looking at the sea: it might have been five minutes—it might have been half an hour. He had no idea how long his wife had been missing. Light and frail though she was, he could scarcely believe that she had been blown away. Even if she had been, someone would surely have called out as she blew by. She could not possibly have fallen into the sea—and yet . . . he looked quickly away with a sudden feeling of coldness. A wave, some distance out—as if in answer to his fears—had raised a little object on its crest—held it up for him to see, then drawn it back into its sullen grey trough. A little dark object, about the size of a hat, vaguely blue in colour.

He turned his eyes away—his heart was thudding madly—and a dull feeling of sickness came over him. He pretended to search the crowd—"What hat did she have on?" he said to Mary in a dry voice.

"The little blue one."

In all of them was growing a panic of remorse. They had been impatient with her all day: they had hurried her—bustled her—they had not said a word about the sandwiches being nice—and then at last—when they should have drawn her into the joy of the holiday, they had looked at her critically because she was so badly dressed for the sea, and almost ignored her—letting her walk behind as they had excitedly made for the promenade. They had been beastly to her all day.

Supposing that suddenly an impulse had come to her—supposing suddenly—in a wave of loneliness and shame, she had resolved to be a drag on them no longer—and quietly crept away to drown her unwanted little body in the sea—

Mary suddenly felt as if she could cry. They were surrounded by hostile strangers—smugly enjoying themselves—neither knowing nor caring where her mother was. Supposing she had stepped back absentmindedly into the road?—she might be miles away now—a mangled little body—bumping along the tarred roads under a charabanc. Ernie nearly cried out: "I'll put my stockings on—I will—I will—if you come back, Mum!"

What could they do? thought Mr. Stevens. He had heard of people disappearing like this: sometimes they were never heard of again. Supposing it really had been her hat—out there: suddenly he felt a loathing—a furious hatred for the sea. The sun had passed beneath a thick grey cloud and the waves looked sullen, and angry, and diabolically sinister. He supposed they would have to go to the police station. A dreadful little notice marked *Missing* would appear on the board outside—*slight build, blue serge coat and skirt—black leather shoes with buttons—hair turning grey*— What was he thinking!—he could not think!—he must take hold of himself! His thoughts became dull, and dreamlike. They would cancel the holiday, he supposed—and return to Corunna Road. No! he couldn't bear the house any longer—if she had gone—there would be morbid whispering over fences—and that empty bedroom.—No! He'd never go back!—but—but what could they do! where—

"There she is," said Dick. "Look."

He was pointing to a small glass shelter—a few yards away, opposite to where they had been standing against the rails. There she was—standing behind one of its recesses—gazing vacantly across the road. An occasional eddy of wind was stirring the grey wisps of hair that escaped from beneath her hat. Scarcely a minute had passed since they had missed her—but it seemed an eternity.

"What's she doing there?" said Mr. Stevens gruffly.

He stepped across to the shelter—"Come on! we've been looking for you!"

She gave a start—turned round and smiled. "I never saw you go on. I came over here to get out of the wind."

"Thought you were drowned," said Mr. Stevens. His body was tingling, and suddenly he felt hungry for his tea. He took her by the arm, and as he led her away, glanced down at her little buttoned shoes.

"Feet all right?"

"Yes, thanks—lovely."

They were protected when they got to leeward of the pier, and the gale, no longer occupying all their thoughts, gave them leisure to look round.

The sun had returned, and Bognor seethed with restless, bustling energy. The high tide had driven the holidaymakers with deck chairs into a solid mass upon the narrow strip of shingle that remained above the sea. Soon the tide would turn, and as the sea gave back the gleaming sands, the people would gradually spread out again. At present they were as tightly packed on their strip of beach as the blight upon Mr. Stevens's beans.

Other, less adventurous people crowded the seats on the promenade, or walked to and fro in clusters, trios, pairs—and, very occasionally, alone. Fat women, thin women, tall men, short men, big children, tiny children— what a crowd!—all dressed in the defiant splendour of their whims.

You cannot help feeling a little out of it when first you mingle with them. Lots of them have probably only just arrived, like you—and yet you feel you are the only novices amongst crowds of sun-baked veterans. It is far better not to take buckets and spades, yachts, or even kites on your first day's visit to the sands. It is best simply to stroll along, to get your sea legs, and look at things.

Sometimes a party went by, boldly strung arm in arm across the promenade, with one or two, who had been squeezed out, vainly trying to push in from behind. Some were in pairs: young people, very close together: old couples walked solidly side by side, with a narrow strip of unvarying daylight between them. Now and then a family passed who had got on each other's nerves, walking slowly, strung out singly, a few yards behind each other, with the leader (usually the father) waiting impatiently now and then for the others to catch up. But then the others would go slower and wait till he went on, and readjust the distance once again. There were rows of strangers packed on seats together—

squashed as close as lovers, yet all staring aloofly in front of them at the sea. Babies fell down and upset buckets of slimy seaweed: old men tottered by in morning coats, panama hats, and white shoes.

It was fun to guess the relationships of the groups that passed: mothers and fathers were easy—and married daughters, but aunts were a little more difficult to spot, and sometimes there would be a grown-up in a group who refused to fit in with any scheme of family relationship—possibly an uncle by marriage—or an old friend—possibly a bore, who, being lonely, was allowed to join a party on payment of a little more than his normal share.

But over all lay a spirit of joyful, unrestrained freedom. There were no servants—no masters: no clerks—no managers—just men and women whose common profession was Holidaymaker. Round pegs resting sore places that had chafed against the sides of tight square holes—and pegs that had altered their shape, through softness or sheer willpower, so that they felt no aching places on their sides.

No one cared who their fellows were: if they smiled, you smiled—if they spoke, you spoke—spoke of the things around you and not of the things that lay behind or ahead. It might have been a tax collector who helped up that child and gathered its seaweed back into its bucket: the father who thanked him might have been in the courts a week ago, because he could not pay. But who cares?—at the sea.

They were opposite the old hotel that lies back from the promenade with a sweep of green turf before it, and Mr. Stevens paused, and looked at his watch.

"Now then!" he said. "The trunk!"

"Oh, bother the trunk!" cried Mary.

"I know—but let's get it over and done with."

Past the pier again they struck the full force of the wind: they leant against it, and sometimes it suddenly gave and nearly pitched them forward on the path. When they turned into the calm of St. Matthews Road, they paused, looked at one another, and laughed.

"What a gale!"

"Ought to be some wrecks."

"Yes. We must look out for rockets tonight."

The sitting-room seemed smaller when they returned to it—perhaps because they all felt so much bigger: they felt hollow and light inside, and although their faces were smooth and cool, their bodies were tingling with warmth.

CHAPTER FOURTEEN

Mr. and Mrs. Stevens had the big double room that looked out over the portico. It had electric light, and a large, dull-green carpet that was clammy, in places, to the bare feet. But it was a good spacious room, with a long window through which Molly sometimes climbed to water the geraniums over the front door.

The children were on the third floor: Dick and Ernie sharing a room that overlooked the back garden, and Mary in a small room to herself. They only had gas in their rooms, for when, some years ago, electric light had been installed at Seaview the Huggetts had not thought fit to extend the expense beyond the second floor. It was a great pity they had not had the foresight to lay it on throughout the house.

Molly, the maid, slept somewhere still higher up—in a kind of attic bedroom, to which even the gas had not penetrated, and there was another room up there where Mrs. Huggett slept when the house was full. Beyond the rooms held by the Stevenses there were two more bedrooms and a sitting-room on the second floor, and a small bedroom on the third, but these had not been fully occupied for some years past— during September.

There were only two other people in Seaview this year, and both had been before. There was Mr. Burnup, who occupied the other third-floor bedroom and had been there regularly for five or six years. The Stevenses understood him to be a barber, who came down to relieve the pressure at a local saloon during the rush months. He left very early after a hurried breakfast in his room, and generally returned after the Stevenses had gone to bed.

He was a quiet, respectable young fellow whom Mr. Stevens had only once met (at the gate) one Sunday afternoon. He had stood back, smiled, and with a gallant gesture said, "After you." Mr. Stevens had done the same, and after a pause they had both got wedged in the gate together. Beyond this one meeting the Stevenses would scarcely have known that Mr. Burnup was in the house except for the chink of his breakfast tray going up in the early morning, and the click of the gate just before eight o'clock, when the Stevenses were still luxuriously in bed.

The other visitor was a schoolmistress named Miss Kennedy Armstrong. She had been at Seaview last year and was again occupying the side room on the second floor which was specially converted into a bed-sitting room. Mrs. Huggett told the Stevenses, in a hushed voice, that Miss Kennedy Armstrong was a lady, and very well connected, but there was something slightly mysterious about her all the same. She moved softly and slowly, and although the Stevenses saw her almost every day, they had never seen her face. She was always just disappearing into her bedroom, or just disappearing into the bathroom—or moving silently away from them down the passage. She disappeared sometimes so mysteriously that Ernie thought she must have a way of vanishing through the wall.

Even when on one or two occasions they had seen her going out, they never saw her face as they watched from their sitting-room window. She would walk deliberately to the gate, open and shut it with her eyes cast dreamily ahead, and up St. Matthews Road without a glance to either side.

Mrs. Huggett told them that she was a quiet, kind lady, very shy— and rather sad to look at.

To all intents and purposes, therefore, the house belonged entirely to the Stevenses during their stay. They paid £3 10s. od. per week, including service and cooking, with the small extra of a shilling per week for cruet. In any case you would have thought the house belonged to them as they unpacked the trunk on the landing. Mr. Stevens stood over it in his shirtsleeves and called the owner's name to each article as he pulled it out. There was a great deal of running to and fro—up and down the stairs to the children's rooms, and more than once Mrs. Stevens had to call out, "Ssh!"

Dick and Mary had brought their own small bags, so most of the stuff in the trunk belonged to the others. The bathing towels, bathing dresses, and shoes were on top: then the woolen coats, sweaters, and scarves (wise precautions against a cold spell). Below these lay the spare underwear, and socks, while farther down came smaller articles—the fruit salts—the camera, the clothes brush, and Mrs. Stevens's slippers, containing in one her toothpaste and in the other (carefully wrapped in a handkerchief) her blue-tinted sunglasses. Last of all, flat on the bottom of the trunk, lay the kite.

Mr. Stevens stood up—wiped his brow and gently lowered the lid. There was just room for the trunk under the landing table, where stood the stuffed fish in its glass case. Mrs. Stevens had been running backwards and forwards, packing her own and her husband's things in the wide drawer of the wardrobe. Ernie's spare clothes were stored in a special corner of the chest of drawers, for there was only room for Dick's things in the room above. She laid out her toilet requisites on one side of the large, marble-topped washstand, and her husband's on the other.

The sitting-room clock was thinly announcing half past four as they filed downstairs with the job completed—more than ever appreciating the wisdom and firmness of Mr. Stevens in getting it finished before tea. Tea was always a big meal with the Stevenses when they were together. On ordinary days, of course, Ernie and Mrs. Stevens had it together, as none of the others got back till nearly seven, but on Saturdays and Sundays there was generally a cake, besides the bread and butter, marmalade, and jam. It was a big meal during the holiday, too—for supper at eight o'clock was quite a light affair.

There was a fresh, uncut cottage loaf on a wooden platter—a large, generous slab of butter (yellower than the kind they had at home), and the jam and marmalade stood in their original, attractively labelled jars. The Stevenses liked it better this way: they did not like it put out in small glass dishes, and they preferred to cut their own bread rather than having it brought in in slices. It was these little things, remembered by Mrs. Huggett from other years, and done by her without having to be told, that made up for other little things that could not be helped.

For Dick and Mary, going once more into their old, familiar little bedrooms, had wondered with sinking hearts why they had never noticed in other years how dreadfully dingy and terribly poor they were.

Was it a growing desire for better things?—or had these little rooms suddenly shrunk—become darker—and almost squalid? They looked at the little blackened gas brackets that would give them a feeble, fan-shaped glimmer of naked yellow light—that would go up in a thin blue squeak if turned too high: the battered chests of drawers: the rickety little wash-hand stands whose thin legs seemed to totter under the heavy imitation-marble tops: the ponderous china jugs and basins: the cracked toothbrush jars, and the poor little white-grey soap dishes—they were clean only in a way that suggested a grim battle fought by Mrs. Huggett against encroaching age and dirt that prowled more boldly every year.

The lace curtains that used once to be looped up gracefully by narrow cords, were now drawn tightly back by broad stiff bands of imitation blue silk—broad to hide as much as possible of the curtains' frayed edges and holes. The bedclothes were clean, but so tightly stretched, through smallness, over their iron frames, that creeping between them looked almost an impossible task.

The window catches were bent upwards, blackened and coated with verdigris: in Mary's room a narrow strip of the linoleum had been cut from the edge nearest the door, leaving a strip of the bare boards, and the released linoleum had been used to lay under the holes that had worn in the centre.

For many years it had been Mrs. Huggett's ambition and pride to renew something every spring, and this year the old yellow patterned linoleum on the stairs had been replaced by a brightly coloured carpet that glared with cheap insolence at the old, faded banisters. Dick and Mary dared not think of the scraping and saving that must have gone to the purchase of this carpet, yet its cheap, gaudy colours seemed to jeer and scoff at Mrs. Huggett, and turn the nobility of her striving into something paltry and almost comic.

It was the only new thing in the house this year, and its glaring vulgarity seemed somehow to have made the old things around it lose all heart, and give up trying.

And yet all through the Stevenses strove to keep these things beneath their notice. They knew the silent battle that Mrs. Huggett fought against the attractive places that called themselves residential hotels—that hung out fairy lights and blared their radio music across the roads. They knew how return-day charabanc trips, and bungalows were sapping the strength from Mrs. Huggett's heart—and they knew that Mrs. Huggett never breathed a word of complaint; that she carried on, thin-lipped and determined—scrubbing—polishing—cooking— smiling—knowing deep down in her heart that an appearance of cheerfulness, ease, and prosperity was the last frail cord that held her people to her house.

So the Stevenses came breezing hungrily into the little sitting-room—with its faint, sour atmosphere, as if apples had been stored in it: they laughed when Mrs. Huggett smilingly congratulated them on getting their unpacking done so quick—and sat down to good thick slices of bread and jam—striving to keep their eyes off the rubber spout that had appeared on the old pink teapot since the holiday last year.

And after all—what did these trivial things matter? They were out of the house all day, and only returned to eat and sleep. Even if the beds were a little lumpy, the sheets were clean, and what did a few lumps matter to a body that was drugged by fresh air, washed by the sea, and tingling from the sun and wind? Even if sometimes the gravy was a bit greasy and the rice pudding rather pale, they had at least the comfort and pleasure of Mrs. Huggett's scrupulous honesty. Not even the smallest and most unobtrusive chop had ever disappeared from their loin of mutton, which of all joints is the easiest for a dishonest landlady to tamper with—and never once, in all their years at Seaview, had they found cause to secretly mark the level of their lime juice.

It is stupid to allow a fretting irritation over a crack in a plate, if the plate is clean, and Mr. Stevens no more than glanced at his before covering it with a slice of bread, which in turn he covered with a good thick layer of jam.

There was one harsh note during tea, for Ernie suggested taking the yacht down afterwards to try a sail.

Dick said: "What! in *this* sea! It'll be smashed to bits"—at which a shade of approval passed over Mr. Stevens's face. The unpleasant incident of the morning was still very near and Mr. Stevens wanted his feelings about the yacht to be completely unprejudiced when it was given its first trial of the year. He was glad that Dick had squashed the idea, instead of leaving it to him: if he had done it himself it would have looked as if he had a spiteful rankling, and actually he had no such thoughts, either of the yacht or of Ernie.

He merely wanted to avoid talking about the yacht—or even seeing it, until at least a night had passed.

Ernie made a feeble attempt to defend the seaworthiness of the boat and then to everyone's relief let the matter drop.

The walk after tea, on the day of arrival, is perhaps the hardest of all things in the holiday to really enjoy. The fatigue of the journey is beginning to tell, and you are still a little shy and embarrassed amongst the other holidaymakers, who look so thoroughly at home. It would be running before you could walk if you went down on the sands to try a game of cricket on your first evening—or even a little tentative cross-touch, and Mr. Stevens never employed the telescope until his interest in the things around him had begun to wear off.

The first fine inspiration of seeing the sea has passed, and the soles of your feet are beginning to grow a little sore after their first spell in canvas shoes.

But this is not to say that the walk after tea was dull; it is only to say that it was the solitary occasion in the holiday when the Stevenses found just a little exertion necessary to enjoy themselves.

Mr. Stevens was very quiet as they walked from Seaview down to the front: he was struggling to make a final decision upon a matter that had been occupying all their minds for some time past.

There are two kinds of bathing hut at Bognor: the ordinary little hut, shaped like a large sentry box, and the better kind, much roomier—with a small balcony in front. Five years ago, when Mr. Stevens had made ten pounds in overtime during the winter, they had boldly taken a hut with a balcony. It had been a splendid luxury: there was something very stimulating to the self-respect in sitting on the balcony—cool and aloof from the sweating crowd on the beach. They had not all been able to sit on it at once, but it was a place to hang about round, to lean against—to come in and out of—and even when it was not Mr. Stevens's turn to sit on it, he could always knock his pipe out against the rails.

But it cost a good deal more than the small huts, and they had dropped it the following year, and every year since—until a month or two ago. Dick and Mary were both paying a little to the holiday now, and the question was whether to spend the extra upon luxuries of a smaller type, or go all-out, and have a hut with a balcony.

It would cost fifteen shillings more each week, and a lot could be done with thirty shillings: two eggs for breakfast; an extra charabanc ride; shrimp paste for tea; and possibly an extra theatre—but good as these things were, they did not give quite the same feeling as sitting on your own private balcony.

They had threshed it out from every point of view and each time it had ended by someone saying, "Let's decide later on."

But there was no "later on" now: the booking of the bathing hut was always done on their first evening walk—and although no one spoke, each knew what was in the others' minds.

So when Mr. Stevens paused, and said, "What about it?" they knew exactly what he meant. They had turned onto the promenade and were within a stone's throw of the little office where they arranged the booking of the huts.

"You mean—a balcony or not?" asked Mary.

"Yes."

They had stopped now. It was no use going any farther till a decision had been made, and they lingered by the rails, with only the pier between them and the bathing hut office.

The front was not so crowded now, but people were just beginning to straggle back from tea. The wind had fallen to a gentle breeze and the sea had given back to the children a strip of shining sand. Here and there you could trace the remnants of proud castles that the sea had washed to ruins in the afternoon: smooth humps from which the battlements had gone, and shallow silted moats.

None of the family seemed willing to commit themselves. They knew they were on the verge of a decision that might make or mar the holiday. If the hut were taken, and it were not a success, they would be haunted at every corner by things that could have been done with the money, and yet if they did not take it they might be haunted just as horribly by the smug faces of people who had got one: they would sneak by, shamefaced—feeling poor, and common—

It was Dick who decided them at last. He had been standing very still, gazing out to sea, and suddenly he turned—

"Why not?—It's only once a year."

"Yes—let's!" cried Mary—and in a second the whole family knew beyond doubt that there was only one course to take.

Ernie was delighted. His yacht could stand proudly in the hut all night—like a boat in dry dock; it would no longer be a futile toy in the cupboard beneath the stairs at Seaview.

Mrs. Stevens did not really mind, one way or another: she did not bathe, so would not feel the greater comfort of a larger hut, and in her heart of hearts she preferred to sit in her deck chair on the beach, with the seething life around her. She did not have people about her during her daily work at home, like the others did, and on holiday it came as a change to be amongst the crowd—

"All right," said Mr. Stevens—"Carried unanimously."

Their heads were higher as they walked to the office beyond the pier. They felt that sudden excited happiness—that sudden pride that comes to cautious people when on rare occasions they boldly step beyond the ranks of those around them. They no longer viewed the passing holidaymakers with shyness and envy: their decision had suddenly raised them far beyond the mass, and they looked with pity, and a trace of contempt, at a fat, bald man who emerged from a small, common, cheap little hut without a balcony.

But suddenly their hopes came crashing round their ears, for when Mr. Stevens went to the window of the office, they saw the man shake his head. They had forgotten how few large huts there were in comparison with the vast crowd of people on holiday at this time of the year. That headshake meant they were all taken, and suddenly they knew the holiday would be hateful without one: they felt furiously angry with themselves for not having decided a month ago and written to reserve one—amazed at themselves for ever having thought the holiday possible without it. They looked at the hateful, sordid little huts on the beach below them—dark and cramped—then at the distant line of shining roofs below the fringe of trees: at the gleaming little balconies dotted with good-looking people—they *must* have one!—they'd bribe somebody to go out—they'd give up every penny—sell something precious if only they could get one!

They saw Mr. Stevens turn with a look of dismay, then they saw his mouth set grimly as suddenly he turned back and talked rapidly and earnestly to the man behind the opening. They saw the man listening, gazing over his glasses with a shade of impatience and a faint touch of suspicion. They saw him doubtfully turn the pages of a book before him and Mr. Stevens almost breaking his neck to see what was written in it.

They watched breathlessly as the man looked up to say something that made Mr. Stevens nod vigorously half a dozen times—they saw him dive into his breast pocket, pull out his wallet, and extract a note with trembling fingers; and suddenly the spirits of the children rose till their feet seemed scarcely on the ground. *Something* had happened!—something good—for Mr. Stevens turned and gave them a radiant smile.

They crowded round him as he came away from the office.

"What happened?"

"Wasn't there one?"

"Could you?"

Mr. Stevens thought of saying "Guess!"—but it would have been rather a silly thing to do.

"It's going to be all right," he said. "They're all taken now—booked right up—there's been an awful rush on them this year—but some people are going out of one on Tuesday—it'll be free Tuesday evening—and we can get the key at seven o'clock."

"Oh, splendid!"

"Which is it?"

"'The Cuddy': the third from the end."

"Let's go and look at it!"

They walked along the front and had a look from the back: the names were mostly over the doors, and they could only judge from the position which was theirs. Then they got down onto the beach and walked slowly along in front.

"There it is—'The Cuddy'!" said Mary in a hushed voice.

"That's right—that's the one."

It was better than the others, they decided. It looked fresher, and the balcony was a bit higher than its neighbour's.

"We save five shillings by going in on Tuesday," said Mr. Stevens— "We'll do an extra charabanc ride—to Arundel."

It could not possibly have worked out better: they would not only save five shillings, but they would enjoy the hut much more through having to wait for it. It was theirs now, to all intents and purposes: they would stroll by and look at it tomorrow: they would picture themselves grouped round it—sitting on the balcony, hanging their bathing dresses over the rails—and then on Tuesday night they would unlock the door and go in: they would sit just inside and look out over the moonlit sea, and the soft music of the band would come to them faintly on the wind.

They strolled a long way down the beach: past Aldwick—nearly to Pagham. They hung a tin over a stick, and a shout went up as Mrs. Stevens hit it with a big stone and knocked it down with her first try. Ernie rolled over and slapped his feet together in the air, and when Mr. Stevens patted his wife on the back she knew that her lucky shot was the omen of a golden holiday.

Towards sunset they strolled quietly back, their shadows stretching out before them, a long way over the sands.

CHAPTER FIFTEEN

Ernie fell asleep during supper, although he feebly but indignantly denied it.

They had pressed beef, the cold rice pudding, bread and butter, and cheese, not much more than a snack after their big tea. Mr. Stevens's crate of dinner ale had arrived, and during the walk a time-honoured luxury had been installed in the corner of the fireplace.

This was a large stone jar of draught ginger beer: delicious on hot days and warming on chilly evenings, giving too an extraordinary sense of satisfaction when you turned on the tap and drew off a glass without having to pay anything—or put a penny in a slot.

They had decided to give up lime juice this year, because they rather thought it was the lime juice that had given them stomachaches last September. They resolved to have two jars of the ginger beer instead, which would just last the fortnight if they regulated their consumption by unscrewing the top now and then, and measuring the depth with a piece of stick. When Ernie was a smaller and more evil boy, he used to contrive (when no one was in the room) to screw his head round in such a way as to fill his mouth when he turned the tap on. But he no longer did this: growing experience had taught him that the amount he got in his mouth never compensated for the wastage and discomfort down his neck when he could not swallow quick enough to cope with the supply.

They had to turn the light on before they had finished their supper. In the last days of the holiday they would have to turn it on before they even sat down, but one of the pleasures of a September holiday lies in that final hour of darkness, beneath the lights of the promenade, and the blaze of the pier.

In full summer the sunlight can become well-nigh a burden towards the end of a long day in the open air. You almost resent the pale glow that clings stubbornly to the western sky right up till the time you go to bed: you draw the curtains, but even then your bedroom is not altogether dark.

But the encroaching nights of September add a new scene to the panorama of the day: the music from the band seems to flow from a crown of sparkling jewels: the murmur of voices and the soft padding of rubber shoes along the promenade—the fairy lights of the pleasure grounds and the glitter of the stars in the sea bring a soft romance to the blaring spirits of the day.

The Stevenses had their own ideas about spending this final hour before bed, when the heat of the day had been drawn inland and a cool breeze came up from the sea to fan their burning faces.

Dick and Mary generally went together for a stroll. They never planned this walk in advance, but purposely went without aim, allowing themselves to be guided by the impulse and thoughts that came to them, yard by yard. Sometimes they simply wandered up and down the promenade: sometimes they sat and listened to the band or had a cup of coffee in a gay-lit café. If the tide were out they would go down onto the sands and stroll among vague lumps of rock and seaweed which glittered balefully from the lights of the pier. It was dark and mysterious down there. At other times they would strike inland through the town and walk a long way down the narrow country lanes.

When supper was over, Mary got her coat and Dick went up to put his sweater on underneath his blazer.

"Shan't be long this evening," said Mary. "Good night, Mum— I expect you'll be gone to bed."

"I expect I shall," said Mrs. Stevens, quite fervently.

No one wanted to do much more on this first day: they had all been strung up, on the go, since seven in the morning, and the talk towards the end of supper had been drowned in yawns. Ernie was unashamedly asleep now, and Mrs. Stevens was very near the same condition.

"I'll go right up," she said. "Come on, Ernie. Bedtime."

"I'll be up in half an hour myself," said Mr. Stevens, pulling out his pipe. Ernie was asleep almost as his head dropped onto the pillow in the little room on the second floor. Mrs. Stevens mechanically tucked him up, turned the gas to a glimmer, and went down to the big double bedroom below. It was an effort even to undress, and she crept into the broad, lumpy bed with a contented sigh.

They always laid a bolster down the middle of this bed—not so much through motives of aloofness, but because the bed sloped rather steeply down to the centre, and she and her husband were inclined to get badly heaped up together in the valley. The bolster had been a good idea, and served as a support for both of them.

She was too tired to worry about the lumps tonight, but tomorrow, when she got into bed, she would work the lumps carefully about with her hands and feet, and get them into the right positions. For luckily the lumps in the bed at Seaview were the kind that could be moved about and kneaded into different shapes, and if properly disposed could be made into an additional comfort.

In the sitting-room below, Mr. Stevens was slowly filling his pipe. He, too, had plans for the after-supper hour: plans that took him down quiet paths of his own. There was nothing secret about them, for they were perfectly straight and aboveboard, but he never discussed them with the family, and the family never asked him questions. He liked some little time of the day entirely to himself, and in some respects this final hour was the most looked forward to of all.

The Clarendon Arms stood a little inland from the sea, in a corner position that looked out to one side upon the busy High Street and to the other upon a by-lane that was narrow and old-fashioned. It was an ornate, but comfortable place: a little above the ordinary public house, and yet not quite an hotel. The saloon bar was on the side that faced the by-lane; there were plenty of inviting plush seats, and a very happy hour could be spent in the big window alcove with a pipe and a glass of beer. The room was sufficiently near the High Street to catch the life and bustle of the town, but just far enough away to have the restfulness of a backwater. The heavy, tobacco-laden air was soothing to braced-up, invigorated nerves, and closing time just coincided with Mr. Stevens's desire for bed.

For many years it had been his custom to stroll down after supper to the Clarendon Arms; going by St. Matthews Road and the High Street, returning along the promenade for a last breath of sea air before turning in.

It had never been his habit at home to go into the saloon bar of the Unicorn, or any other local public house—not because he disapproved, but simply because he preferred his glass of beer with his supper, and, after a day in the office, liked a walk in the open air before going to bed.

But on holiday it is the reversing of normal habits that does one so much good. Most years he struck up acquaintance with one or two men of the same kind as his own: men who had no desire to addle themselves with perpetual "rounds" of drinks, but who sensibly preferred to buy their own and be beholden to no one: who liked a peaceful chat, with now and then a friendly, good-humoured argument. Sometimes the same friends would turn up for another year, or even two or three, but the circle was always a little different, and Mr. Stevens alone came regularly every season.

Last September had been particularly pleasant at the Clarendon Arms. Four of them had come together on the very first evening of Mr. Stevens's arrival. As if ordained for friendship by some higher power, they had drifted into the alcove corner with tankards of beer and greeted each other quietly and naturally, like lifelong friends. Never before had Mr. Stevens so resented the barman's monotonous "Time, gentlemen, please!"—every evening it cut into the alcove corner so crudely that all four would look up sharply at the clock and say, "Surely not—yet!"

There had been Mr. Montagu, the solicitor—one of the nicest men Mr. Stevens had ever known, who had left a lingering memory of friendship throughout the year.

He must have been a swell in private life, and Mr. Stevens had never met a man like this before, on such easy, friendly terms. He had asked Mr. Stevens, on the last evening, to go down and visit him at his home near Godalming, and his card showed *The Manor House* as his address. He had renewed the invitation by letter a few weeks afterwards, but a subconscious instinct had fought and beaten Mr. Stevens's excited desire to go.

It was not the instinct of the man who "knows his place" in the world—nor was the desire to go inflamed by snobbery, for never in his life had Mr. Stevens felt such pleasure and pride when slowly he had discovered his mental kinship with Mr. Montagu.

But it was this very sympathy, this easy interchange of thought that made Mr. Stevens decline the invitation. Another man would have gone out of sheer desire to tell his friends, but no such thought crossed Mr. Stevens's mind. He wrote three drafts of his reply before he was satisfied: he finally dismissed business ties and eagerly grasped Ernie's chicken-pox that had arrived most opportunely to form the basis of an excuse.

Then he put Mr. Montagu's letter away in his private drawer, to wait the time when he could go to The Manor House, and return the invitation without shame. For his meeting with Mr. Montagu had shown him that he had within him the stuff that takes men to Manor Houses—directly the chance came their way. How it would come, and when, he did not know, but something within him had whispered all the year that he would not end his life in Corunna Road. The whisper had begun with his friendship with Mr. Montagu.

Then there had been Mr. Sanderson, the cheery old commercial traveller, of very different kidney to Mr. Bennett who had pestered them on their way to the station in the morning—and the fourth had been the very jolly, very fat, very bald man who asked that the others should simply call him "Joe." No four men could have come by such widely divergent paths to the smooth road of good fellowship in the alcove seat at the Clarendon Arms.

Mr. Stevens hoped one or two of them would be there again: it was too much to expect them all, but even so he might possibly find some very interesting new friends to take their places.

He went into the passage and drew his stout walking stick from the hall stand. He paused at the gate to relight his pipe, and set off down St. Matthews Road in the gathering darkness. For a long time he had wondered if Mr. Montagu would be there again: sometimes hoping he would be—sometimes hoping he would not. . . .

Then of course there was Rosie: she was almost certain to be there, and he smiled slowly to himself as he turned into the bright-lit High Street.

Rosie, the barmaid, drew him in a way that was almost frightening in its contrast to the magnetism of Mr. Montagu—yet she did draw him, and he liked it—quite a lot.

It was scarcely a physical attraction, for Rosie was very large, and no longer really young—yet he could not deny, in fact he had no wish to deny that she appealed to the baser instincts of his nature. He was satisfied that his baser instincts were not of the same baseness as those of other types of men, so he felt neither fear nor shame in his feelings towards Rosie.

She thrilled him, and gave him a sense of happiness because somehow she brought him into pulsing touch with reckless instincts without the humiliation and danger of indulging them. Her bold blue eyes seemed to hold beneath them a tremendous, almost fearful knowledge of everything by which hot blood linked man and woman; they were the eyes of an adventuress: generous, unscrupulous—remorseless, yet he could look into their impudent depths and laugh, because she made him conscious of his own quiet strength.

She had a lovely sidelong way of looking at him with pouting lips that made him feel like a high-spirited, mischievous little boy who was telling fibs to pull her leg. He liked her because, when he spoke frankly and simply, with exaggerated innocence, she would not believe a word he said, and her eyes would answer: "Don't you play that stuff across me!—*I* know you!—You're one of the quiet ones, you are: the quiet, dangerous ones. *You* talking about a holiday with your wife and kids!— I like that!—Now, come on—tell me who she *really* is!"

She gave him a pleasant sensation of feeling wicked, and he liked the way she artfully suggested that a trail of wrecked homes lay behind him. He would pick up his pint of beer and walk away with a look that said: "Oh, well, Rosie—it's no good trying to keep anything from *you*!"

It made him slightly uneasy to think of the scorn her eyes would hold if she knew the kind of man he really was, and yet he felt her scorn would only come to hide an admiration for him: the admiration that all women of her sort must secretly hold for a simple straightforward man with nothing to hide.

Yes. He liked Rosie. She added a lot to the holiday. It was exciting, too, that the family knew nothing about it.

He had passed the Clarendon Arms with the family on their way from the station, but he had scarcely glanced at it then. It was dull and uninteresting by daylight, and even Rosie, he thought, would not look quite the same as she did in the gay illumination of the evening.

But as he now drew near, he suddenly and quite unexpectedly decided that he would not go in tonight. He was feeling very tired, and the mental stress of the day had made him dull.

With Rosie, and more especially with any new friends he was to meet, a very great deal depended upon his first appearance. A flash of wit amongst new acquaintances upon first meeting them would establish him as a humourist for the whole fortnight, but he was certain he would think of nothing clever this evening. He might, through his tiredness, be labelled a bore, and be shunned every subsequent evening by the men he would most like to join.

It was not worth risking: he would just walk by, and look to make certain that Rosie was still there.

The lower part of the saloon windows was frosted, and the people sitting at the tables would be hidden from view, but the place where Rosie stood was a little raised, and if she were there he would be able to see her quite easily from the other side of the road.

He crossed over a little before he reached the door lest he should come face to face with one of the old crowd and be drawn inside. He stopped directly opposite, but had to wait a moment until a bus moved off, and cleared his view.

Everything was as bright and as cheerful as ever: shadows of customers moved to and fro among the silhouettes of glasses of beer. Yes, there was Rosie!—he just caught sight of her between the heads of two men standing at the bar. Rosie—in a bright-blue blouse, with the magnificent bar fittings rising behind her, each ornamental compartment packed with bottles, cigarettes, and glasses, with little mirrors behind each shelf and a superb cash register picked out in red and gold—so fine and scintillating that he half expected to see the whole thing slowly start to revolve and grind out music.

He watched her for a little while, talking to a man with a bald head: then she moved off down the counter to serve another customer and disappeared from his line of vision.

He had felt practically certain she would be there: she had become almost part of the Clarendon Arms, and he could not imagine it without her. The sight of her through the window removed the last anxiety of the day, and now all he wanted was bed.

He crossed the road, walked through the arcade, past the theatre, and down to the front where the sea was murmuring a long way out across the sands. The band was playing, but he did not pause beyond dropping into step with its lively march. As he drew away from it the crowd grew thinner; the fresh night air braced his body, but seemed to drowse his mind. The moon had not risen yet, and it was very dark in St. Matthews Road after the glare of the promenade. Well as he knew Seaview, he stopped once before reaching it, thinking he had arrived.

Mary's coat was hanging in the hall, so the children had returned, and gone up to bed. He went into the sitting-room, took a little ale from the bottle he had opened for supper, and sat down for a few minutes to finish his pipe.

A few holidaymakers passed now and then, laughing and talking, but as their voices died away it grew so quiet that he could catch a far-away, bell-like ripple in his ears.

This time last evening he had been finishing his pipe in the sitting-room at home. It was very hard to believe. It seemed a week—a month ago. He thought over the things that had passed since the morning, and marvelled how so much could happen in the span of a day. Ruislip the porter, Mr. Bennett the traveller, the people in the train—they seemed like misty figures of a half-forgotten past. Even Corunna Road seemed a distant place of memory.

But he knew that time only moved evenly upon the hands of clocks: to men it can linger and almost stop dead, race on, leap chasms, and linger again. He knew, with a little sadness, that it always made up its distance in the end. Today it had travelled gropingly, like an engine in a fog, but now, with each passing hour of the holiday it would gather speed, and the days would flash by like little wayside stations. In a fortnight he would be sitting in this room on the last evening, thinking how the first night of the holiday seemed like yesterday—full of regrets at wasted time. . . .

But it was foolish to think of it like that: far better think in hours and minutes—hundreds of hours—thousands of minutes, each packed tightly with interests of its own.

It was splendid about the weather. The forecasts said it would hold.

Something told him that the holiday would be the best they had ever had.

He finished his beer, laid his pipe on the mantelpiece, and tidied a few things in the room. Then he went to the door and turned out the light.

The moon had risen now, and was shining at its full through the red part of the coloured window in the passage. It made him think of it as he had seen it last night—shining over the Crystal Palace at home, and as he went quietly up to bed, he thought of the silent little house in Corunna Road, with the stair boards cracking out into the quietness now and then, as they shrunk with the coolness that followed the day.

CHAPTER SIXTEEN

Two fishermen, in a solitary little dinghy, were the only folk to see the sunrise over Bognor on Sunday's dawn: two little dark-jerseyed figures—jerking their boat through the twilight over a smooth, bottle-green sea. They ran their dinghy up the beach with a crunch that echoed down the silent coast, and pulled it clear of the ebbing tide. They slung their baskets over their shoulders and went up onto the deserted promenade, their breath hanging in little frosty clouds.

Bognor lay slumbering from its long, hectic day in Saturday's sun: not a window on the whole front so much as blinked a curtained eye as the fishermen passed with the soft clump of their gum boots. The pier stood black and gaunt behind them, like the skeleton of a gigantic monster with its front legs planted in the sea. The stars were fading, and far away down the coast—half from the sea and half from the sloping arm of the downs, came a very delicate amber glow, smudged with tiny streaks of cloud.

Fishermen are not by nature cynical, or the lips of these two solitary men might have curled at the sight of the sleeping rows of pale-grey houses: they might have thought how, in two hours' time when the day was already upon the verge of maturity, people on every side would be leaping from bed, drawing the blinds, and shouting delightedly for others to come and look, as if the sun had leapt from the sea precisely as they scrambled from their beds.

A solitary policeman leant against the rails of the promenade, and watched the tip of the sun rise over the faraway black shoulder of Beachy Head, where the rocks came down to meet the sea. Presently he slowly turned his back, as if satisfied that it wasn't going to do any harm. He yawned, and pulled out his watch.

The sea began to sparkle, and tiny figures in overalls began to move along the promenade: a little army of housemaids come to clear away the litter and put the place tidy for the people who still slept upstairs.

The turf round the bandstand was speckled with crumpled programmes, empty cigarette boxes, and sweet-bags, and the gathering light revealed a lady's umbrella beneath one of the chairs. A few bottles lay on the higher parts of the beach—a few banana skins, and an occasional half-eaten bun.

The little overalled figures moved quietly to and fro, gathering the refuse and bumping it into carts. One found the umbrella, looked at it suspiciously, and put it to one side. He pointed it out to a mate, and after a pause, said: "Somebody's umbrella."

A man in uniform came briskly down the promenade, jingling some keys: he unlocked a door and went onto the pier.

A milk cart turned onto the front and went rattling along towards the bandstand. The noise made people turn upon their backs, sigh contentedly, and fall asleep upon their other sides.

The sun gathered strength, and drove away the little clouds that threatened it. A seaplane droned along the coastline; transparent as a tiny fish in the clear sky. Bognor slowly stirred, and rubbed its eyes.

It was close upon eight o'clock when Mr. Stevens did exactly what the fishermen—had they been cynics—would have expected him to do. His sleep had gradually grown lighter, and in passing moments of vague consciousness something had told him that the morning was brilliantly fine. At last he stirred more definitely and opened his eyes. Mrs. Stevens was still asleep in the undulating territory beyond the bolster: he did not wake her, but rolled softly from the bed, tiptoed to the window, and let the blind up.

The road was blazing in the morning sun. He gently pushed up the window and leant out in his pyjamas to drink the air. His face was still burning from the buffeting wind of yesterday, and the sun today would carry his skin a step forward to the splendid, mellow brown that would be the envy of the office on his return. He was pleasantly hungry: he wanted to sing, but restrained himself and turned briskly to go to the bathroom for his shave.

He had a slight shock when he stepped forward, for as he bent his legs a sharp, stiff pain darted up the backs of them.

He had paused, and lowered his hand to the brass bed knob before he remembered. It was the canvas shoes, of course. He had forgotten for the moment: he had the same stiffness last year. The shoes had no heels, and the first walk in them always stretched the muscles at the backs of the legs. It was only a little healthy stiffness that would soon wear off, but the first feel of it had certainly frightened him— rheumatism and lumbago had shot through his mind: cruel things to develop on a holiday. He went into the bathroom very relieved.

People were already passing on their way to the sea as the family sat down to breakfast: a girl in the house opposite was sunning herself on the stone balustrade, swinging a long sunburnt leg to and fro. At several windows they could see the heads of people gathered round tables at their morning meal.

There is a feeling about the beginning of a cloudless day on holiday; an excited rustling as if invisible hands were rubbing together in antici- pation over the rooftops: a droning murmur that seems to come from crowds of people collecting together buckets and spades, magazines and bath towels: all trying to assure themselves that there is no need to hurry—but trying frantically all the same to free themselves from the petty little things that hold them within the shade of their rooms.

Every now and then a party would emerge from one of the houses in St. Matthews Road: one by one they would come out of the gate and gather in a group outside—generally someone would run back to get something, and then they would move off in a bunch towards the promenade, the ones in front almost walking backwards to keep in with the talk.

Directly breakfast was over, the Stevenses dispersed to get ready themselves. They did not believe in starting too early, for the best of mornings can be made too long. It was arranged, as usual, that Mrs. Stevens should go up into the town and do the ordering, while the rest went straight down to the sands. Mrs. Stevens would join them towards eleven o'clock, with a bag of buns, after they had had their bathe.

Mrs. Huggett came up the basement stairs with an armful of cricket stumps and a small anaemic bat. They had been left by some other people a year or two ago, and the Stevenses had free use of them during the holiday. It saved the trouble of bringing their own—and any old bat would do for the sands.

"Got the ball?" said Mr. Stevens.

"Here it is," cried Ernie.

"Come on, then!"

Mrs. Huggett watched them go with a smile; then she went into the sitting-room, gathered the breakfast things on a tray, and went down the basement stairs.

Mrs. Stevens turned in the opposite direction from the rest of the family and had gone a little distance when Mr. Stevens called out quietly, "Don't forget your port."

She hesitated—half smiled—and said, "Shall I?"

"Of course," said Mr. Stevens.

"It's an awful expense."

"No it isn't. You get it," and with a nod he turned and followed the others towards the beach.

"You'll be in the same old place?" cried back Mrs. Stevens.

"Yes. The same place—in front of the bandstand."

Mrs. Stevens was swinging her bag almost girlishly as she walked the other way. Some years ago she had not been very well; the doctor had said she was a little run-down: her blood was thin and a pick-me-up would do her good. He recommended a bottle of port.

She had felt recklessly abandoned when she had ordered it from the grocer, but was proud afterwards to find how well she could take it. A glass after supper—a delicious warmth sinking down the throat—a feeling afterwards as if achievement were throbbing in her veins. It was a lovely, lingering experience, and since then Mr. Stevens had insisted upon her having a bottle every holiday. While the others were out upon their evening stroll she would sit back in the armchair and have her glass, clear in conscience because it was medicine; enjoying it because it was port. She took such tiny sips that none ever seemed to reach her lower regions: it seemed to sink warmly into her throat and tongue.

She paused where St. Matthews Road joined the High Street and pulled her shopping list from her bag—*bottle of pickles: sugar: pound of rice: two lbs. neck of mutton: onions*—it gave her pleasure to read down the list and decide which shops she would go to first. She would not be able to get everything today, being Sunday, but several shops opened for an hour or two in the morning. She enjoyed shopping, and although she spent far longer doing it than most women, she never minded people cutting in in front of her, even when sometimes they grossly abused the rules of shopping etiquette.

She liked to linger in the shops, and shopping at the seaside was better than at home because the people were jollier and much more good-tempered. More than once she had been so startled by someone stepping back and saying, "After you," that she had completely forgotten what she wanted, and could only shrink back and murmur, "No!—you!—you next!"

A splendid stretch of sand greeted the others as they reached the promenade and they were glad they had struck the tides so well. It was far better to have the sands in the morning and do their lazing in the afternoon. People were streaming down every road to the front now; hurrying in all directions to get their favourite places, while others, who had arrived, were opening deck chairs and getting them purposely entangled to make their friends laugh. Here and there children had begun their castles—some working silently and alone upon battlements that no one must tamper with, others forming syndicates and working together at vast Norman strongholds with turrets and moats. A tired-looking man in a neckerchief was designing an ornate palace with a view to gain, calling plaintively to people to throw pennies into a sodden upturned cap. A sturdy little team of donkeys had already begun work and had a waiting list of riders. Everywhere people were settling down to the day with a certainty of unclouded sunshine.

The Stevenses paid little heed to the things surrounding them: they kept steadily along the promenade towards the western bandstand before which, on a strip of sand, they yearly staked their claim.

But as they approached it, Mary had an inspiration.

"What about trying to find a good place in front of The Cuddy? It'll be much better for when we get the hut on Tuesday."

"Yes. That would be rather an idea," agreed Mr. Stevens—wondering why he had not thought of it himself.

They passed the old place by a hundred yards or so, and coming to The Cuddy, found the space before it almost clear. The sands of Bognor are very conveniently divided by breakwaters into miniature playing grounds, the wooden barriers stopping the ball and saving a lot of running about. They serve also to confine each party within a definite area, preventing selfish people from taking too much room.

At first they were a little uneasy in front of The Cuddy—feeling they had taken possession of something before their time; but looking at the hut from the corners of their eyes they saw only an old lady and gentleman dozing upon its balcony, and soon got to take no further notice of them. They were sorry for the two old people, because their time was so nearly up—and were glad they didn't know that the people settling on the sands in front of them would be in their places on Tuesday night: they might have resented it, and had their last days spoilt—but of course, they could not possibly know.

Dick put the stumps under the breakwater and Mary piled the bathing dresses and towels together on a dry sunny heap of shingle. They simply played catch to begin with—to get their eyes in, standing round in a wide circle and throwing to one another, sometimes skiers, sometimes straight and low. Now and then Mr. Stevens, instead of throwing the ball on in the usual way, would jerk it quickly back the way it came to make the others keep on the alert, and sometimes when one of the children missed it, and had to chase it down the sands towards the sea, Mr. Stevens would rest his hands on his hips, and gaze round.

He felt radiantly happy: as young and as light as a schoolboy. Everything around him was so unutterably fresh and clean: bronzed faces—open shirts—bare legs—blue sky. Now and then the speedboat would drone by in a haze of spray: dark little rowing boats wandered lazily to and fro: a kite rustled overhead and once or twice swooped playfully down at them, to rise again and frighten the drifting gulls. A man with a small boy hurried down to the sea with a shrimping net.

Mr. Stevens took a deep draught of the air—pressing out his lower ribs to let the ozone penetrate to the lowest part of his lungs: these were the moments that justified every pain in life—every disappointment— every humiliation.

"Look out!" shouted Dick—and Mr. Stevens was just in time to gather the ball as it came soaring down. He twisted himself backwards and flung it high into the air: very pleased to see an old gentleman stop and watch its flight with admiration. He had always been good at throwing, and had lost nothing of his youthful skill.

After a while they pitched the stumps, and Mr. Stevens and Ernie played Dick and Mary. Dick was the best batsman, and made a lot of runs before he recklessly threw his wicket away. He hit Mr. Stevens's slow bowling all over the sands, but Mr. Stevens was more pleased than annoyed, and just a little proud. For Dick seemed suddenly bigger, and altogether different in his open cricket shirt and rolled-up sleeves: a merry schoolboy again, like he was this time last year.

For Mr. Stevens had felt uneasy about Dick—ever since he left school and started work, just on a year ago. He had found the boy a first-rate job with Maplethorpe's, the wholesale stationers off Ludgate Hill: he had pulled strings to get the job, and was very proud. Dick, too, had seemed delighted at the prospect of taking his place in the world and earning his own money. But after a little while a change seemed to have taken place in the boy. He had never been a boisterous fellow— but was always full of quiet good fun, and very good at games at Belvedere College. In his last year he had been Captain of the Cricket Team and Vice-Captain of the Football, and Mr. Barbour, the headmaster, had told Mr. Stevens that Dick was a very good influence at the school and was sorry to lose him. He was good at running, too, and had won the Victor Ludorum at the Sports. It had been a proud year for Mr. and Mrs. Stevens.

He'd started work with Maplethorpe's soon after the holiday last year, and Mr. Stevens had gone with him on the first day. Even then Dick had seemed a little changed. His stiff bowler hat did not sit easily on his wiry brown hair and his new blue serge city suit seemed rather tight, and made him look narrow and thin. In his schooldays he had always knocked about in an old loose blazer and baggy flannel trousers.

And then, in the weeks that followed one another into the winter, Mr. Stevens knew that his son was terribly unhappy—and was fighting very bravely to keep it hidden.

He was uneasy lest Dick had done something foolish at the office, but discreet enquiries proved that the boy was very painstaking and conscientious, though a little slow and sometimes absent-minded.

But gradually he appeared to settle down, and did not seem quite so unhappy. But he was very quiet, and often looked tired and pale.

His hours were long, of course—from nine till often well past six, and he was kept too late on Saturdays to play in any games. He'd entered for the Old Boys' race in the School Sports, and used to go for a run before supper in the dusk of the spring evenings. He had seemed better then, and more like his old self when he sat down to supper in his old school blazer after a rubdown. But he had not done very well in the race.

He did not seem keen on keeping up his old school friends, though sometimes, if he were home early enough on a Saturday, he would change into flannels and go down to the school field to watch a game. But even this he gradually let drop. He read quietly in the evenings, and sometimes went for long walks alone.

But now he was his old self again—driving the ball with strong, well-timed strokes, and dashing quickly between the wickets. When his hair blew over his eyes he tossed his head back in the way that had always, for some reason, made Mr. Stevens proud of him. There was a glow in his cheeks, his eyes were clear, and he was laughing all the time, only looking grim as he brought the bat down to drive the ball.

The innings was over, and they sprawled themselves in a line on a little bank of sloping shingle. The sun was blazing down from a perfect sky, but a cool sea breeze kept fanning the heat from their faces. From all round them came the drowsy, happy sounds of the seaside.

None of them spoke for a long time—then Dick's voice came—almost as if he were talking in a dream.

"I say. Isn't this *grand*?"

His arms were stretched out across the shingle, and a tiny stream of pebbles was running between the fingers of his hands.

CHAPTER SEVENTEEN

People who like arranging things in advance can make themselves a dreadful nuisance on a holiday—but it largely depends on the way they go about it.

Mr. Stevens liked arranging things, but he knew that it had to be done very carefully, and never pressed his plans against general opposition.

It was not that he enjoyed bossing people and running the show: it was simply that he knew how necessary it was to have some general scheme if every hour of the holiday was to be properly enjoyed.

One of his best ideas was to have a set programme for every other day—leaving the days between absolutely free for everyone to do what they liked. It was a wise plan from several points of view. The little squabbles you so often saw happening on the sands in the afternoons were not always due to the heat: more often they came from people being too much together, and getting on each other's nerves.

So Mr. Stevens did all he could to encourage the family to split up on the days when no plans were set. It added tremendously to the pleasure of mealtimes, because each returned with different experiences to describe, and new ideas to exchange. They did not, of course, all go out singly, for neither Ernie nor Mrs. Stevens really enjoyed being on their own—but they did definitely break up, and were no longer doing things together as a family.

It suited Mr. Stevens very well, too—for one thing he always enjoyed on the holiday was a long day's walk alone.

He liked to have a good think—a good, connected think without anything to disturb him, and almost always he came back from this lonely walk with a firmer grip upon himself, and renewed confidence for the future.

It was on Tuesday evening that he announced his intention for the following day. He was sitting with Mrs. Stevens on the little balcony of The Cuddy, which an hour previously had at last become theirs. Dick and Ernie, on the sands below them, were fighting the sea back from the castle of the afternoon, feverishly strengthening its walls as each wave drove more hungrily against it. Dick was now in a pair of old grey football shorts and an open shirt, and as Mr. and Mrs. Stevens watched him they marvelled at the change that had taken place in him in so short a time. The dark rings had gone from under his eyes and his cheeks had a ruddy glow: they were very glad the holiday was doing him such wonderful good. About Ernie they did not so much care: he was always as strong and lusty as a young colt, and no holiday could add much to his shiny red face. Mary, lost in the pages of a magazine, was sitting on the beach nearby—her back against a breakwater.

The sun was fading, and the sands were beginning to gather a golden darkness. People were collecting on the promenade for the band, and a drowsy evening peace had fallen over the coast.

"I'll be off for the walk tomorrow," said Mr. Stevens, "that'll be all right, won't it?"

Mrs. Stevens said she hoped it would not rain—for during the afternoon the sun had clouded for the first time since they'd arrived.

"I think it'll clear," said Mr. Stevens, glancing round the sky. "I'll take my mack, though. Don't want to be caught—right up on those downs."

It did, indeed, rain that night, but it was the kind of rain they welcomed on a holiday. As they walked back to their supper, big heat-drops began to spot the dusty pavement, and patter into the parched leaves like grit falling on dry paper. It grew heavier after dark, and they lay comfortably in bed, listening to the steady fall, welcoming every drop that came down while it did not matter to them. But the morning was clear and fine once more, with everything cool and fresh for another sunlit day.

Mr. Stevens came down in his stout walking boots, put his map on the hall stand before he went in to breakfast, and soon after nine was striding up to the place where the buses started for the villages in the downs.

The buses had made it possible for Mr. Stevens to go farther afield than he used to in the early days, for they took him right up into the country marked in deep brown on his map. He got a front seat on top of the Petworth bus without any trouble, and after a few early halts they began to run steadily and leave the houses behind.

The rain had braced the country for its fight against the autumn, and given a cool, earthy smell to the banks beside the road. As the fresh morning air blew in his face and fluttered in his ears, Mr. Stevens thought of his last ride on a bus, five days ago—returning home from his last evening's work before the holiday. He thought of the traffic blocks; the medley of motorhorns and the incessantly flowing shop windows. What a difference now!

Sometimes they slowed down to squeeze by a swollen hay cart that would draw in for them and streak the tall hedgerow with its hay: now and then it was all the driver could do to get round sharp twists in the narrow lanes, and Mr. Stevens was left wondering what they would have done if they had met a vehicle coming in the opposite direction. Only once or twice they stopped, to pick up a country woman with a basket and a child—or a nondescript, solitary man.

Mr. Stevens sat with his map on his knees, because he liked to pick out the distant church spires and name the clustering houses. He liked to find on the map the streams they would cross before they came in sight. He was fond of maps, and had learnt to read them well. They appealed to him because of the endless pleasure they offered his imagination, the picture they showed him of a country built up through the romantic casualness of centuries.

Broad, metalled roads still turned and twisted to follow the aimless tracks of prehistoric wanderers. They still made detours round long-dried marshes, and turned abruptly and obediently where some old feudal baron had barred the early traffic from his sacred meadows and commanded it to go round.

They crossed the old grass-grown canal, built long ago to carry troops secretly along the coast if Bonaparte had landed. Some men in a field were coaxing a wisp of smoke through a bonfire that had almost died in last night's rain. A pig was squealing its heart out in a farmyard, and Mr. Stevens turned his head the other way. It hurt him to think of pain on this lovely autumn morning. He wanted his mind to be at peace.

At the outskirts of a little village, nestling at the foot of the downs, he left the bus and took the path he had followed last year, and the year before—through the narrow avenue of thorn trees and sharply behind the grey-walled church. He struck the old cart track, worn so deep into the chalk by sheep and rain that at first he was breast-high with its banks. It led him steeply upwards, and soon he could look down on the red roofs of the village.

Then it grew shallower, and as it came out onto the open downs he climbed its edge and walked on the springy turf.

He was quite alone here. Some sheep were nibbling their placid way inch by inch across the grass, but there was no human being as far as the eye could see.

He was fond of the downs because they brought him easily and smoothly in touch with the past. The woods grew and died—the meadows were hedged, and cut, and changed—towns and villages rose and fell: not a day passed but you heard the hammer prizing up old boards;

but this wiry turf, with the chalk glistening underneath, was no thicker nor softer to the feet of Roman Legions than it was to his. They too would have glimpsed the sea when they reached the shoulder of the first hill, and he knew that in another thousand years the downs would still be just the same—quite timeless.

Supposed site of Roman camp, read Mr. Stevens's map, and he could place the spot exactly by the crossing of two paths. He could follow the faint ridge of it in the grass, and he thought of the same soft outlines that remained of Ernie's sandcastles, after the sea had covered them and gone. Just a difference between moments and years.

It was not really time for a rest, but the day was so splendid and the view so fine that he lay for a few minutes on the walls of the camp and looked at the thin strip of distant sea.

He thought of the crowds along its shore: they would be swarming like ants at this time in the morning—clustering round bandstands, rubbing shoulders in deck chairs, seething round refreshment stalls, standing in queues for speedboats, and here he was, alone, right above it all. He thought of the noise—the dusty promenades, and then of this solitude.

He was glad to think that he would be back with the crowd again that evening—walking under the lights, surrounded by human sounds: he would not like to live in a lonely place, miles from everywhere, but he liked to think that he could detach his mind from the crowd—to feel that he had an understanding with nature that allowed him to sit and smoke a pipe with it in silence.

He rose, and went on, right away from the footpath now—across virgin soil. He knew by his map that in a couple of miles he would strike the lane that led him into the valley and through the woods.

He passed a weather-beaten little tree—bent into the shape of a man blown along with his umbrella in front of him, inside out, and his thoughts flashed away from present things to his tumble from the wall of his father's yard, at the rear of their shabby little house in Wandsworth. It was not that this bent little tree had the slightest actual connection with his fall: it was because he had passed the tree last year as he was thinking of it, and now, directly he saw the tree, his thoughts flashed back in the way they have of doing.

How he had got onto the wall, at so early an age, he never knew—but the clatter of the empty paint cans he fell among had become the first concrete recollection of his life.

It had become the starting point of the connected thoughts that he indulged in upon his yearly walk: the point from which he began to draw up the little summary that braced him for another year.

JNO. STEVENS, BUILDER AND DECORATOR, was all that had shown his father's trade—painted in faded gold letters on a pale-blue board over the door that led into the yard.

His father had never had a proper shop, with a showroom. People requiring his services had to come to the front door, and he would interview them in the passage. Some people went through the side door by mistake and wandered unattended round the little yard till Mr. Stevens's mother spotted them through the kitchen window.

The whole of Mr. Stevens's childhood seemed to have centred round that untidy, jumbled little builder's yard. Later there merged with it the Council School across the road, but every one of his earliest recollections began, like his fall among the paint cans, with the bewildering medley of rubbish that his father collected in the tiny walled space behind the house.

There were ball-cocks from cisterns, distorted lengths of leaden pipe, and strange, obscure things that lie concealed beneath the floors of houses, and only plumbers know how to find.

The smaller articles came and went according to the time when the old man found use for them again, but large things sometimes found their way into the yard, and generally remained.

There was a rusty old kitchen range with doors overgrown with straggling creeper; an ancient bath, perpetually full of red-brown water since, years before, its waste hole was choked with leaves; a pile of mouldering planks through which grass sprouted in the spring; an iron gate, a cart wheel, and a statue of Pan.

The garden which had once grown beneath this rubbish never ceased in its feeble efforts to escape: every spring it would push its pallid green suckers through the cracks and crevices of the things that lay upon it.

Once a year the old man had a clear-out, and a cart came from somewhere to take the useless junk away. But old Mr. Stevens loved hoarding rubbish and it well-nigh broke his heart to see any of it go. He only sent stuff away when the yard was too choked to get new rubbish in, but often, at the last moment, he would be filled with remorse, run after the disappearing cart, and return triumphantly with a piece of ornamental ironwork or a blackened chimney cowl which he would return almost tenderly to its old corner to rot for another year.

But everything in due course seemed to go, except the bath, the kitchen range, and the statue of Pan.

The statue dominated the little yard—a pale-grey giant among small, rusty things. From the back bedroom where he slept as a child Mr. Stevens could look down upon the horned forehead and just see the tip of its pipes and its crossed, cloven feet.

It had come years ago from the garden of a large house in Brixton—how and why Mr. Stevens never knew: it was the only thing in the yard his father resented; he often tried to give it away, but nobody wanted it any more than he did—and there it sat through Mr. Stevens's childhood—eternally playing its pipes to unresponsive lavatory seats and door scrapers.

He often wondered what had happened to it in the end—he'd passed the old house on a bus a few years ago, and saw a large garage where the yard used to be. It was not until he was a young man, and the old place was ten years behind him, that he'd found the mystic story of Pan in a greasy book from the secondhand shop in Vauxhall Bridge Road. He had read the story one evening when the lengthening days just gave him power to read by daylight at his window, and, conjuring back the statue in the yard, he had understood for the first time the beauty of its meaning.

Strangely little remained in his memory of the school: a few hard, unfriendly benches: the weekly smell of carbolic on the day they scrubbed the floor: a shadowy memory of Mr. Perkins, the teacher, with his red-lidded, lashless eyes and the tight, shiny trousers on his bandy legs: a few distant shouts in a high-walled asphalt playground, and the memory of his own schooldays faded into the big square house in Belvedere Road, Herne Hill—Belvedere College—to which he had been able to send his boys.

He held his head a little higher, smiled, and slashed the thistle heads with his stick.

His own schooldays were behind him before he had turned fourteen. He was helping his father, and he thought of the hours at the bottom of the ladder, steadying it, with one foot on the lower rung while his father worked above.

It was the clearest recollection of his boyhood—the circular rubber heels on his father's boots, and the "Bill-low, laddie!" from his father before a piece of rusty guttering plopped on the ground beside him.

He paused as he reached the path that led into the valley. In a hundred yards he would be in the shadow of the trees, and he was sorry to leave the open downs behind.

It had been the little chance things—like his discovery of Pan—that made him aware of his yearning to understand far more than had come his way: little chance things that seemed to raise a curtain and reveal almost frightening depths beyond. He was glad that he had always had the instinct to step forward and not shrink back—to go groping on—exploring and probing for another curtain beyond.

A crudely written notice *Strong boy wanted* did not always bring a man to the leisured freedom of a fortnight's holiday by the sea—a family sitting in a hut with a balcony before it—a house that in twelve more payments would be his.

Three years a handy boy—three years a packer—at twenty-three a clerk. He remembered the evening in the hall of the warehouse when he rolled down his sleeves for the last time and said good-bye to manual labour. And his walk home, when he bought two shirts, and four pairs of stiff cuffs. Very few packers in the firm of Jackson & Tidmarsh rose from the warehouse to the office: still fewer at the age of twenty-three.

Step by step his rise had come—slow but very sure. Two pounds a week—two pounds ten—three pounds; ten pounds in the Savings Bank, fifteen pounds—twenty—the day he took the bigger room: the first ride on his bicycle—his meeting with Flossie and his marriage—the taking of their house in Corunna Road—everything building up, slowly but very surely.

He came to the memory of his first day's walk at Bognor, when things during the year had been happening to make his thoughts a jumble of excitement and expectancy.

He was about to begin his second season as Secretary of the Football Club, which was rising in prestige and power. Two men from a bank had joined and new fixtures arranged with better clubs. He was on tiptoe for the beginning of the season on the Saturday of his return. He'd cut a day off his holiday to be at the first match—which showed the way he thought about things then.

But an even greater thing was dominating his thoughts on that first ramble on the downs: a thing that had happened in the office in the summer. Chief invoice clerk—at thirty-seven—with four men under him and a place of influence in the big warehouse behind the office.

There were two other clerks with the same standing as his own: two elderly men with bent shoulders and hesitating, timid eyes. He had looked at them, watched them, and realised with a thrill that the ball was at his feet.

The secretary sat in a private office—nearing sixty and certain to retire within ten years. Mr. Stevens, at thirty-seven, could wait if necessary for twelve, but it would come sooner than that now. Five hundred pounds a year—an office of his own—a daily talk with the directors—control of forty men—and once a handy boy!

There had been a magnificent sunset on the way home from that first walk fifteen years ago—and every step towards it took him nearer to the secretaryship and one of the big houses in College Road. He knew exactly the kind of house it would be: through the thick holly hedge people would glimpse quiet shrubberies and a smooth, secluded lawn.

He had reached home that evening with an exhilaration that determined him to repeat the walk each year: to summarise the past—to collect and carry forward the things that had brought him to the verge of this splendid future—to add the significant happenings of the past twelve months, and to probe the future with every increasing confidence.

It was not that he had nursed a too inflated opinion of himself, it was a fight to conquer his shortcomings—to convince himself of his ability to hold the position he looked forward to. The Football Club had confirmed what he hoped lay in his power: they would not applaud him so when he rose at meetings if he lacked the instinct for leadership and the understanding of men.

It gave keen satisfaction to use this power for the good of a healthy sport—but far greater pleasure to know that soon he would be able to use his gifts to their utmost, in the material and important business of life. His present clerkship gave few opportunities—but the secretaryship—that would be an infinitely different thing. . . .

He often wondered whether the trouble that led to his resignation from the Football Club had anything to do with what happened at the office.

The football trouble had shaken him far more deeply than he first had thought: the terrible injustice of it—the heartless way in which they threw him aside as if he were a worn-out tool. It had been a crashing blow to his confidence and spirit: a terrible struggle to keep himself from bitterness and self-pity. It might possibly have affected his work at a critical time, but he would never believe the two disasters were really connected.

The directors had shown him every courtesy when he had applied for the secretaryship.

"It's not that we are in any way dissatisfied, Mr. Stevens—on the contrary, you are one of the most valued members of our staff. But we've got to look ahead: we've got to face very heavy competition. We must find new markets, and Mr. Wolsey has a very wide experience of the retail trade. We're certain you will find Mr. Wolsey a very excellent man to work under."

It was the last word that cut like a whiplash—"under."

For a wild moment he had felt like throwing the gauntlet down, and resigning—but he remembered what had happened at the Football Club—and this was his living—not merely sport—"I'm sorry, sir—I'll . . ."

—and the director was speaking again, of some trivial matter of routine—

It was lucky his boots were stout, for the grass under the trees was sopping wet from the rain. But the ferns were magnificent, down here in the shade. The sun always seemed to dry the delicacy of their lace-work.

He was through the valley now, and presently he was out on the ridge that marked the summit of his journey. The view was magnificent. To the north the country stretched out as far as his eye could see, with the old towns of Petworth and Midhurst snuggling amongst the distant trees. Here and there the sun glittered on the narrow river that wound across the plain.

For some years past he had planned to come out on this ridge as his thoughts had reached the twin disasters of his life—for the view that lay ahead seemed to stretch out its arms, raise its eyebrows, and say laughingly to him—"Does it really matter?"

It was not that he had lost the secretaryship of the Football Club—or the secretaryship of Jackson & Tidmarsh—through dishonour: he had lost the first through injustice—through jealousy perhaps—and he must try and forget—and harbour no bitter thoughts: the second he had lost because no man can drive beyond the uttermost limits of his opportunities. He'd started as a handy boy—and that was the beginning and end.

He had little thought, when he had married Flossie and taken their house in Corunna Road, that he was building the refuge that saved him after each of his disasters.

His home had never looked so friendly—his garden never so restful as on the night he returned from the office with the knowledge that he was not to be secretary—that he was never, perhaps, to have the big house in College Road, with its lawns and shrubberies.

He had seen the fire flickering through the front-room curtains, and in the hall hung Dick's blue cap, with the yellow stripes of Belvedere College.

He had made the utmost of his chances: he was proud of the fine opportunities he had fought to gain for his boys.

He struck the path that would lead him into the lane with the Woodman's Arms a mile ahead: he was relieved to think that the wet season had kept away the wasps that last year had plagued him at his lunch outside the Inn—settling on the lip of his tankard of beer.

He would meet the four o'clock bus at Singleton, and on the walk home he would probe, as he always did, into the future—planning the things he would do when his stroke of big luck came.

For he knew, as surely as there were cart ruts in the lane, that one day something would happen—something would come to reward his striving in the past.

CHAPTER EIGHTEEN

It would be unfair to say that the family were glad to see Mr. Stevens start off for his day's walk alone: it was not his absence they enjoyed; it was the difference they noticed in him when he returned.

The trouble was that during the first few days of the holiday he was always a little overanxious to make things go with a swing—he was inclined to be artificially boisterous: he clapped his hands together and said, "Now then!" too many times.

It was all so obviously well-meant that the family could not possibly resent it, for when, in their turn, they became boisterous, Mr. Stevens would grow quiet, and draw aside as if afraid to do anything to spoil it. He seemed to tiptoe away, as he tiptoed backwards from the dining-room clock at home when he got it to go after a long and obstinate stoppage.

This year he had rather increased his efforts, although Dick and Mary knew it was quite unnecessary. They knew perfectly well that the holiday would go all right if it were left alone—it was only that as you grow older you naturally take longer to work up the swing of it. Mr. Stevens appeared to forget this—he still seemed to take as his standard the holidays of five years ago, when the children dived into it headfirst directly they arrived. Several times, when Dick and Mary were in a quiet and thoughtful mood, they had caught him looking at them with an uneasy, puzzled expression, as if he were afraid that Bognor was losing its hold, and had disappointed them this year.

But his day's walk would take all this away. He would return, as he always did, in an entirely different mood—quieter and more natural. He would enter into everything more as one of them than as leader and organiser, and the holiday would settle pleasantly down.

It was this reason, and this alone that pleased them to see him go, for they were genuinely sorry that he was not with them to enjoy the first bathe from The Cuddy. Dick and Ernie thought how much their father would have enjoyed pulling off his shirt without taking the skin off his elbows, as he invariably did in the cramped space of the small huts: and how majestic he would have looked, issuing from the interior onto the balcony, in his blue costume with its yellow edgings.

The morning was so hot that they had no need for towels: for half an hour they swam, and splashed, and floated, and wallowed in the clear, tepid water—then they lay out in the sun and let the salt dry in.

When Mrs. Stevens arrived soon after eleven with a bag of macaroons, she was shocked to find the children sprawled out on the beach with nothing on but their bathing dresses. She said they would catch their death of colds—which made them roll over, and laugh.

Mary had brought down a bottle of olive oil to rub over the scarlet patches on their chests and backs, for there was no point in getting sunburnt merely to have the skin come peeling painfully off in a few days' time. A little oil prevented the skin from cracking, and helped it towards that rich mellow brown that everyone likes to bring back from a holiday.

If Mr. Stevens was finding it warm, right up on the downs, with the wind blowing freely about him—the others found it scorching down on the beach, too hot for cricket, too hot even for sandcastles. Everyone around them seemed to have collapsed, and the drone of the speedboat, and the bathers calling to one another in the hazy, far-out sea, were the only sounds to break the silence.

People were squeezed up into every little crack of shade, or sprawled grotesquely under newspapers: an old gentleman nearby was feebly sucking a banana, while his red-faced wife, propped up beside him against a breakwater, furtively loosened her stays.

"Indian summer—that's what it's goin' to be," said an old sailor, resting on the edge of his boat.

But the Stevenses sat in luxury—just within the shade of The Cuddy, the doors flung open to catch what gentle breeze came by. It was very fine to sit there, crunching macaroons—watching other, less fortunate people sweltering in the sun. The Cuddy was worth its price—ten times worth it.

"Fancy us sitting here, like this!" said Mrs. Stevens.

But the best part of the morning was the end of it: going back to the shady sitting-room of Seaview, which seemed no more than twilit after the glaring sands—turning on the tap of the stone jar in the corner by the bookcase, and watching the clear, cool ginger beer slowly fill their glasses.

They drank down half of it right off—for macaroons are thirsty things—then they filled their glasses again and set them on the table for the meal.

The long bathe in the sea, with the sun and the air, had given their bodies a triumphant, tolerant feeling of contempt for their clothes—so utterly different from the feeling on a miserable winter day, when the clothes seem to have the body cringing within their power.

They lay back in the armchairs, tired and stiff after their bathe, and waited for their dinner to arrive. The gramophone was playing in the house across the way, and gusts of laughter kept floating over to them: they seemed a jolly crowd at "The Sycamores": three young men, apparently, and three girls—with no old people at all. . . .

Soon after the meal was over, Dick put on his blazer, and said he was off for a stroll by himself.

"I'll be back to tea," he said.

The others were a little surprised. Dick had never gone off like this before. Sometimes he had gone on long rambles with Ernie, or

Mary, but never alone, except perhaps to run up to the shops for something.

"Dad'll be in about five," said Mrs. Stevens, as Dick went out of the room.

"Righto. I'll be back."

"Which way are you going?"

"Along the beach, I expect."

He waved to them and smiled as he passed the sitting-room window. Ever since he'd arrived at Bognor the urge had been growing stronger to get off by himself. He wanted to think out one or two things, and he knew that no clear reasoning would come unless he were quite alone.

The sands and the promenade were unusually clear, for most people had decided upon forty winks in their bedrooms as the coolest and most desirable way of spending the afternoon. But a fresh southerly breeze had come with the rising tide, and blew in Dick's face as he walked along the sands.

He passed the last outlying houses, then the last bathing huts, and came to the stretch of coast between Aldwick and Pagham, which even in September was quiet, and free from people. For big private houses lay back from the shore along this part, and their gardens ran down to the beach.

The groups of holidaymakers grew more scattered until presently he was quite alone. He found a place by a broken mass of concrete that had once protected a garden from the encroaching sea, and lay down in its shade.

It was only vaguely that Dick understood this urge to come out alone. He only knew that in every dark hour of the past year— whenever his mind was groping panic-stricken in the troubled mists that surrounded it, the same thought always came to his relief—"Wait till you get to Bognor again—get out along the beach—and think it out, facing the sea."

And here he was: sitting just as he had pictured himself so many times. He wondered whether now the mists would clear—whether he could rise to a calm detachment that would help him to understand.

It was something that had happened to him since he was on this coast last year—something that had brought him deep unhappiness—at times despair—yet something very hard to reflect upon and clearly define.

And he ought to be happy, that was the perplexing root of it all—far happier than last year, by all the rules of reason.

Last year he had been a schoolboy—costing his father money and doing nothing useful in return. Now he went to London every day: he was earning money—helping the house, keeping himself, and doing a useful job in the world.

True, thirty shillings a week was not a great deal, but it was a fortune compared with the pocket money of a year ago. The grey flannel trousers he was wearing were bought out of his own money—his hat—his overcoat at home had come from what he had earned by his own hand. He was helping to pay the rent of The Cuddy: the whole family was better off because of what had happened to him since last September. Oughtn't he to be satisfied—and quite contented? Reason said: "Yes—certainly, yes."

For months now he had fought bitterly against this strange unhappiness, that closed upon him one winter evening as he came home from his work—which had clung to him unceasingly ever since: he wanted to try to understand the cause of it, so that he could fight it better, and perhaps, one day, drive it right out of his mind.

What had happened since last year? He had left school, and started work in London. That was all. Gone to Maplethorpe's, the wholesale stationers. A clerk at Maplethorpe's. Ten months of it—and then this holiday. Back at Bognor: back in his old loose flannels and school blazer.

The blazer, somehow, held the key to it all—worn over his flannels as Captain of the school Cricket team—over his light running-clothes when he had gone up to take the Victor Ludorum at the Sports in June last year.

BELVEDERE COLLEGE SPORTS

Stevens I. wins Victor Ludorum

... a promising young athlete of whom we should hear again. ...

The cutting from the local paper lay in the drawer of his dressing table at home. It thrilled him to think some man he had never seen—whom he did not even know—had written that about him.

The holiday last year had closed a golden chapter in his life: he had left Belvedere College in the flush of complete achievement, for he had, indeed, accomplished everything he most desired—Captain of Cricket—Victor Ludorum—a deuce of a fellow on holiday last year—strutting about in this blazer—dreaming through the memories of his triumphs: keyed up with anticipation of his coming work in London. Maplethorpe's sounded tremendously grand, and his father's great pride in getting him the job only served to increase his excitement.

"Settled for life, my boy—in a good, sound job."

That was the irony of it. His father thought it such a splendid job. "Settled for life—settled for life!"—proud words echoing back in pitiless mockery.

If only he could tell his father—or if only his father had known, and said to him, "Look here, old chap—it's not a first-class job—it's rather a second-rate firm, really—but it's the very best I can do for you." What a difference that would have made! He would have said, "Righto, Dad. Thanks. I'll tackle it for all I'm worth, and try my best to get a better place later on."

He could have done it, with his father on his side.

But there it was. It couldn't be helped. His father was proud of it: it would break his heart if he knew that his son looked down upon the job, and hated it. Maplethorpe's—its dusty barrenness—its commonness—

the shame of its squalid side street. It had dawned upon Dick only gradually, as the bewilderment of his first few weeks had ebbed away. He had had to keep his disappointment so utterly to himself, for his mother would never have understood and he had no friend who would understand. In the shock of disillusion he had recoiled upon his schooldays—seeking security and courage from memories—from Belvedere College—and he had found that no firm ground lay even there.

Just a big ugly converted private house: forlorn bare windows: a worn-out garden trampled bare by boys. That was all that remained when he turned his eyes back to it—the veneer of boyish romance peeled off, and a skeleton of pathetic, pretentious make-belief grinned at him and said, "Now you know."

Incredible that he had never known before!

A smouldering anger grew up against the way he had been deceived; every day, in some roundabout manner—it was hinted to the boys that Belvedere College stood shoulder to shoulder with the greatest schools of the land—just because they were boys: young and impressionable.

If only the masters had been honest—if only Mr. Barbour had said—"Look here, boys, Belvedere College is only fifteen years old. I started it myself—it hasn't got any traditions, like other schools—it's only a small place—but we don't charge much, and we do the best we can. We're sorry about it: the College can't make you proud—it's up to you to make the College proud."

How he would have knuckled down to defend it—and work for it!

"All right—let's jolly well do our damnedest to make it as good as the best!"

But that was the pity of it. Belvedere College was wrapped in a tawdry little blanket of self-deception. It really did think it was a splendid place. The masters honestly thought that old boys ought to be proud of it—and immensely grateful!—the hopeless futility of it all!

It was not a great deal that he asked of it: only that it could have given him a few proud lingering memories—a dignity that he could cling to—a strong, understanding hand to give him the courage to face the crumbling path ahead—

A crunching of pebbles broke into his thoughts. His eyes had been on the hazy outline of a tramp steamer—right out on the horizon, and he did not see the group that passed, until they were almost on him.

A tall man, smoking a pipe, and two boys—not brothers, Dick thought—just friends—boys of about eighteen. They were wearing plus fours, and striped blazers with coats of arms on the pockets: both had the same coloured tie—some Old Boys' tie.

He followed the little group with his eyes until they passed round a bend of the coast behind some trees, and suddenly he was intensely lonely. There was no old boy of Belvedere College whom he wanted as a friend.

He glanced down at his blazer. Just *B.C.* on the pocket—*B.C.*—Belvedere College, woven in hard green thread. The badge had been given him when he got into the Cricket team—mounted on a piece of cardboard, to be sewn onto a blazer that was bought separately—any old blazer that you fancied.

Would it have been too much to have asked of Belvedere College, that it should have a proud striped blazer—with a coat of arms—and perhaps an Old Boys' tie?

But he knew it did not matter, really: he knew that he would never have worn the tie if there had been one. Butler would have worn it, serving in his father's tobacconist's shop: Cheesman would wear it, driving his uncle's furniture van. They would be proud of it—not ashamed, like he would be.

Would they have been proud of it because they were loyal, and true to their old school?—or would they merely have tried to extract from it a vague social advancement?

He knew quite well that he had no right to be ashamed. He had no greater claim than Butler—or Cheesman. Their fathers were better off, probably—than his own. He ought to go down to the school field on

Saturdays, stand with Butler and Cheesman, and shout, "Play up, the College!"—"Good old College!"

"A boy who speaks against his old school is no better than a worm." A bishop had said that. It had been printed in one of the papers—and it made him feel despicably mean.

He was ashamed of his job—ashamed of his old school—and the job and the school were the proud achievements of his father's life. He was disloyal: he knew that was the very core of his unhappiness. If he were to avoid being a lonely outsider he must pretend all his life to be proud of what in his heart he secretly despised—of what he knew was second-rate—not good enough.

Was that the meaning of loyalty?—that a man must drown all native pride and crush himself to a level from which he could look up at the pitiful little standard set for him to serve?—even if he knew beyond doubt that a prouder standard should be his?

Was it shameful for a man to feel superior to his station—to prefer loneliness to the association of men who were not good enough for him?

White horses were flecking the sea as it drove in with the breeze behind it, and as Dick lay watching them a ray of new light broke in upon him.

Suddenly he began to think quite clearly: his thoughts no longer eddied sluggishly round a vortex of self-pity. When, a few weeks ago, he had read those words "self-pity" in a newspaper article, they stung with the cruelty of a gibe at a physical deformity—but now suddenly they took a different meaning. He felt strangely excited—he could no longer lie listlessly on the beach. He rose, and walked on, until he came within sight of a line of bungalows—then he turned and walked back. In sight of Bognor he turned again: he strode up and down the lonely mile of beach that had given him this sudden ray of hope.

It was growing clearer every moment, and his newfound excitement mixed itself with the consciousness of his physical fitness: the holiday had scarcely begun! Five—seven—ten—splendid days ahead! . . . but he must not let his thoughts run wild . . . keep them to the point!

What an absolute fool! No wonder he had felt so miserable—and mean! He deserved it—

He had got the wrong idea about this loyalty business—loyalty didn't mean a passive cringing to something second-rate: it meant a tremendous determination to raise the things he was connected with to a finer level.

His anger at Belvedere College melted into something that was neither pride nor shame—a vague sense of possession—a sense of guardianship—a sense of obligation. He no longer felt contemptuous of Mr. Barbour, and the futile pride he sought to drum into his boys—it had been his only course—the right course—and suddenly Dick knew that a patient nobility lay behind it—

Supposing he could do something to turn the sham pride of Belvedere College into a fine reality! It was the boys who made a school and built up its traditions—

Vague recollections came tumbling over each other—jostling and scrambling to shape clear outlines and encourage him—a great lawyer had begun life in his father's little jeweller's shop—Cabinet Ministers had been mill-hands and engine drivers. A famous doctor had begun life in a labourer's hut—scraps he had read in papers sprang to life: incredible that they had brought no message to him at the time!

The tramp steamer was now no more than a funnel and a sluggish wisp of smoke. He stood for a long time watching it.

He would do nothing hasty, nor stupid: he would not despise Maplethorpe's and slapdash through his work: he would stick to it until he was ready to go.

Careers for Boys: how on earth had he passed that bookseller's window a hundred times without the urge to go in and buy that book?

He would get it directly he got home: quietly study it and choose his course. He would fix up a table in his bedroom, to work in winter evenings: in the summer he would take his books out and read under the trees of the recreation ground. Already his fingers were itching to cut the white leaves of those books.

Seventeen—he had years and years ahead! One day he would go down to Belvedere College to give away the prizes—or open the new pavilion he had presented—he would tell them what a hopeless fellow he was at school. All successful men did that.

He would turn up on Saturdays when he could get away in time—and cheer the boys on. . . . What a splendid thing this holiday had done! . . . cleared his mind and set his course . . . ten splendid days of it to come, every day getting fit to begin directly he got home. Maplethorpe's no longer lay ahead like an ominous black cloud.

He knew now that the tawdryness of Belvedere College—the commonness of Maplethorpe's—these things that had drowned the past winter in such dark bitterness had now become incentives to his success. A prouder school—a happier job—might have lulled him into a smug self-satisfaction from which he would never have risen. It had all been set for him—to test him—and now he had won—

Better get back to tea. He turned and faced the distant houses of Bognor with a sigh of regret. He would never forget this silent piece of coast, and all that it had done for him.

On his way he passed the little group that had gone by him when he was resting under the broken wall. He passed close to them and the two boys smiled at him in a friendly way. Dick smiled back—and hurried his steps to be in time for tea.

CHAPTER NINETEEN

"You'd hardly believe it," said Mr. Stevens, cutting himself another slice of bread—"I must have walked a couple of miles once, without seeing a soul—not even a house. And they say England's crowded!" He reached for the jam, and dropped an extravagant blob on the side of his plate.

Mrs. Stevens was quite prepared to believe it: she believed everything her husband said—but she couldn't picture it. She couldn't imagine a place where you could twist round without seeing somebody, somewhere, or at least a house. If ever she found herself in such a situation she knew for certain she would scream, but she admired her husband for the bold way he plunged into such frightening vacancies.

"It must have been lovely. Aren't you tired?"

"I bet I'll be stiff tomorrow."

"Did you make a good lunch?"

"Oh, just bread and cheese, and beer—good healthy stuff and plenty of it."

"You haven't half caught the sun!" said Mary.

He certainly had—he'd noticed his face in the mirror over the fireplace as he had sat down—it looked like a lobster, sticking out of the neck of his cricket shirt.

"Better put some of my cold cream on your nose," suggested Mary—and everybody laughed—not because it was frightfully funny—

but because they were having such an extraordinarily cheerful tea. It was by a long way the most animated meal they had had since they arrived, and was due of course to their different ways of spending the day. Mrs. Stevens began with a curious incident which had happened in the morning. She had ordered half a pound of petit beurre biscuits and was certain she saw the man weigh them out and put them in a bag. But when she opened the bag on her return she'd found it full of dried apricots.

"Can't think how it happened," she declared. "He must have put my bag beside another, and taken his eyes off it when he wrote the bill. Then picked up the wrong one. The man was at his dinner when I took it back—but they changed it, even though I wasn't known there."

"Must have been a conjurer," said Dick—"wonder who got the biscuits?"

Mary related the luxury of the first morning's bathe from The Cuddy, and painted it so alluringly that Mr. Stevens declared he would have a quick dip before supper that very evening. Ernie had found a friend—a boy with a green cap and ginger hair—and Dick described how splendid the coast was, out beyond Aldwick, and what a fine walk he had had that afternoon. It had been a most successful day.

"What an appetite it gives you," declared Mr. Stevens, halfway through his third slice of bread and jam. "Never want more than a biscuit with my cup of tea at the office." He reckoned from the map that he had walked nearly fifteen miles, for having arrived early for the bus, he had come on along the road at least another mile before it caught him up.

As tea was ending, Mrs. Stevens persuaded her husband not to have a bathe before supper: it did no good when the body was tired, and easily brought on a chill. Mr. Stevens pooh-poohed his wife's suggestion to start with, but was secretly rather glad, and gave in to her as soon as his dignity allowed. It would certainly be a bit dull, going in alone, when everyone else had finished, so instead he went up to his room, took off his heavy walking boots, and sat for a few minutes on the edge of the bath, dangling his feet in warm water. Then he put on lighter socks and his canvas shoes, and came down feeling as fresh as paint. He just caught sight of Miss Kennedy Armstrong as he turned on the landing—just her back, and then her thin pale knuckles as she closed her door. What a pity it was that she was so retiring, and shy.

After such a strenuous day the vote was unanimous to stroll down and listen to the band. They decided to pay and go into the enclosure, for although they could hear the band quite well from the balcony of The Cuddy they did not get the pleasure of watching it, and after all, you must see a band to really enjoy it.

They arrived in such good time that they got comfortable deck chairs in the second row. It was a lovely, placid evening: so warm that Mr. Stevens opened his coat over the woolly he had taken the precaution of putting on. The sea was right in, but so smooth and quiet that it gave an uncanny feeling to look over the promenade and find the still water just beneath them. They lay back in their chairs, rested their feet on the grass, and watched the bandsmen arriving.

It was interesting to see them come along in twos and threes, go up the steps into the bandstand to get their instruments in place, and carefully set their chairs and music stands. It was a Military Band, and the men looked much smarter than the ordinary kind. The band last year was not a military one, and some of the men had had long draggling moustaches, which made them look as if they did something else during the day. It spoilt the crispness of it all.

One by one the soldiers completed their arrangements in the bandstand and came down, lit cigarettes, and stood about, waiting. Two good-looking young bandsmen sidled over to the railings and began to talk and laugh with two girls on the opposite side. Mary watched them, enviously. Two tall girls, one dark, the other fair—both attractive and interesting in their light summer frocks and deep-brown arms. They must have been at Bognor quite a time to get their arms that beautiful colour. She looked down at her own, which were still no more than flushed. She glanced to one side of her, at her father's knees, grey flannel trousers and canvas shoes: to the other side, at her mother's little blue serge lap with her purse upon it—and suddenly she felt hemmed in—a prisoner. It was ungrateful and mean to think of it in that way, but she couldn't help it. The girls over there looked so free, and cool—and easy. She wondered how they got to know the bandsmen, and hoped, for some absurd, vague reason, that they were old friends—or relatives.

A man came round with programmes. Mr. Stevens bought two, and passed one down with a slight flourish to the others. It was one of the things Dick and Mary liked about their father—the way he always bought two programmes of everything they went to see. It had a way of bringing them into more familiar touch with the performers: one programme made you feel just one of a crowd, listening by sufferance: two programmes gave you a sense of giving the band your influential and valued patronage.

"Good!" said Mr. Stevens. "'Poet and Peasant'"—(he particularly enjoyed the things they had on the gramophone at home)—"'Blue Danube'—that's a catchy old favourite of mine—*Mikado* selection"—

It was an interesting programme, finishing with "Pot Pourri" which was Ernie's favourite, because now and then amid the medley, excitingly and without warning, a tune would turn up that he whistled at home, and the hearing of it, played authentically by the band, gave him an opportunity of correcting his own version which had usually gone astray through constant repetition.

"I do like a Military Band," said Mr. Stevens—"always plays things with a bit of go in them."

"Is there any Gilbert and Sullivan?" enquired Mrs. Stevens, who had left her glasses on her bed when she had gone up to put her coat on.

"Yes. *Mikado*."

"That's lovely."

Suddenly a stir went through the waiting bandsmen: they took a last hard puff or two at their cigarettes, and pressed the stumps into the grass: looking round, the Stevenses saw the reason: the Bandmaster had arrived and was standing just outside the ring of chairs in conversation with a lady and gentleman: a fine, military-looking man, with a fierce, iron-grey moustache, a long, black braided coat, and a red sash. Ernie could not take his eyes off him: suddenly the men who shot the showers of pennies from automatic machines into small black bags became sweating, labouring little animals in greasy bowler hats—doing paltry jobs. Why had he never realised before that to be a Bandmaster was the one and only thing for him to do? He had one amongst his soldiers at home and used him as a General, but only now did he see the splendour and romance of a living one.

The bandsmen were trooping up to their places—busily adjusting their music stands and seats while one of their number handed round the music for the first selection—yet all the Bandmaster had had to do to make this happen was simply to appear, and stand with his back to it all! The power of it!

After a minute or two he glanced at his watch, smartly saluted the lady and gentleman he had been conversing with, and walked through the passage between the chairs. A lady clapped, and he bowed to her gravely and courteously before mounting the steps. He spoke a word to the bandsman nearest him on the right, but the Stevenses could not quite catch what he said; he tapped the stand in front of him and raised his baton firmly but lightly with his thumb and forefinger: very softly the band began to play. . . .

The Stevenses settled themselves with half-closed eyes: the sea was lapping drowsily against the wall, and the soft breeze turned its gentle murmur into the rustling of distant elms. They could hear the evening train puffing out from the station, the murmur of voices on the promenade, and the padding of feet—but the music of the band seemed to gather these other sounds and weave them into its symphony.

It was strange how this unplanned evening stood out—long after the holiday ended—as the happiest time of all. Mr. Stevens had been quite prepared for a restless, unsatisfactory evening after the exhilaration of his walk—but now, as he lay stretched in his chair, he scarcely stirred lest he should break the exquisite drowsiness that had stolen over him. He relaxed every muscle, and was scarcely conscious of his body beyond the healthy ache of his legs. Almost always, at home, there was some trivial pain, in the forehead or eyes—a sore tendon in the throat—a touch of tightness across the chest or a twinge of rheumatism somewhere: nothing, of course, to worry about, but just enough to remind him that he possessed a body which demanded a little thought and care. But it was different here, at the seaside: he was only conscious that his mind was peacefully reflecting—his body a friendly covering—as light and as cool as air.

Mrs. Stevens was very fond of music, although not in the sense of knowing the names of pieces and their composers. She had, probably, a more sensitive ear than any of the family, and was easily the first to recognise that the second piece played by the band was the thing they had on the other side of their "Destiny" record at home, and had only once played—in mistake for "Destiny."

The pieces on the other sides of favourite records are always unfairly treated—they are looked upon as something thrown in as a make-weight, and only come into their own if by chance they are given the dignity of a rendering by an orchestra. This was a case in point—for as the piece finished, the whole family resolved to play it when they returned, and give "Destiny" a rest.

Mrs. Stevens liked music of a soft, flowing kind, and while "The Blue Danube" came gently to her ears, she nestled a little deeper in her chair, and lay back smiling at her shoes. She rested the heel of one upon the toe of the other, so that she could the better enjoy its polish. Of all her many duties in the home, the cleaning of her shoes was the only one of which she was ashamed. She did it secretly in the scullery, and never in the garden, for fear that some acquaintance might see her from a passing train, and if a tradesman unexpectedly arrived at the back door she would hastily conceal the shoes beneath the sink.

But at Bognor, by paying a trifle extra, they had their shoes cleaned for them, and nothing in the holiday gave Mrs. Stevens greater pleasure, and a keener sense of that atmosphere of well-being which a little spare money can buy.

As each selection ended, people would give a round of scattered applause, turn and speak to one another, or get up to stretch their legs—but several times, when the band stopped, Dick remained quite still and silent in his chair.

It had come to him quite suddenly—this new flash of inspiration—how and from whence he could not tell. He had, in fact, made up his mind that afternoon to think no more about the future until he returned home and got *Careers for Boys.* He wanted to study it with a clear, unprejudiced mind—cutting out the paths that offered nothing to his natural desires, bringing them down to three or four that really attracted him. These he looked forward to exploring further until one gradually surged away from the others, set fire to his imagination, and carried him to success. He was certain that somewhere in that book there lay a course that would capture his ambition and bring him great achievement—he was content to wait till he returned; he had resolved to enjoy the anticipation of it during the holiday; and it was no conscious effort of his that flashed this new inspiration before him—said, "Here it is!—you know it's the only course—why did you never see it before!"

He was lying back with his hands clasped behind his head: his eyes on the row of little houses beyond the green—little old-world houses that must have been among the very first to settle themselves along this shore. Behind rose tall grey buildings that said "Sour grapes" to the little first arrivals, and sought contemptuously to look over their heads.

Dreamily his eyes took in their straight, strong walls, the little details of ornament, and suddenly he was among the cool white mansions which on country walks he had seen on distant hills, shining in the sun, glittering in the moon: he was among the master hands that shaped them—the keen minds that chose their positions among billowy clouds of trees—and suddenly—in a flash, it came.

He would build—not with the grinding, wooden obedience of the man who follows the plan—he would be the conceiver—an architect—

Architect!—the very word revealed a hidden music as he murmured it softly to himself: and every other path crumpled away before his eyes into flat uninspiring dreariness.

He knew that he could do it: he was fond of drawing and designing. At school, when the drawing master piled up wooden boxes and cones for them to sketch, he alone amongst the boys had felt the urge to master their elusive angles and shade them into life.

He knew that with patience and study he could achieve the elementary slogging part, and he pushed it aside, for his mind was shouting excitedly to him to follow it among graceful towers that swayed in the passing clouds—to see the mighty strength of the great buildings he passed in the City on his way to Maplethorpe's—the delicate grace of country mansions, rising from their banks of trees.

To build meant courage: deep faith in yourself—rugged strength in conception—the gentlest touch in detail—magnificent mountains of stone rose out of the inspiration of a solitary brain—and stood for all time to inspire unborn distant eyes.

"You see the splendid view you will get all round—and how the house will seem to have grown out of the hillside—"

He was standing, plan in hand, beside the man whose house he was about to build—he was in the office—throwing into the model stray seeds that dropped from his brain—he was standing by—in rough tweeds—watching the men cut and roll up the first strips of turf—he watched the house grow, foot by foot—until one day it would begin to breathe. . . .

It dawned upon him that the music had stopped—the interval had come, for some of the bandsmen were standing on the grass. He looked around him at the people. They were standing about—aimlessly chatting—making silly talk to pass the time. Nothing had happened to them: they were just the same as when they arrived an hour ago— they would always be the same—nothing would ever happen to them. He alone of all these dreary prisoners had seen the narrow gate, and glimpsed the shining sky.

To his joy he found that his sudden inspiration had not died with the music of the band—it had not clattered down with the bandsmen's instruments like lesser inspirations did: he knew this was no fleeting daydream—

Perhaps it was a good thing that the music had stopped—it might have led him too far into flights of fancy—and above everything he would have to be cool, and practical.

He was certain to find some book in one of the shops in the town— just an elementary book to start with, that he could read on the sands. Even that would be filled with excitement: even if it only spoke of foundations, and the strength of different stone. He would wait till he got home before he started seriously, and although he was sitting back as if half-asleep something was urging him to get up and stride along the promenade—passing everybody—passed by no one—striding up the pier beyond everybody—to the little platform at the very end where you looked round and only saw the sea.

"I always like the good old tunes," remarked Mr. Stevens.

"So do I," said Dick. He wondered what good old tunes the band had just been playing.

"It's gone seven," said Mr. Stevens, "we'll just be able to hear *Mikado* and then we'll have to leg it back."

"Oh, let's stay on till the end," protested Mary—"it's only a cold supper."

" 'Pot Pourri' isn't till the end!" cried Ernie.

But Mrs. Stevens was not like some women who have no servant of their own, who revel in taking a fleeting advantage of someone in their power.

"It isn't fair to be late," she said, "Molly's got to clear away and wash up before she goes to bed."

And so, when *Mikado* died away the Stevenses sadly rose, filed down the narrow strip of grass between the chairs, and gently edged their way through the standing crowd. It had been a lovely interlude: it would linger into many winter evenings as the year grew old, and they hurried when they reached the promenade, not only because they were late for supper, but because they wanted to be out of earshot of the tantalising music before it started again.

CHAPTER TWENTY

In the early days of the cinematograph—when a perspiring opera-tor, in a small dark box, worked the machine by hand—the first few pictures would linger visibly on the screen, and remain for a moment stationary before the shutter passed over them—*flick—flick—flick—*

But gradually, as the operator worked up speed, you were no longer conscious of the dark interval between each picture, and the rapidity of their passage lulled you into a deception of slow movement, clear and smooth.

A holiday is like that. The first days linger almost endlessly. The sun, towards evening, settles itself in a hollow of the downs and stub-bornly defies the night. Sunday—Monday—Tuesday: you feel you have been at the sea for weeks and weeks—

But gradually, relentlessly—time gathers speed. At night you sleep so soundly that you scarcely notice the darkness that flicks across to reveal the picture of another day. The hours go racing by—impossible to check—

On Thursday the Stevenses took the kite out into a stubble field, and lay under the trees in a corner where the grass was thick, listen-ing to the rustle of the paper tail, high above them. In the afternoon they lashed the telescope to one of the balcony posts of The Cuddy—so that they could swing it easily round to reveal the whole horizon. They picked out people on the point of Selsey Bill, and could almost see the name on the Lifeboat. They saw that a fisherman far out in a small boat had a dark moustache, and read the time the band would play on a poster nearly half a mile along the promenade.

"Wonderful bargain," muttered Mr. Stevens as, nearing teatime, he untied it, and carefully wiped its lenses. . . .

Long hours of cricket in the baking sun: arms and faces turning from pink to scarlet—scarlet to Indian brown: invigorating plunges in the sea—placid floating on the surface with toes just sticking up into the breeze: pleasant lounging in cool cake shops with feet sprawled out: boisterous buffetings on the pier and silent evening rambles into the sunset—mixed together with the jingle of the pierrots' piano, the Bandmaster's baton, and the cry of gulls; smoothly linked by drowsy hours of shade. Three nights running they went down after supper and sat on their balcony in the light of the moon. They would talk in undertones then—with their eyes on the glittering path across the sea. The evening sounds eddied round them on breaths of wind that were cooled by the autumn dew, and in the fragments of silence they would hear the sea whispering and the faint, rhythmic pop of Mr. Stevens's lips as they opened to let out small puffs of blue tobacco smoke.

But the dawn of Saturday filtered through a leaden sky and a steady drizzling rain. The banisters were clammy as the Stevenses came rather heavily down to breakfast, and the sitting-room had a slight recurrence of the mustiness which they thought they had long ago dispersed through the window. Time rested in its flight for an hour or two, and the family fidgeted backwards and forwards, to and from the window—searching again and again the strip of dull grey sky above St. Matthews Road.

They fidgeted with the sheets of their picture paper, peevishly wanting to exchange their bits when others wanted to keep the sheet they had. Mr. Stevens sat at the table and made up his accounts, worrying Dick and Mary by continually counting a little pile of silver and copper, looking thoughtful, and searching all his pockets, again and again.

Mrs. Stevens mended a snag in Dick's blazer, where he had caught it getting through a barbed wire fence, and Ernie whiled away a little of the time by the coloured window in the passage—first making the forlorn back garden look blue, as though bathed in extravagant moonlight, and then, by going a few steps up the stairs, making it glow a lurid red, like the film he had once seen, of the burning of Rome.

But suddenly, towards the end of lunch, the sun broke through, and the vinegar in the cruet lit up and glowed like wine. It brought them eagerly to their feet, upstairs for their thick boots, and away with a basket, through the town and out to the hedgerows and the tangled, neglected corners of fields, where they found unpillaged blackberries. They came back with a basket nearly full—still glistening from the morning rain. Blackberry pie—and cream—with an egg cup in the centre to keep the pastry up.

On Saturday night—as Mr. Stevens sat back in his favourite chair before knocking out his pipe and going to bed, it came to him with a sigh of regret that half the holiday had gone. Gone, it seemed, in no time—in a flash, for though their last morning in Corunna Road might easily have been a year ago, it seemed scarcely a day since he had sat in this same chair on the evening of their arrival, thinking of the unbroken holiday ahead.

Still, there was a whole week yet: Sunday—Monday—Tuesday, Wednesday—Thursday: five clear days at least before they need think of packing. But even as he reviewed the days remaining, a pile of ragged invoice ledgers loomed out from where, a few days ago—only the sea, and the downs had lain. He had to blink, and give his head a shake before the dusty, unpalatable vision would fade away. He was letting an attack of the blues get hold of him—a futile thing to allow—

That order form from Warrington's! Why couldn't he forget the beastly thing? It had arrived just as he was clearing up to go on his last evening before the holiday: he was almost certain he'd put it on Mr. Rogers's desk to be dealt with in the morning; he'd stuck a pin through it to prevent it fluttering to the ground and being swept up by the char-woman. And yet just as definitely he remembered it lying on his blot-ting pad beside some papers he was to put in his desk to be dealt with on his return. Supposing he had shut the order in the pad? It might be lying in his desk, unattended to—a big order—and Warrington's were just the sort of people who would kick up a row. It had occurred to him on his way home on the bus, but his thoughts had been too full of the holiday to worry then. And now the confounded thing kept intruding itself—again and again—even when he was undressing for his bathe that morning. He ought to have dropped Rogers a line—just to make sure—but it was too late now: Warrington's would have been fuming on the telephone early last week—probably cancelling all their busi-ness. It would mean a black mark against his name—possibly some-thing worse. Again he shook his head to get rid of it: of course he'd put it on Rogers's desk: it was probably quite all right—and here he was worrying himself to death over nothing.

And now he was thinking about the garden. He wished he had re-minded Mrs. Bullevant to watch the gate, and see that it was kept shut. A big dog had wrought havoc once, with its scratching. He would make a note of the gate and put it down in Marching Orders for other years.

Other years? Of course there would be other years: why was it that this queer, disturbing thought kept worrying him? He looked round the little sitting-room and tried to believe for the hundredth time that everything at Seaview was just as it had always been. It was Dick and Mary, he knew—that were somewhere behind his thoughts: Dick and Mary—with their unspoken words, their patience at the little things that had happened at Seaview this year—things which had never hap-pened before—things they could even still overlook, but for Dick and Mary.

They had never, in other years, sat round the table waiting for meals that seemed as if they would never come: and the chops on Thursday—they were almost raw. It was the first time they had ever sent anything back to the kitchen, and Mrs. Huggett's hands were quivering when she brought the chops back with the raw edges fried over. She had stood at the door and been almost maddening with her apologies, and Mr. and Mrs. Stevens had said, "It's quite all right," so many times that they began to wish that they had shut their eyes and swallowed the raw meat without a word. It was so unlike Mrs. Huggett: she had always been so punctual, and good with the meals before.

Could it really be a cold she had in that eye? She'd said, three years ago, when the Stevenses had first noticed it, that she had caught a chill in it through the cutting March winds—but that was three years ago, and it was still red, and drawn. Whenever she brought anything in to them at meals, they heard her stop outside the door, quite still for a moment before she turned the handle—and they knew she was wiping her eye with the handkerchief that was always ready in her blouse.

It was terribly mean and cruel to let this repel them—but Mr. Stevens, in his heart, knew the others felt as he did. He had caught Ernie looking up at Mrs. Huggett's eye, furtively and somehow ashamed, and sometimes he thought that Dick and Mary, hungry for their meal, finicked and ate almost against their will as Mrs. Huggett left the room.

And yet it was only a funny, red eye from which a tear trickled now and then. Mr. Stevens felt hot with anger at himself: it was caddish to feel this urge to slink away and leave a woman because she was ill—that was the trouble, and the pity of it: she was ill, and was fighting to conceal it from them. She need not worry, though: they would stand by her all right. They would not let her down.

He rose and knocked out his pipe—switched the light out and briskly left the room.

It was very dark in the passage, for the waning moon had not yet risen. He could scarcely distinguish which part of the passage window was blue and which was red. Softly he groped his way upstairs.

The second part of the holiday was the best.

Of course it was the best.

CHAPTER TWENTY-ONE

Sunday morning entirely cleared away the depression that had surrounded Mr. Stevens on Saturday night. Sunday brings a fleet of charabancs into Bognor—packed with people on a day's excursion, and although they crowd the sands and overrun the promenade, they make up for it by giving the genuine holidaymakers a very comfortable feeling of superiority and possession.

You can tell the excursion people by their relatively pale faces, their slightly frowsy, travel-stained appearance, and their eager, ferret-like glances to and fro. The regular holidaymakers are obvious by their brown skins, their slow, leisurely movements, their open clothes, and the tolerant amusement with which they watch the excursionists. They are good-humoured, and never resentful when they find their regular places on the beach taken by querulous, banana-laden parties in sticky suburban clothes, for they know quite well that towards sunset these parties will climb back into their motor coaches: they know that before dusk the whining low gears of the last coaches will have died away up the London Road, to leave the regular people in quiet possession of a cool, untroubled evening.

When the Stevenses arrived at The Cuddy towards eleven o'clock they found their usual strip of sand occupied by the members of a Bicycling Club, all of them, both girls and men, clad in knickerbockers and untidy, rumpled stockings. They were rather common people, and were noisily playing football with a tennis ball.

By opening the doors of The Cuddy to their fullest extent, the Stevenses found it possible for all of them to sit within its boundaries. Two of them had to sit well back inside, and two on the balcony, and Ernie was quite happy on the floor beside his yacht.

"I can't think how we ever managed without one of these huts," said Mr. Stevens, as he lit his pipe and looked from his seclusion at the seething crowd.

"Don't you remember how we used to sit along under that wall?" said Mary—"frightful on hot days—in the crowd—"

"Why, yes—of course," replied Mr. Stevens, looking curiously at the spot over his glasses. "How hot they do look. Just look at the heat sizzling off the sand."

Mrs. Stevens, free from her morning shopping trip on this day of rest, had come straight down with them, and towards midday had to move her chair onto the beach so that the others could close the doors and take their turns to get their bathing dresses on. She found herself next to a stout lady who smelt of camphor balls; undoubtedly on a day's excursion. But she sympathised with people who took steps to keep the moths out of their holiday clothes. Camphor balls were old-fashioned, and smelt rather strong when you perspired, but none of the newfangled things were really as good.

It was during the bathe, on this Sunday morning, that the exciting thing began to happen to Mary.

The family always split up when they went in to bathe, for they did not believe in the rather childish idea of forming a ring and bobbing up and down.

Dick and Mary usually ran out as hard as they could, prancing forward until the deepening sea tripped them up and threw them headlong into it.

Ernie's way was to run in, twist round, and fall backwards, but Mr. Stevens was inclined to be sedate. He walked down rather grimly: stopped at the edge and took three deep breaths according to the Bathing Hints he had read in his morning paper. This done, he waded out a little way and paused to wet his forehead to prevent a sudden rush of blood to the head. Reaching a point where the sea was up to his hips, he fell forward, puffed out his cheeks, and struck off with one foot gently and secretly assisting him by its contact with the shingle.

He had never been a good swimmer, and was a little self-conscious in the sea. If at the end of a swim he found himself in very shallow water, he would stand up with his knees bent beneath the surface, giving on-lookers the impression that it was much deeper than it actually was. Floating was his speciality and he floated most of the time.

On this particular morning, Mary, who swam well, had just completed a wide circle, and was getting to her feet when someone's head collided with her knees beneath the surface. The collision overturned Mary: she fell backwards to swim again, and found herself alongside the culprit, who had risen coughing and spluttering.

"Sorry!" said the culprit—laughing close to Mary's face.

"All right," said Mary, "I thought it was a shark or something."

The other girl laughed again—an easy, merry laugh, and the two stood up together breast-high in the sea. The girl's face was vaguely familiar to Mary—and then, with a pleasant thrill, she remembered. It was the tall, fair girl who had attracted Mary's interest that evening at the band: the girl who had stood with a friend and talked to the soldiers across the railings. Mary had watched her that evening, envying her, but liking her. Several times she had thought about her, wondering who she was and rather hoping she might catch sight of her again—and here they were, face to face. It was embarrassing, but strangely exciting: for this girl was so different to the kind that Mary knew at home. She was so utterly free, and boyish, and easy: she must have known that lots of eyes were on her while she stood that evening laughing and joking with those two good-looking soldiers—but she had been quite natural, and had not shown off like most girls would have done—

"What an awful crowd you get here on Sundays," said the girl. "It's these ghastly charabanc people."

"I know," said Mary, pleasantly surprised and flattered. The girl had guessed at a glance that Mary was not one of the ghastly charabanc people—"Still, they all clear off in the evening."

"Staying long?" enquired the girl.

"Another week."

"Same here, worse luck. I could do a month, couldn't you?"

"I should think I could!"

They were wading towards the shore, side by side, quite naturally, as if they were old friends. Mary's heart was thudding as though she had been running hard: she felt extraordinarily happy and excited.

"D'you dry in the sun?" asked the girl.

"Rather!" said Mary.

They found a place on the crowded sands and lay down side by side. Dick was swimming by some distance out, his dark mop of hair rising and disappearing with the rhythm of his stroke; and occasionally, through the groups of surf bathers, Mary caught a glimpse of the yellow edgings of her father's bathing dress.

She was glad the family had not seen her with this pleasant, newfound friend, although she scarcely knew why she would feel embarrassed if they had. The Stevenses kept themselves very much to themselves at Bognor, not so much through shyness of strangers as through a vague, underlying shyness of each other.

As children, Dick and Mary had often mixed with other children playing nearby, but as they had grown older they had gradually withdrawn from these chance acquaintances and spent the holiday entirely within the family circle. It had become their habit to shrink from the friendly advances of strangers, although they always felt a secret pang of regret. Mr. Stevens was as bad as any of them, for if when walking with the family he passed one of his evening friends of the Clarendon Arms, he would take the most absurd precautions to avoid the embarrassment of introducing his family: he would edge by with a feeble nod and a guilty smile.

All families who live a great deal together are like the Stevenses in this respect: they unconsciously develop two separate personalities; one for family use, the other for use with strangers. The family one is restrained below their natural selves—the one revealed to strangers is inclined to be jaunty and artificially buoyant. They consequently become uneasy and embarrassed when by force of chance they have to reveal themselves before strangers and family at one and the same time, and they go to the most unreasonable pains to avoid it.

Many a time, in the holidays of the past few years, Mary had wistfully picked out girls from the crowded sands and promenade, girls whom she felt instinctively were the kind she would like to have as friends, but with whom she never dared to strike up acquaintance. She would watch out for them during the holiday, and see them, perhaps, several times, but never before had anything happened like this: never before had she come face to face with such a girl—and talked to her. For the first time in her life she became aware of fate's uncanny hand. She was disturbed—vaguely frightened—but intensely excited.

Often she had weaved fanciful pictures round the girls she saw and liked the look of. She would paint a background of romance and adventure; but generally, in the end, she consoled her hunger for companionship with the thought that quite probably they were dull and commonplace girls in reality, and had only attracted her by their outward appearance.

She shyly turned her head and stole a glance at the girl beside her. She lay with closed eyes—her hands beneath her head, a few shining beads of seawater on her brown legs and arms.

It was scarcely believable that they could lie here side by side without speaking, confident and at ease in each other's presence—scarcely believable that this girl was everything that Mary had pictured in her most romantic dreams—and then something more. She was even more attractive in this bright sun, in her light bathing dress, than she had been when first she had captured Mary's interest, in the twilight, in her graceful summer frock.

But far more exciting was the strange, magnetic charm that surrounded her. Mary had pictured rather a shallow, flitting brain beneath this fascinating, tomboyish face: a girl too keen on attracting men to find much interest in other girls, but here was something far deeper and finer than she'd dared to hope for. Her impulse was to talk: to talk rapidly—to strain every ounce of her mind to be witty and amusing, for she knew beyond all shadow of doubt that here at last was the girl she longed for as a friend.

She reminded her a little of Betty Pawson, who went to the St. John's Hall dances; but the very comparison made poor Betty shrivel up and become a languid little ghost. This girl was much taller than Betty: she had a far finer profile: Betty was dead beside this girl's vitality—a timid, pale-eyed little person beside the bold, laughing candour of this girl's glance—a puny little governess-cart pony beside a wild horse of the prairie.

"Golly! It's hot!" muttered the girl.

She spoke it to the sky—to the blazing sun, and Mary liked it better than if the girl had turned her head and spoken it to her. Mary wondered why she had thought "golly" a silly word. It *was* silly, of course, as some people said it: Betty would have made it silly: Maisie Johnson would have said it so that you would simply have had to laugh.

"Golly! It was hot!" She knew that she, too, could say it and give vibrant life to the words: she would say it when they gathered round their cup of tea in the basement kitchen at Madam Lupont's on the first evening of her return. The girls were certain to ask her what the weather was like—

"Isn't it!" was all she could reply—and she too spoke without taking her closed eyes from the sun.

"Staying here alone?" enquired the girl.

"With the family," said Mary. For a moment she thought of adding, "worse luck!"—but she knew it would sound stupid and rather mean. She knew, too, instinctively, that it would lower her in this girl's estimation: it would have raised her in the eyes of some, but not, she knew, with the girl beside her. She even thought of pointing out Dick, who was just then swimming by, quite close in—but something urged her to keep this friendship entirely to herself.

Suddenly the girl rolled over on her side, and lay gazing at Mary with wide grey eyes. Mary returned the gaze: and quite spontaneously they laughed. She knew this girl, through and through—there was a thrilling bond between them: she was pulsing with excitement: pictures flashed through her mind—pictures of things they would do together when their friendship was firmly sealed.

"Just your mum and dad?"

"Two brothers as well."

"My chum's gone back," said the girl, and for a fraction of a second Mary felt hurt—unreasonably, but acutely hurt—

"You staying alone?" she asked.

"Just with my aunt—and Nunky. They live here. I come down and stay for the holidays. I'd come here, though, even if it was just ordinary digs. What d'you do in the evenings?"

"I?—oh, I—well—generally we take a stroll, you know."

"With the family?" This time there was a fleeting shadow of mockery behind the girl's eyes: Mary felt herself struggling for a defence.

"Not always. Sometimes I go with Dick, my brother. It's fun, along the promenade at night."

"What d'you want to take your brother for?"

There was something so utterly disarming in the girl's impudent, laughing eyes that Mary could say nothing: she just laughed—

But beneath her laugh were tumultuous thoughts: something strangely like panic was calling her to escape: something quite different was mocking her and whispering, "Timid little frump!"

"Look here," went on the girl. "Come along with me tonight. You don't know what fun it is!"

A gauntlet had been thrown down: could she possibly, conceivably leave it there—and lose her friend—because she was afraid? The promenade, at night: the blazing lamps—the dark backwaters of mysterious, impelling fascination—the throbbing life—

"It's an awful job to get away. You know—the family—"

"You aren't going to tie yourself like that, are you? Why should you? Why shouldn't you have a bit of fun?"

The girl's eyes were still on hers: they held something that no longer mocked at her: something that urged courage—life—bold adventure—

"You can easily say you've met an old chum."

What awful fascination there was—in every word—yet what tantalising, hopeless impotence! The family would ask which friend it was. The girl spoke as if Mary had dozens of friends the family did not know! They would ask if it was Maggy—then if it was Polly, and finding it was neither they would look dumbly at her, startled and suspicious.

"You've got a job, I s'pose?"

"Yes."

"Well—say you've met a girl who used to work with you: won't that wash?"

"But it's—it's a lie!" gasped Mary—and as soon as the words were out of her mouth she could have bitten her tongue for its stupidity—its childishness.

"A lie!—of course it isn't. A lie's only a thing you tell to get yourself out of trouble. This isn't trouble."

Mary's mind was settled: if the difficulties had been a hundredfold they would not have swerved her now. It was good enough: a girl who used to be at Madam Lupont's.

"What name shall I say?"

"Jessica Marshall."

"Righto. That your real name?"

"Sure."

"Mine's Mary. Mary Stevens."

The girl nodded, looked at her thoughtfully, and smiled.

"You needn't worry," she said—"I'm not the sort that picks up with anybody."

"I'm not worrying about that!" laughed Mary.

"Good for you!—but I mean it—I'm not the kind that goes messing round with office boys."

They both laughed, and the girl dropped her hand over Mary's wrist—held it and pressed it.

"Can you manage nine o'clock?"

"That'll do me."

"Righto. Nine o'clock—at the sweetshop by the pier."

"At the entrance on the right?"

"Yes."

"Righto."

They rose, and the girl smiled down at her. She was a head taller than Mary—as tall as a boy—

"Cheerio, then. Nine o'clock"—and she waved a hand as she went up the beach towards her bathing hut.

CHAPTER TWENTY-TWO

The others had returned from their bathe, and were dressing behind the closed doors of The Cuddy as Mary came slowly up from the sea.

"Who was it?" asked Mrs. Stevens, craning eagerly forward from her deck chair.

"Oh—just a friend," said Mary.

She sat on the steps of the hut and slowly undid the laces of her bathing shoes. She hoped the others would be quick in dressing: it would be easier to think inside the darkened hut—away from the glare of the sands. She knew the family had seen, for as she had risen with the girl she had glanced towards The Cuddy and caught a glimpse of her father and mother, with their heads close together, gazing curiously through the crowd.

But it scarcely mattered now: small difficulties so quickly melt away in the blaze of greater ones. The mere fact of her having met a strange girl: the mere embarrassment of being seen by the family talking with a stranger was nothing now, compared with the terrific complications that had overshadowed everything else.

Her brain was far too excited to give chance of any logical, reasoned thought: just one powerful impulse gripped her: an impulse to jump to her feet and rush away to find the girl—to tell her that after all she would not be able to meet her by the pier that night. For in a strange, frightening way the girl had taken with her all the romance and adventure that the evening seemed to hold, and left Mary with nothing but its lurking dangers—its bewildering difficulties.

How could she ever tell the family? As she had lain there in the sun beside that fascinating girl the whole thing had seemed so absurdly easy and natural—just a word that she had met a girlfriend and was going for a stroll with her—a casual "Cheerio—won't be late."—

But now, as she sat tugging the laces of her shoes, it came to her with overwhelming certainty that her father and mother would guess—and something would happen. They would not try to prevent her: her father would not lock her in her bedroom like fathers she had read about: he would just look at her with his round grey eyes, and say, "Oh. All right,"—and silently, relentlessly, a chasm would open between her and the family—a chasm of doubt and suspicion that would never close—and things would never be quite the same again—ever—

Pleasant memories of all the quiet evenings with the family rose softly up to taunt her: placid, carefree evenings, strolling together along the promenade. How could she ever have thought those evenings dull, and looked with resentful, envious eyes at the groups of giggling girls and boys in the shadows?—they were such comfortable, happy evenings—

And beneath her fears lay an aching disappointment. The first moments of her friendship with this girl had throbbed with almost unbearable excitement, and now, quite suddenly, it had wriggled elusively away into a disappointing, dangerous side track. If only they could have arranged to meet, and just go for a quiet walk together along the coast! If only they could have sat together, somewhere alone, and talked quietly in the gathering dusk—quietly and firmly building up their friendship and understanding of each other! For even though this girl had carried away with her all the bold spirit of romance and adventure, she had left Mary with an admiration and a longing for her friendship that grew deeper through every passing moment. Never before had she felt this exulting determination to win the friendship of another human being, for deep down in her she knew, beyond all shadow of doubt, that a lifelong, treasured friendship lay within her grasp—a friendship that would alter her life and carry her into undreamt-of happiness—

"You're quite pale! Rub yourself down, dear—and wrap your towel round you. What a time they are in there!"

Mary pulled herself back to her surroundings—to the crowded beach—to her mother's anxious voice—

"I'm all right, Mum!"

"Sure you aren't cold?"

"How could I be—on a day like this!"

The Cuddy door opened a few inches, a bare arm emerged, and a wet bathing dress dropped with a soggy plop on the balcony.

"Don't be long," called Mrs. Stevens: "Mary's waiting."

"Won't be half a tick," came a muffled voice from within.

Mr. Stevens's half tick was actually about five minutes, but he made up for it by bouncing out of the hut in Ernie's little school cap, with the boys laughing behind. Mary smiled at them, and passed almost guiltily into the hut.

She dressed slowly, pausing now and then, sitting back rigidly on the little bench with a piece of clothing in her hands. There was a warm, woody smell inside the hut: a small frosted skylight at the back flooded the little room with a pale-yellow glow. She leant down, and slowly and thoughtfully rubbed the sand from between her toes.

Wasn't it rather absurd to be afraid—or even ashamed? Hundreds of girls went out every night and enjoyed the excitement of the promenade: quite decent, healthy girls—just enjoying the fun of meeting boys and having a bit of a rag with them. What earthly harm was there in that?

Cheerful sounds crept through the cracks of the darkened hut—a dog barking in shrill, excited little bursts—the lazy *chock* of rowlocks—stray fragments of talk and laughter. Gradually her depression faded, and then, quite suddenly, her fears and forebodings were swept away in a flood of buoyant confidence. The promenade at night—the tingling excitement of it—the freedom!—footsteps hurrying—footsteps slowing down—lingering—and stopping! Quiet voices from patches of dark, mysterious shadow! Her breath came quickly—her heart seemed to thud and call through the doors that concealed her shrinking spirit, excitedly urging it to rouse itself—to assert its pride and courage. A lucky thing that she had brought her best flowered frock—that her cheeks were bronzed, and her eyes were clear! As nearly as anything she had left that frock at home, and brought only her blue one of last year, which in ordinary ways would have been quite good enough for anything she was likely to do with the family.

Another thought came to help and reassure her: there would be no need for her father and mother to know. She would take Dick into her confidence. Dick would rather enjoy the fun of it. They would go out just as usual, for their evening stroll: they would leave each other at the corner of St. Matthews Road and fix up to meet again at a definite time. Dick would be quite happy on a roaming walk alone—

"Come on, Mary! If you want a bun!"

A bun? Yes, of course—they had buns after the morning bathe.

"Just coming," she called out, scrambling with her stockings.

What was the matter with the bun?—It felt like a lump of putty in her mouth, and after swallowing a small piece of it she left the remainder lying on the step of the hut.

"Dry?" asked Mr. Stevens.

"It is a bit."

Her father looked over his glasses at the half-eaten bun and turned to his wife with a shade of disapproval.

"I told you they would get dry in this weather. There's no need at all to get Sunday's buns on Saturday—there's plenty of cake shops open today."

"Yes—I'll remember another time," said Mrs. Stevens. "It *was* silly"—and she guiltily brushed the stale crumbs of her own bun off her lap.

CHAPTER TWENTY-THREE

During the afternoon another unexpected thing occurred, this time involving the whole family and slightly upsetting them in different ways, according to their particular points of view.

They were playing an afternoon game of cricket, and as Dick was in a hitting mood Mr. Stevens had retired some distance away in the hope of bringing off a spectacular catch. Ernie was bowling and Mary was behind the wicket when Dick sent the ball soaring into the sky. Ernie shouted, "There you are, Dad—catch it!"—but to their surprise Mr. Stevens had disappeared from the place where he had been fielding, and the ball bounced harmlessly on the sands beside a girl in yellow beach pyjamas.

It was the more surprising because Mr. Stevens was always so careful to observe the rules of any games he played. He would not dream of casually wandering off in the middle of an innings.

But the mystery, or at least part of the mystery, was quickly solved, for a glance round the sands revealed Mr. Stevens standing beside a breakwater in conversation with an extremely fat, red-faced gentleman, strikingly dressed in a light-grey flannel suit. He was wearing a large, very white panama hat and carried a malacca cane. A broad red belt of some soft material was round his waist and his dapper brown-and-white, leather and canvas shoes were pointed, and small out of all proportion to his bulk.

He was so unlike Mr. Stevens, and so completely different from the kind of men their father usually had as friends, that the children stared in curiosity and wonder. The cricket match came to a sudden halt, and they stood round waiting, pretending not to be curious, but stealing sidelong glances at the place where their father stood. The stout man's hat came so far over his eyes that they could only see a large red double chin and the end of a broad fat nose: he held his hat on with the curved handle of his walking stick, and as he stood with his legs together and his knees braced back his clothes fluttered behind him and made him look like the figurehead of an old battleship ploughing triumphantly through a storm.

The conversation continued for some little time: the children could hear the fat man's loud voice, but the words were blown away. Their father seemed rather embarrassed and ill at ease—almost like a guilty little boy. He pulled up his trousers, tucked in his shirt and once or twice smoothed down a few thin straying wisps of hair.

At last the fat man pushed out an enormous hand; Mr. Stevens limply grasped it, and the fat man went briskly off along the beach, swaying buoyantly like a captive balloon.

Then Mr. Stevens turned, and slowly approached his children. His head was lowered as if he were deep in thought, but suddenly he seemed to remember. He looked up with a feeble smile, called out, "Carry on," and went back to the place where he had been standing for the cricket.

But his attempt at casualness did not deceive the children: they knew instinctively that something had happened, and although they were burning to know they turned back to the game and carried on.

But the life had gone out of it: they played in a preoccupied way, and when at the end of Ernie's spell of bowling, Mr. Stevens came up to take his turn, Dick could stand the suspense no longer.

"Who was it, Dad?"

"That," said Mr. Stevens with a touch of importance, "was Mr. Montgomery."

"Who's Mr. Montgomery?"

"He's a very important customer of the firm."

Dick felt a sudden relief. For one anxious moment he had pictured the stranger as the Managing Director of his father's firm who had come down to Bognor to give his father the sack.

"He's in a very big way of business," went on Mr. Stevens—"and he's asked us all over to tea tomorrow at his house in Aldwick Road."

He paused and looked at each member of his family in turn, wondering how they would take it. Mrs. Stevens, who had watched the whole affair from The Cuddy balcony, had come down to hear what it was about, and it was she who broke the somewhat awkward silence.

"That's a very kind thing to do!—Is there a Mrs. Mont—?"

"—gomery? Oh, yes. He said his wife would be at home."

The first impulse of the children was naturally one of annoyance—but they concealed it for their father's sake. They knew that they would have to go, for to refuse might hurt their father at the office: it would be very dangerous to decline the invitation of such an important customer of his firm. But the first week of the holiday had passed, and every speeding hour was becoming more precious. There were dozens of things they wanted to do tomorrow, and this stupid invitation would ruin the whole day. The morning would be spent in worrying about it—the early afternoon in getting ready—polishing shoes—putting on wretched collars and ties and hot, tight clothes, and at least part of the evening would be gone before they got back and dressed comfortably again. Why—*why* did aggravating things like this turn up to spoil their precious days? What had they done to deserve it?—Still, it was no good worrying—it couldn't be helped—they would have to make the best of it.

But Mr. Stevens had wisely kept something up his sleeve. He knew exactly how the family would feel about it, and he wanted to get the worst over before he revealed his surprise.

"He's sending his chauffeur—with the car to fetch us," he announced, "and afterwards the chauffeur's going to drive us back!"

"Not—reely!" gasped Mrs. Stevens, but her husband gravely nodded. "Well—I do call that kind!"

The news acted electrically upon Mrs. Stevens, Ernie, and Mary. Only twice had Mrs. Stevens been in a private motorcar, once in a small, noisy little thing belonging to her brother-in-law, and once at her uncle's funeral. The grandeur of a car drawing up at Seaview and throbbing, with a chauffeur at the wheel, outside the gate! She was glad for Mrs. Huggett's sake as well as for her own: it was certain to be seen by other landladies in St. Matthews Road, and even if only one or two saw it the news would rapidly get round—specially as it was bound to be a grand car.

Even Mary could not resist the hope that the showy-off boys and girls at The Sycamores would see: she felt certain it would quieten them down and make them look with more interested, respectful eyes in the days that followed.

Ernie was naturally excited, but to Dick the news brought little to curb his annoyance. A sturdy independence in him was always ready to rise at anything that sounded patronising: he would rather walk—there and back—and only have one "thank you" to give, for his tea. He had taken a dislike to Mr. Montgomery: even from a distance he had summed him up as a bounder: he resented the strange, unpleasant way in which the man had made his father look silly, and small, and ill at ease. Certainly he would rather walk—

Mr. Stevens went on. He knew that he was responsible for the trouble and was determined to do everything in his power to make the occasion as interesting as possible.

"He's just built a new house of his own—and we are his first guests."

"Is he very rich?" enquired Ernie.

"Rich! I should just think he is! He's a very big wholesale sweet manufacturer."

"What sort?" asked Ernie, in a voice that was hushed and awed.

"Buttered sweets mostly—and boiled sweets. I don't think he does much in chocolate. You must have seen them in shops? Montgomery's Butter Nuts? In glass jars, with red and white labels."

Ernie gazed at his father with wide-open eyes: he could only murmur an incredulous "Coo!" He was enthralled—in ecstasy: visions floated before his eyes of the fat man wading knee-deep in assorted fruit balls—of him lazily sprawled on the beach, playing ducks and drakes with Butter Nuts.

"D'you think he'll have some sweets there—tomorrow?"

Mr. Stevens laughed. "I expect he's sick of sweets on his holiday."

Try as he would, Ernie could not remember ever having seen Mr. Montgomery's distinctive bottles in the sweetshops—but he resolved to leave no stone unturned to find them, next time he was in the town.

The others began to catch a little of Ernie's enthusiasm: at any rate they might just as well make the best of it: they laid bets on the colour of the car, and its make. Mary was certain it would be a Rolls, but Ernie stood out for a big Buick. Dick thought a bright-yellow Daimler. After all, it might be rather fun.

Mrs. Stevens hoped that as it was a new house they might be shown all over it. She was always keen on getting new ideas for curtains, and even if she could never hope for any big alterations to the kitchen, she was very interested in seeing the wonderful new inventions people were having now, for keeping things hot and keeping things cold.

Mr. Stevens's own personal feelings were very mixed. It was natural that he should feel irritated and resentful at this unexpected stroke of fate, for no man likes the atmosphere of his office to intrude suddenly upon his holiday. The appearance of Mr. Montgomery had given him quite a shock. He had been caught so completely off his guard, and felt such an awful tramp in his grubby cricket shirt, his old flannel trousers, his untidy hair. It was as if he had gone absent-mindedly to the office like that, for as he stood talking with Mr. Montgomery by the breakwater he felt as though the office, with all its musty files and bleak corners, had suddenly swept down and enveloped him. He would scarcely have been surprised to see a door open in the promenade wall, for one of the Directors to walk out and say, "Ah, Mr. Montgomery! Come along in!"

Tomorrow's journey to Mr. Montgomery's house, even in the comfort and importance of a large motorcar, would be like a journey to his work. He felt sure that he would watch the clock, and feel rightfully entitled to go as it struck six.

But there was another side to it: a very important side. Mr. Montgomery was one of the biggest and most valued customers of the firm: his monthly orders for boxes were regular and considerable, while his order just before Christmas was very large indeed. The Directors, without exception, treated him with great respect when he called at the office, and always conducted him to the door in person, and bowed him out on his departure. He was so important that he often took no notice of Mr. Stevens at all, but sometimes, if he chanced to call after lunch, with a specially red face and a long cigar, he would nod to Mr. Stevens and give him a smile. On one occasion he had even asked Mr. Stevens how he was.

First of all, then, it was a pleasant compliment that Mr. Montgomery should have stopped and spoken to him at all; a still greater compliment that he should have asked them all to tea.

Secondly, it might do Mr. Stevens a lot of good at the office if the tea party went off well, and Mr. Montgomery was left with a favourable impression. He would probably mention the meeting to one of the Directors at his next call, and the Directors would gain a higher estimation of Mr. Stevens, not only because this important customer had thought him good enough to ask to tea, but because he had done something to cement a valued business relationship at the expense of a part of his holiday. It would leave a good mark against his name.

Yes. Certainly the meeting was not without its favourable side—if only the tea party went off well. He knew that he would be proud of Dick and Mary: they would both look smart, both were good-looking and had pleasant manners. He was sure that his wife would try hard and would flatter Mrs. Montgomery about the cakes, and the house, and everything. Ernie was the only doubtful quantity and Mr. Stevens could only hope that he would not fidget or say anything awful about sweets. But after all, he was young, and might even amuse Mr. and Mrs. Montgomery with his funny ways.

He found himself already getting anxious, and he tried to forget it for the time being in the cricket match. But try as they would, they all found the shadow of Mr. Montgomery—his car and his chauffeur—hovering over the pitch and obscuring their sight of the ball.

The walk back to tea was lengthened in order that they could pass through the town and look for Montgomery's Buttered Sweets in the confectioners' windows. They did not find any, however, and Mr. Stevens suggested that Mr. Montgomery probably confined his activities to London and the larger towns. Ernie was disappointed, but Dick was glad that their own little Bognor had ignored this unpleasant fat man's Butter Nuts. They were still discussing Mr. Montgomery, his chauffeur, and his Butter Nuts as they filed through the gate of Seaview for their tea.

As far as Mary was concerned Mr. Montgomery had arrived as a pleasant diversion—a relief to a day that was becoming unbearable in its lingering uncertainty. After lunch and all through the afternoon she had watched for a chance to get hold of Dick and take him into her confidence, to arrange the evening walk and the place where they should part, and meet again. But somehow the opportunity had never come. There was indeed a moment at lunch when she felt the courage to tell her father: he asked a question about the girl, and as Mary told him the story of them having once worked together at Madam Lupont's it was on the tip of her tongue to say that they were meeting that evening for a stroll: it seemed perfectly natural and reasonable that they should meet again, but even as she was framing the words the conversation had turned to something else and her chance had gone.

And now they were at tea—with only a few hours to go, and nothing yet arranged. The talk kept coming back to Mr. Montgomery, and she joined in it mechanically—laughing when the others laughed—but thinking all the while of the coming evening. There was only one thing for it now: directly after tea she would go up to her room, and make an excuse to call Dick up to her, it would be . . . suddenly her train of thought stopped dead—

Tea was over and Mr. Stevens had pushed back his chair and stretched out his legs.

"I tell you what! We'll go along to the pierrots tonight—after supper."

Was there a demon of punishment that hovered over those with guilty secrets?—that waited its chance to dig its fingers into the delicate tissues of deception and tear them apart? Or was it possible that her father had guessed the truth, and done this to thwart her—possibly to save her? But as she looked at him she could see no shadow behind his eyes—just a smile of pleasure at offering a happy evening to his children and his wife—

It scarcely seemed like her own voice that was speaking—it sounded so muffled, and strange.

"I'm sorry, Dad. I fixed up this morning to go for a stroll tonight with Jessica—"

The gilt clock on the mantelpiece, under its glass case, did its utmost to dispel the silence with its thin, metallic tick. Mary felt eyes upon her—four pairs of curious, penetrating eyes—

"I'm awfully sorry—I didn't know you—you thought about anything this evening."

An ice cream man trundled by the window, discordantly jangling his bicycle bell: the faint tinkle of the gramophone came from The Sycamores across the road, and Mary sat hunched in her chair. When her father spoke, the calm naturalness of his voice sounded almost unreal.

"Oh. Oh, well, we can easily go another night."

"I'm frightfully sorry, Dad—"

"Don't be silly! Why shouldn't you go out with her? It'll be a nice change. I thought she looked a very nice girl."

Mary could not reply—she could only raise her head and smile at him. Her gratitude was beyond words.

She ran up to her room directly she could get away, took her best frock from its drawer, and laid it out on the bed: she had taken it out once earlier that day—just after lunch, but then she had only given it a shake, and guiltily returned it to its hiding place. Now she left it where it lay, and put her best shoes and stockings out on the floor beneath it. She left her door open when she came downstairs: there was no guilt to hide now—the frock lay there for anyone to see, and the evening lay ahead, with all its excitement and breathless adventure waiting with outstretched hands. She would never forget her father's trust in her: he had raised her confidence, and given her a new feeling of pride. He had said, with a wink at his wife, that two pretty girls had got to look after themselves in Bognor after dark, and there was something in his voice that showed he had no fear of danger. The evening seemed to have grown lighter: even her gloomy little bedroom caught a stray beam of sun.

The time between tea and supper sped quickly by: the boys went with Mr. Stevens for a stroll along the sands while Mary and Mrs. Stevens walked into Bognor to find a present to take back to Mrs. Haykin. They had sent Mrs. Haykin two coloured cards during the week: of the pier, and one of the bungalows, marking The Cuddy with a cross. Mrs. Haykin had replied with a picture of the Thames Embankment, and said that Joe was quite well and singing beautifully in the mornings. The seed was getting low, but would just about last the time.

It was their annual custom to take back to her a piece of china, with the arms of the town and *A present from Bognor* engraved on it. They took pains each year to get a piece to match the others, and so far had given her two egg cups, a candlestick, a butter dish, an ashtray, and a cream jug. This year they thought a china toast rack would be a pleasant surprise, and found one, after a good deal of searching, in a shop just off the London Road. The shop was shut on Sundays but they resolved to get the rack first thing in the morning.

Dusk was falling as they walked back to Seaview—the dusk that Mary had been waiting for through the long sunlit day, at moments with intense longing, at other times with shrinking fear.

CHAPTER TWENTY-FOUR

Supper, being a cold meal, was soon over, although their jar of ginger beer caused a little anxiety and delay. It began to show signs of giving up the ghost, and a good deal of coaxing, squeezing, and tilting was necessary before their glasses were filled. But it had done very well, and lasted its proper time, for the second jar was due in the morning.

The delay worried Mary because she had decided not to change until after the meal. It would be foolish to flaunt her adventure in the family's eyes, for even though all need for secrecy had been so happily dispersed, it would seem like a challenge to her father and mother if she sat down to supper in her best flowered frock. It would challenge them to reconsider their first generous impulse, it might even arouse second thoughts of an uneasy kind. She tried to conceal her excitement, and talked quite freely of the evening when her parents spoke of it.

It was strange to dress in the glimmering gaslight of her bedroom: it was something she had never done before at Seaview, for after supper in the normal way it was just a matter of running up and groping in the dark for a coat or a hat. It reminded her of winter evenings, dressing in her bedroom at home for the Thursday Dances at St. John's Hall, except that here the light was so terribly bad and so far away from her looking-glass.

A streak of sunset was fading behind the houses on the other side of the road, but the house fronts were very dark, and lights glimmered in windows here and there. She imagined other girls dressing for the evening behind those curtained windows; it gave her courage, and helped her to dispel the loneliness that kept creeping in upon her. She used her lipstick and then decided to rub it off; it was unnecessary, rather incongruous upon a healthy, sunburnt face. It was ten minutes to nine: she pulled on her hat, took a glance in the dingy mirror, and went softly down to her mother's room, where the light was better and the looking-glass less tarnished.

A small, half-empty pot of cold cream stood on her mother's dressing table, beside a bottle of mosquito lotion and a partly knitted sock that bristled with gleaming needles. She took a last glance at herself, flicked off the light, and stood for a moment in the darkness. She would not see herself again until she returned: she wondered what would happen before she lit the gas in her room and went across to her looking-glass to see her face once more. The darkness began to soften, and the window appeared in ghostly grey: the houses opposite rose in black silhouette against the fading remnants of the sunset. She stole softly to the door and downstairs to the hall.

St. Matthews Road was gathering the heavy blackness that falls between the setting sun and the rising moon, but lights were glimmering at the far end, along the promenade. She enjoyed these friendly lights as a rule, but now, as she came out into Marine Parade she shrank from them, and hurried along the pavement on the far side of the road. Even here she felt terribly conspicuous in her bright flowered frock: she had the uneasy feeling that people, as they passed, were stopping and looking back at her.

The entrance to the pier was always a crowded place because of its blaze of lights and enticing automatic machines. In the evenings it became the hub of Bognor, and there looked to be a huge crowd there as Mary anxiously drew near. She thought what a pity it was they had not arranged a quieter meeting place, and with a touch of dismay she wondered if she would ever find her friend in such a throng. A clock was striking in the town as she began to cross the road. The crowd was not really as big as it had looked from a distance, and a glance round showed Mary that her friend had not yet come.

She began to wonder whether they would recognise each other—she hoped she would not be long—it was so glaring, and unprotected where she stood. . . .

Two boys came out of the gloom, into the circle of lights: boys in tight blue blazers, drawn in at the waists, and baggy grey flannel trousers. They stared at her, slowly and impudently, from head to foot, and as they drew away they glanced over their shoulders, spoke to each other, and laughed. Mary felt the blood surge to her cheeks—a sudden impulse to rush off into the night and find her way home through darkened roads. Boys had often looked at her before, but shyly, in a way that pleased her—never had this brazen rudeness happened. She was not angry with the boys, but with herself: Wasn't she asking for it? Wasn't it for this she had come? If only the lights were not so glaring . . . if only the minutes would not drag so eternally. . . .

A strange feeling began to steal over her—a strange, frightening feeling of unreality—the Arcade—the slowly passing crowd became remote, and dreamy: the footsteps and the clang of the automatic machines grew hollow and echoing: her feet were no longer pressing on the pavement—the pavement seemed swollen, and was pressing up against her feet. She felt neither faint nor giddy—it was just a strangeness that would not go. She fought against it, desperately—her heart was hammering—was it madness coming on—was her memory failing? Only a grizzled little man selling papers in the gutter, outside the ring of lights, remained of the world she knew: she gazed at him, trying to draw back, through his placid wrinkled face, the old friendly world of a minute ago. Then he too gradually changed: he too went over and joined this blurred, terrifying unreality.

She took a deep breath, and lowered her head. "It's all right," she whispered.—"It's Bognor!—Dear old Bognor—don't worry—*you* know

Bognor!" "You!" Whose tongue was it, framing the word? "Mary, of course—Mary Stevens!"—And then she was struggling in terror— "Who *is* Mary Stevens? You, of course, and you're staying at Seaview with the family—Seaview—halfway up on the right in St. Matthews Road—remember that!—For heaven's sake remember!" But it was not Mary Stevens any longer—it was a strange, terribly unknown girl in a blazing coloured frock—standing by herself in a blinding glare of light—surrounded by unreal, hollow sounds.

In a minute she would grope her way to Seaview—halfway up on the right in St. Matthews Road—they would wonder who she was— she would plead that she was Mary Stevens—beg them to believe it— unless—unless, of course, Mary Stevens was there. . . .

She was dreamily conscious of an old man passing her—he was looking at her as the boys had looked, shamelessly—impudently—with a half-smiling, hungry stare. She felt herself turning round—walking up the Arcade—facing a shop—a dark shop that was closed. The shadowed window was crowded with knickknacks—beaded purses—little calendars—and there on a shelf stood a row of little china pieces, with a coat of arms upon them, and *A present from Bognor.*

She stared at the little pieces, and a calmness began to come: Wasn't it all right? Hadn't she stood with her mother that very afternoon, before a shop in the town, and looked at little china pieces like this? Of course it was all right—and they were going to buy a china toast rack tomorrow—for Mrs. Haykin. It was just the excitement— getting strung up and anxious, that made her feel so funny. Her eyes rested gratefully on the darkened window, away from the glare. The knickknacks and the beaded purses were helping her—things were becoming normal again: softly and cheerfully real—

An arm slipped round her waist, and made her jump.

"Sorry I'm late!"

"Hullo!" said Mary. "You're—you're not late."

"I say—what a stunning frock!"

"D'you like it?" said Mary with a glow of pleasure.

"Like it! It's lovely! But what chance d'you suppose I'm going to have against that!"

Mary laughed. "Shouldn't think *you* need worry!"

Her friend was wearing a simple white frock, with a little red belt of shining leather. It looked superbly fresh and cool beside the gaudy coloured posters and automatic machines, and it thrilled Mary to think of the evening she had first seen her friend wearing it, by the railings at the band. It thrilled her to remember how she had sat watching the girl that evening, in wistful admiration and envy, from her seat between her father and mother—how restless and dispirited she had felt because she never knew any girls of that kind. Had she dozed in her chair that evening could she ever have dreamt such a wonderful thing as this? The girl's hand was resting lightly on her arm—her eyes were laughing down on her—the eyes of the one girl—above all others in Bognor. . . . If she lived a hundred years she would never cease to wonder at this moment, and treasure it as a fairy story beautifully come true. . . .

"Let's wander along, shall we?"

"Righto."

CHAPTER TWENTY-FIVE

They went out of the Arcade, away from the warm smell of sweets and people, into the open air of the promenade. The breeze was fresh, but it came from the south and carried a softness with it. Mary felt splendidly well again now: all trace of the frightening sense of unreality had passed with the arrival of her friend and Bognor had become its good old friendly self again. It did not lift its eyebrows in surprise—it did not edge away from her because of the boldness of her adventure—it welcomed her as it always did, and drew her softly into its drowsy evening life.

The usual crowds were passing to and fro, sauntering aimlessly and lazily after their day in the sun: the charabanc people had gone and the promenade was in the hands of its rightful owners. A few children dodged amongst the crowd and a few dogs mingled with the passing legs.

After a little way the girl took Mary's arm and glanced down at her with a smile.

"Look here," she said—"What am I going to call you?"

"Mary's what I'm generally called."

"Righto: you're Mary to me now. My name's Jessica—but it's too starchy for most people. Most people call me Billie."

"Shall *I* call you Billie?"

"Yes. Rather."

They walked on in silence, Billie glancing easily and happily to and fro. Mary walked close beside her—resolving to do as Billie did—yet holding her head up and glancing round without fear or shyness. She was happily surprised to find that she was not afraid: the crowd was so friendly and good-spirited: she felt nothing but a bracing urge for fun and adventure.

Boys passed in groups—sauntering with their hands in the pockets of their baggy flannel trousers—idly kicking stones and bits of paper—laughing, talking loudly, sometimes whispering. All turned round and looked as the girls went by: sometimes a boy would say "Good evening" or "Hullo!"—and Billie would reply with a friendly word and smile: sometimes they passed boys who looked in silence, with genuine admiration in their eyes, for even amongst a crowd of girls all dressed for the occasion, there was just a shade of difference about Billie and her friend. Billie was so much taller than most of the girls who passed, and yet it was a tallness that carried grace and poise. Mary could not help noticing that none of the boys came boldly and crudely up to them as they did to other girls; there was a touch of shyness in their manner towards Billie, and although she always returned a friendly smile she showed quite clearly that her nets were made to jerk out the little fish in slouch caps and baggy trousers.

They came to the Western Bandstand and listened beside the railings for a while. It was pleasant to turn for a moment from the glaring lights and the shuffling crowds, and look into the cool peace of the darkened enclosure with its soft green turf and quiet people lying back in deck chairs. But something happened as they stood there listening: Mary became conscious of a solitary man who sidled up nearby. She saw the pale blur of his face intently turned their way, and gradually a little touch of fear crept over her. There was something uncanny in that silent stare, something rather ominous, and evil.

But Billie quickly reassured her by very pointedly turning her back on the man and starting a casual conversation with Mary about the bandsmen.

"Nice boys, some of them," she said—"You see those two on the right of the Bandmaster—playing flutes?—they're brothers. We had a bit of fun with them last week—but they're country boys and get frightfully stodgy after an hour or so. Come on." She rapped out the last two words so abruptly that Mary was quite startled.

"Be careful of men who're out by themselves—like that one," she announced to Mary as they walked away: "There's often something queer about men out alone—always go for boys who're together. You can tell they're decent if they've got friends."

They had nearly reached the end of the promenade, and were thinking of turning back when Billie gave Mary a gentle but expressive nudge. They were out of the main crowd here, and Mary, glancing quickly up at her friend, saw that she was looking intently between the scattered, sauntering people at a seat some little distance ahead. It was just where the promenade ended—where the sea front narrowed into a path beside some trees. Two men were sitting there, side by side.

"Don't stare too hard," whispered Billie.

They drew abreast of the seat, and Mary, from the corner of her eye, could see enough to understand the sign her friend had given her: two well-dressed men were sitting there—in plus fours and smart, soft felt hats—very different from the baggy-trousered, tight-jacketed boys they had been passing.

The two men made no sign as the girls went by: they seemed, in fact, scarcely conscious of them at all, for they went on talking quietly to each other. But Mary, with a stirring excitement, felt the men's eyes upon her as she drew away—felt the men had stopped talking, and were watching them—

The two girls neither glanced back nor checked their pace: they went beyond the promenade—into the narrow path between the trees. It was not until they had gone a hundred yards, and were well out of sight of the men on the seat, that Billie stopped and looked down at her friend.

"What d'you think?" she asked. "D'you like 'em?"

"I think so," whispered Mary. "They look quite nice."

She was wondering, as far as her excitement would allow, whether the men, in their turn, had liked the look of Billie and her. She had not seen much, really, for the brims of their hats had thrown their faces into shadow—she had only judged them by their clothes, and the easy look about them that made her sure that they were gentlemen—

Billie appeared to have no doubt about the two men's feelings—she pondered a moment, and then said: "We'll just stroll back, just as we came. Don't look at them or stop till we're a good bit past them. Then we'll go up to the railings and look at the sea. They'll come up then, and we can make up our minds."

A couple passed, arm in arm, but they took no notice of the lingering girls.

Billie raised her hand, brushed the hair back from her forehead, and firmly took Mary by the arm. The promenade was hidden, and it was only when they left the dark, wind-bent trees that it came in view again. It would have been a sad anti-climax if the men had gone since the girls had passed them, and Mary's heart began to race when she saw the same four legs sprawled out from the shadows round the seat. She could never have passed the men again if Billie had not been with her, but she took courage from her friend's leisurely unconcern and walked as calmly as she could. The two men still seemed wrapped in conversation as the girls drew opposite, but Mary felt more keenly than before the searching eyes that followed them—cool, discriminating eyes—

They must have gone some thirty yards before Billie gently steered her friend towards the railings. "This'll do," she whispered—and then in a normal, unconcerned voice she began to talk of trivial things.

"Isn't it a lovely night?—That must be a boat out there—d'you see the cabin lights? It must be a big boat to have so many—"

Mary marvelled at Billie's self-control: there was something inspiring about her absolute knowledge and understanding of the thing to do, there was boldness and courage, but Mary herself could scarcely force a word: she had to fight an overwhelming fascination to look over her shoulder at the seat. . . .

The sea was feeling its dark way across the sands, a fragment of the black horizon was faintly smeared with tarnished gold where the waning moon was resting behind the clouds. They seemed to wait ages by the railings, and gradually Mary felt the indignity of it, an anger against herself, and against the men—were they just playing with them? It had not occurred to her till now that Billie might have made a mistake: she traced uneasiness in Billie's voice—the airy casualness of it began to take on a note that was strained and artificial.

And then it happened—just as Mary had given up all hope. Billie was prattling about the Fun Fair and the Crazy Cars when suddenly her voice died, and Mary felt an urgent little nudge. "Here they come," she whispered.

There were steps behind—sauntering, casual steps that seemed to last an eternity: Mary's heart was pounding somewhere in her throat—she nearly screamed at the strain of it—and then, mercifully, a quiet, pleasant voice broke in to snap the intolerable silence—

"Sorry to keep you waiting," said the voice, "we had something important to talk about. We're free now: at your service."

Mary was too bewildered to feel either anger or shame: it was so utterly unexpected; there was something so utterly deserved in the taunt—yet something in the pleasant voice that took all the rudeness from the words. It was Billie who flared up: Mary could see the flushed cheeks of her friend: she had drawn herself up and was standing with her back to the railings as though the man had struck her in the face.

"How *dare* you! . . . Who are you! . . ."

"Don't be silly," came the smooth, friendly voice.

"If you don't leave us alone—I'll—"

"—tell a policeman?"

"Yes! I'll tell a policeman!"

The man raised his arms in comic terror.

"Don't shoot," he pleaded—"Don't give us up!—It'd be the last straw. Look at us! Two poor men who were just thinking there wasn't a solitary good-looking girl in Bognor."

"Then what d'you mean—talking like that!" There was still an effort at anger in Billie's voice—but Mary knew that every shadow of true anger had fled.

"I'm sorry," said the man, "I'm an absolute idiot—I didn't mean it—really—"

There was something so disarming about the way the words were said that before they realised it, all four of them were laughing.

Mary had said nothing: she had just stood by—her face half turned towards the sea. The waning moon had pushed its way through a film of cloud—but it seemed like the moon of some other world. Every glance she had shyly taken had strengthened her admiration of Billie's knowledge, for beside her stood by far the two best-looking men she had seen that night.

The man who had spoken was tall and fair: his friend was shorter and younger—scarcely more than a boy. In a strange way they seemed the male counterparts of Billie and herself—for the tall fair one seemed obviously the leader of the shy dark-haired boy beside him. The boy was rather like Dick in a way, though a little broader in the shoulders and rounder in the face. She could see his eyes now, beneath the turned-down brim of his hat—dark, friendly eyes, and a large, good-natured mouth that showed a line of white teeth as he stood there smiling.

But the leader it was who sent a prickle of excitement through her body: there was something so immensely strong about him although he was not physically a ponderous man. His rough brown suit was so perfectly in keeping with him, and although there was a rugged look about his face there was no trace of coarseness in it. Perhaps it was his voice that held her most of all—there was music in it she had rarely heard before—anywhere—not even on the stage—and while his words were spoken lightly and flippantly, there lay a strong sincerity beneath.

She never quite knew how it happened—perhaps because it was so easy and natural—but there was Billie, strolling along in front with the boy beside her—and here was she, a few yards behind, strolling beside this splendid man. She had felt certain it would be the other way about; and that she would have been with the boy, for Billie and this tall man seemed made for one another. Perhaps it was that very likeness that brought about this different scheme—Billie would certainly get more admiration from the boy . . . but what did the hows and whys of it matter?—it had happened—just happened. . . .

"Let's go the other way. We're walking along like a girl's school!"

It was the first thing he had said to her, or at least, the first words of his that came intelligibly to her bewildered brain: she turned with him as if some mighty power had reached out and twisted her with its little finger.

He did not attempt to take her arm: he just walked beside her as Dick might have done. Only once, when three rowdy boys approached, did he gently place his hand upon her shoulder as if to protect her, and the boys, who had been strung out arm in arm, broke up and went quietly by on either side.

He talked of casual things in a light, joking way, and when they came to the seat where he had been sitting with his friend, he paused and looked at it, and gave a little laugh.

"I'll have to buy this seat—and keep it as a souvenir!"

He smilingly motioned to Mary to sit down, and it was not until he had seated himself beside her that a deep, vibrant meaning flashed from the words he had said, and left her for a moment quite breathless—

The golden hours of life leave no sharp outlines to which the memory can cling: no spoken words remain—nor even little gestures and thoughts; only a deep gratitude that lingers on impervious to time.

Pat was his name. Pat Mackenzie: an actor who was playing a week at the Theatre in the town. He preferred playing in London, but he always enjoyed the rag of a seaside tour in the summer: it gave him a holiday without interrupting his work. He had only arrived that afternoon from Hastings, and they opened at the Theatre tomorrow night: an awful play, he said, with a wry little smile—but it wasn't bad fun—a thriller called *The Crimson Dagger*.

He sat a little away from Mary—but he was facing her—leaning a little towards her with one arm stretched along the back of the seat, behind her shoulders.

For a while Mary sat quite silent—scarcely listening, thinking only—a little sadly—"I'll wake up in a minute."

It could only be a dream. No one in her waking life had ever spoken to her like this: his bantering, joking voice had gone: he was talking to her intensely and earnestly. Not a word of silly teasing or flattery—just about himself—his life—his art—the stage. Yet never a word of conceit or self-esteem; he told her of his life because he wanted her sympathy and understanding, and now and then he would pause and say very softly—"What would you have done?"—or "Would you—if you were me?"

Slowly the incredible wonder of it began to dawn on her: this was no dream after all: it was true—all exquisitely true!

He tried to belittle his achievements: he tried to show that his life was just a work-a-day one, like her own—but nothing could stem the romance of it: nothing could shatter its enchantment. Freedom—wanderlust—thrilling loyalty—poverty and wealth—rehearsals that ached their way into the dawn—bitter failure—thunderous applause—

Then suddenly Mary realised that he was growing silent, and she was speaking. He was asking her about her life—about herself—and she told him everything, with his steady, thoughtful eyes upon her, with now and then a little nod of understanding and a flashing smile—

She was aghast when he pulled out his watch and asked what time she wanted to get in.

"I *must* be in by ten," she said.

He threw back his head with a laugh. "It's gone the half hour!"

"What—nine!"

"No—ten!"

She begged him not to trouble about seeing her home—but he insisted upon guarding her to the corner of St. Matthews Road—and all the time while his long legs strode evenly beside her hurrying footsteps he was talking of tomorrow—eagerly of tomorrow. His part was all over in the first act and he was free by ten past nine—would she come round to the stage door, and meet him there? She could wait just inside.

And then, at the corner of St. Matthews Road he gently took her hand, and held it for the first time.

"I wonder if you know," he said—"what this evening has meant to me?"

The front door was ajar—she remembered looking into the sitting-room and seeing her father there, finishing his pipe: she saw the blue smoke curling in the air, and smelt the scent of it. She heard his voice asking if she had had a nice time, and her own voice saying, "Lovely—thanks, Dad. Good night."

She remembered the gas in her bedroom, squeaking its blue jet towards the dark-brown ring on the ceiling—of crushing her face into her pillow and whispering—"Go to sleep!—Don't think!—If you start thinking you'll never—never sleep!"

CHAPTER TWENTY-SIX

The Monday of the second and last week of the holiday went down in the history of the Stevens family as Montgomery Day.

In a sense the tea party began before dawn, for twice, while it was still dark, Mr. Stevens woke up and lay thinking about it. Each time he realised with keener anxiety how much its success or failure would affect him at the office, and once, when he dozed, he dreamt that Ernie called Mr. Montgomery a brandy ball, and Mr. Montgomery telephoned straight up to Jackson & Tidmarsh and took all his business away, and Jackson & Tidmarsh telephoned straight back, giving Mr. Stevens the sack. It was a very unpleasant dream, and he woke up in a cold sweat.

The tea party hung like a cloud over breakfast, and took the heart out of the morning on the sands. It was not that anyone objected to the tea party simply as a tea party, with plenty of cakes and sandwiches— much less to being called for in a large car with a chauffeur. As far as that went it was all right: even exciting. But the thing that no one could help regretting was the way it broke into one of the precious remaining days of the holiday.

Only five full days remained to them now, and they would have given almost anything to have this Monday entirely free. They would not have done anything special: they would have spent just a quiet, ordinary kind of day—the kind they enjoyed most of all—morning cricket, with half an hour's interval in the sea, a deliciously lazy afternoon, dozing round The Cuddy, then a peaceful ramble along the sands. If only Mr. Montgomery, in a fit of divine understanding, would send the tea—packed in cardboard boxes—all sorts of cakes and sandwiches—for the family to eat quietly and happily round their own table! But things like that do not happen in this world. They did their best to forget the afternoon in a game of rounders, but Mr. Montgomery's bulky shadow still seemed to loom across the flight of the ball, and there were many fumbled catches and mistimed hits.

It was useless to start doing anything seriously after lunch, for they would have to begin getting ready at three, so Mr. Stevens, with Dick and Ernie, walked up into the town to call at the chemist's for a roll of film he was developing for them. They had taken their first lot of snaps on the previous Wednesday—nearly a week ago, and they were keenly looking forward to opening the packet when they got outside the shop. So much had happened since the day they were taken that it was impossible to remember exactly what each picture was until they pulled them out and looked at them.

"All right?" enquired Mr. Stevens rather anxiously.

The chemist nodded and smiled as he handed over the packet. They were very relieved when he charged them for developing six negatives and printing six pictures: it showed that they had all come out, for he never printed from negatives that were failures. He was a tactful man, too—a man of understanding, for he did not pull the pictures out, like the chemist did at home, and spoil the Stevenses' pleasure by handing them the photos, one by one, between the bottles on his counter: he knew how much more exciting it was for people to go away with the closed envelope, and open it, quietly, in a secluded corner.

"This'll do," said Mr. Stevens, and they drew into a recess a few yards down the street. Dick and Ernie watched their father's fingers fumbling inside the envelope; he was quite excited as he drew out the pictures and passed them round.

The first was wonderfully clear—but then, of course, it had been a beautiful day. It was a family group, with everybody except Dick, who had taken it. There was Mr. Stevens, leaning against the balcony, smoking his pipe, with Mary beside him, leaning over the rails. Mrs. Stevens was rather too far back, in the shadow, and only her face and a V-shaped piece of neck showed up. Ernie was sitting on the steps so near to the camera that his knees looked enormous, and Mr. Stevens laughed and cried out, "Look at old Jumbo!" Mary had come out best— she was laughing, and looked splendid. Mr. Stevens was secretly a little disappointed about himself, for the bright light made his hair look so thin—much balder than he really was. It was a pity that he always seemed to come out like that.

Next came a merry picture of Dick and Mary, arm in arm, in their bathing dresses—roaring with laughter at something Dick could not now call to mind. There was one of Ernie, with his yacht under his arm—scowling in a most unnecessary way, and a comic picture of Mr. Stevens in Ernie's little striped cap, with a shrimping net in one hand and a bun in the other. Ernie doubled up and laughed so much at this picture that Mr. Stevens got rather quiet, and looked at it again. He wondered whether by some mishap it was funnier than he meant it to be.

There was an awfully good snap of Mrs. Stevens, taken when she didn't know; sitting in her deck chair on the sands, knitting—and they looked forward to surprising her with it when they got back. The last was simply a picture of The Cuddy, with no one in it, the doors thrown open to make it look as big as possible.

"Look at that!" said Dick—"You can read the name as clearly as anything over the door!"

"I've never seen such a clear photo," remarked Mr. Stevens—"It's better than the one of Puss on the cushion."

"You mean the one we took on the lawn?"

"Yes—the one we took last year."

"Oh—this is much better—it's so clear-cut—you can almost count the pebbles."

It was a most successful batch altogether: there was a funny little straggling thing, like a blade of grass, dangling down from the right top corner of all the pictures—it must have been something on the lens, for it was just the same in all of them—not enough to spoil the pictures, but Mr. Stevens decided to have a look at the camera before taking any more.

Dick and Ernie took one final glance, then Mr. Stevens pushed the pictures into the envelope and dropped them into his pocket with a sigh. What a pity it was about the tea party. It would have been so much jollier, lazing round the dear old Cuddy, drowsily watching the crowd. Tea in their own sitting-room, even without cake, would be a hundred times nicer—but there it was: it couldn't be helped—

"Come on, boys," he said, "We'll have to go and spruce up now. It's nearly three." He spoke cheerfully, and thought how splendid it would be in the cool of the evening—when they were free once more: specially if the party went off well—

There is nothing more horrible than putting on a stiff collar after a week's freedom in an open cricket shirt. The neck seems so rough and warm—the collar so stiff and cold. Mr. Stevens decided not to dress up too much—just a collar and tie, and his blue serge coat instead of his sports jacket: he decided to wear his grey flannel trousers and white shoes, for it would be silly to look too Londony at the seaside, even at a tea party. It took him a long time to get his hair smooth and properly parted, because he had let it run wild for a week. He always hoped it would grow by leaving it free to the wind and sun, but somehow, when the day came to brush and oil it once more, it always seemed thinner and quite a lot came out on the comb.

Dick also put on a collar and tie—but he wore his blazer and flannels, and Mr. Stevens felt very proud of his son when he came down to the sitting-room. He looked so fresh, and healthy.

Mrs. Stevens, with a clean lace collar over her best blouse, was disappointed when Mary came down in her light-blue frock.

"Why ever not your new flowered one?" she exclaimed.

"It's all right, Mum," said Mary, with a little smile—"It'd never do to dress up too smartly. It's only afternoon tea."

Mrs. Stevens looked hesitatingly at Mary, and finally agreed: Mary had a knack of looking nice in anything, so it didn't really matter. It was silly, though, not to wear that beautiful flowered one—an important tea party like this was just the time for it.

Ernie made himself an abominable nuisance. His seaside clothes were impossible for a smart tea party—and he was ordered to wear the blue serge suit that he came in: his best suit, which he hated and loathed.

It was certainly growing a bit too small for him—for Ernie threatened to be the largest of the family in a few years' time, but Mrs. Stevens was certain that he deliberately puffed himself out through sheer obstinacy. "Look at it!" he kept wailing—"It won't meet! Do let's wear the other things, Mum!"

"You've got to look smart," repeated Mrs. Stevens for the twentieth time. "D'you want your dad to be ashamed of you? Don't stick yourself out—you naughty boy!"

They were ready by half past three, and the little sitting-room looked like the waiting-room at a railway station: they sat round silently—anxiously gazing towards the window at every sound of a distant car. Twice they heard cars actually coming down the road, but they were only tradesmen's vans. Dick and Mr. Stevens occasionally smoothed their hair, and passed a finger uncomfortably round the inside of their collars. The car was not actually due till a quarter to four, but as Mrs. Stevens very sensibly reminded them, cars are such quick things, you never know.

But a quarter to four came: it chimed out thinly from the mantelpiece clock: it died—yet no car came in sight.

"He'll come down the road from the High Street end, I expect," said Mr. Stevens, strolling to the window.

"Unless he comes up from the promenade end," suggested Mrs. Stevens. But he came from neither. Five more minutes dragged by—the feeble conversation sickened and died.

"Wouldn't it be a good idea," said Mrs. Stevens, "if somebody was to walk up to the top of the road—and look?"

Mr. Stevens pooh-poohed the suggestion. Chauffeurs, he said, were specially trained to find places. But nevertheless—as the clock was on the point of four, he rose, and sauntered to the gate.

"It's a funny thing," said Mrs. Stevens, fidgeting with her blouse, and crossing her ankles the other way. She was sitting upright in one of the stiff chairs, her bag and gloves ready beside her on the table.

"I'll just stroll up to the corner," called out Mr. Stevens through the sitting-room window. But even as he stepped through the gate, a large blue car swung round from the High Street and came slowly along the road. Mr. Stevens quickly withdrew to the cover of the thin laurel hedge—then furtively he crept back up the steps. Private cars very seldom came down St. Matthews Road—and he was certain that only a man like Mr. Montgomery would have one as large as the one approaching.

"Here it comes, I think!"—his shoulder brushed against the picture of Grace Darling, making it swing dangerously to and fro. He steadied it and reached for his hat.

Ernie was the first to see the large shining nose of the car glide slowly into view, and stop outside. He was watching, unashamed, from the window, for nobody at the moment had the leisure to pull him away. Then they stood round waiting, but no knock came at the door: no chauffeur came up the path—no chauffeur even got out of the car. Perhaps chauffeurs didn't get out—thought Mr. Stevens—perhaps you just went out and got in. He really couldn't remember what he had seen happen when private motorcars drove up to private houses, and after a moment's reflection he decided to take the initiative.

"Come along," he said.

They trooped out of the little sitting-room, down the dark, narrow passage to the front door. The cricket bat and ball lay on the hall stand; happy relics of their freedom—of the sands that now seemed strangely faraway: the bat seemed to turn its pale face up to them as they passed—it seemed to whisper, "Never mind—it'll all be over soon—I'll wait!"

They saw that the chauffeur had climbed from his seat and had opened the door of the saloon: they also saw him look contemptuously at the faded narrow house—and then at the big, shining car beside him. He was a tall man with thick black eyebrows and a long, hatchet face. His mouth seemed to dangle a long way down from his nose by two dark lines tied to the corners of it—he looked the kind of man who drove ghostly coaches over precipices on dark, stormy nights, but when his face cracked into a frosty smile they saw that he only had two teeth in front, and then, with a stretch of imagination it was possible to think of him as faintly human. Ernie wondered how he had come into the world, for he never could have been a baby.

He made no effort to help the Stevenses as they grouped round the door of the car like an anxious little flock of sheep—he looked on, enjoying their embarrassment. At last Mr. Stevens turned round—placed his hand on the small of his wife's back, and propelled her gently forward—but she lost her nerve, slid off his hand, and shrank away. "Somebody else first!" she whispered.

It was Mary who stepped forward with a laugh, and jumped into the car: there was a trace of anger in her eyes and her cheeks were flushed. She had caught a glimpse of a group of faces at the window of The Sycamores on the other side of the road: the boys and girls who were staying there—and she thought she saw laughter in their faces. The family quickly followed; Mr. and Mrs. Stevens beside Mary—Ernie on a small seat facing them and Dick beside the chauffeur. They ran down to the sea, turned westward, and purred along the promenade.

CHAPTER TWENTY-SEVEN

S everal people glanced at the car as it passed, and Mr. Stevens wondered if they thought it was his own. He hoped they might pass one of his evening friends of the Clarendon Arms, but they had no luck, although once, with mingled hope and fear, he thought he recognised a broad back on the pavement ahead as belonging to Rosie. She certainly might be out at this time in the afternoon and if only she saw him without his having to see her it would be great fun in the evening: she would rag him about it—and he would make up all sorts of nonsense to annoy her . . . but it wasn't Rosie, after all—he looked from the corner of his eye, and saw the hard profile of quite a different sort of woman—

They passed through the outskirts of the town and came into a narrow country lane that held pleasant memories for Mr. Stevens. It was along this lane that he used to start for his day's walk before the buses took him to the higher ground: it used to wind peacefully and beautifully between tall hedgerows and rich pastureland, but of recent years the lane had fallen into builders' hands, gradually the hedgerows had grown bald and dusty—great gaps had opened to let through lorry loads of bricks, and villas had risen where larks used to rise.

It was outside such a villa that the car drew up: they saw the chauffeur lean forward to change gear, then they swung gingerly through a varnished yellow gate and up a new gravel drive that shone brightly in the afternoon sun. The family, craning eagerly through the windows, saw a bright-red house before them, standing shadeless in the glare.

The car pulled up, and the chauffeur suddenly came to life. He jumped alertly from his seat and briskly flung open the saloon door.

Mr. Montgomery himself came out to greet them—"Ha!" he cried in a jovial voice, "Got here all right?—That's fine!"

Mr. Stevens introduced the family as the chauffeur unpacked them and Mr. Montgomery shook them all boisterously by the hand.

He was dressed much about the same as when they had seen him on the sands, but this was the children's first chance of a close view of him. He was also without his hat now, and they saw that he had a very bald, shiny head. His eyes, nose, and mouth were crowded very close and rather meanly together considering the large amount of unused face that lay around them, and as they followed him into the house, Ernie saw that there was ample room for another face on the back of his neck.

It certainly was a very new house indeed: it looked as if it had been finished five minutes before they arrived, and it was hard to think of any of it having been built even a few days before the rest. It was a good-sized house of bright-red brick and dazzling white stucco: two white columns supported the entrance porch, and in the glass panel of the front door was a coloured picture of an old-fashioned ship in full sail. Striped green-and-white sun blinds stuck out over all the windows—and there was something about the whole place that made you feel that since the day it was finished the sun had shone on it: that it would go on shining on it—bakingly and relentlessly—forever and ever—from a hot, pale-blue sky.

"Now then!" said Mr. Montgomery, as they came into the imposing hall, "make yourselves absolutely at home! Nothing stiff about this house!"

"That's what we like," laughed Mr. Stevens, wondering where to put his hat.

There was a large oak chest in one corner, with rare carvings on it, but it looked too good to put a hat on. It was like the kind you saw in Museums, where they took your umbrellas away in case you poked it with them. He saw Ernie stuffing his cap into his pocket, and envied him. He had mildly rebuked Dick for coming bareheaded, but now he wished he had done the same. Then luckily his eye fell upon a window seat, and he pushed his hat furtively into a corner of it.

"Come along into the lounge!" shouted Mr. Montgomery—and the Stevenses followed him into a large, very grand room which made Ernie lick his fingers and smooth his hair. The room was all done in light blue—with lots of brass bowls, and ferns sticking out of them.

"Where's that wife of mine?" boomed Mr. Montgomery. He went out into the hall and called up the stairs—"Daisy!!"

There was a pause: then a thin querulous voice from somewhere above replied, "All right,"—and the tone of the words also included—"What made you go asking these people to the house—without finding out first if it was convenient?"

Tea was already laid out—and it was certainly a generous array. There was a cake stand with chocolate eclairs, small currant buns, a large sponge sandwich, and two kinds of bread and butter—but Ernie could see no sign of Montgomery's Boiled Sweets.

"Now then!" said Mr. Montgomery, returning to the room, "make yourselves quite at home. Free and easy's my motto at the seaside."

There were several very low, very soft-looking armchairs, and a luxurious settee. Mrs. Stevens sat on the edge of one of the chairs—not so much through diffidence, but because in a few moments she would have to rest her teacup on her knee, but Mr. Stevens, lacking his wife's foresight, sat right back in his: he sank down and down until he felt his feet jerk off the ground as the edge of the chair straightened out his knees. Ernie watched his father's struggles with mingled curiosity and dismay: he had a vague feeling that he ought to run and look for a life belt, but Mr. Stevens soon recovered himself, and was just in time to rise as Mrs. Montgomery came in.

He was surprised at Mrs. Montgomery—in fact they were all surprised. During supper the previous night they had decided that she would be a fat, rosy-cheeked woman, rather like Mrs. Bullevant at home, only grander, of course, and easier on her feet. But they saw in front of them a woman neither fat nor thin: a faded woman with yellow hair, bright-red lips, and rosy cheekbones. She looked as if she had been boiled in too much water, then artificially flavoured. She gave a soft, limp hand to Mr. and Mrs. Stevens, smiled languidly at the children, then sat down and tinkled a small bell on the tray.

"So hot," she murmured with a heavy sigh—"the sun seems to get everywhere, doesn't it?"

"It does," agreed Mr. Stevens, his eyes wandering out to the shade-less garden. He could see some small, scraggy trees, with labels round their thin, parched necks. They looked as if they had been set five minutes ago, and were crying down the road in panic to the man who put them in—begging him to return and take them away with him.

A maid arrived with a shining tea service, and as their hostess began to pour out tea Dick stood up and offered Mr. Montgomery the plate of brown bread and butter. It pleased Mr. Stevens to see his son do this without any prompting: he did it so quietly and modestly, and looked up at Mr. Montgomery with a friendly little smile. Mr. Stevens saw Mr. Montgomery look down at his son with a curious expression in his little eyes—then he reached for a slice of bread and butter, folded it up, and took it. He did not eat it: he just took it, and it made Ernie, who was watching, very interested in Mr. Montgomery. The little piece of bread and butter had disappeared like a trick, and Ernie half expected Mr. Montgomery to produce it from his ear. He watched, but was disappointed to find that nothing further happened.

Mr. Stevens had felt happy and confident as they had jumped from the car and followed their host up the drive, but now, as tea began, he felt an uneasiness stealing over him. It was nothing to do with the family, for they had behaved perfectly and he was pleased and proud of them up till now: it was something else that made him restless and uneasy—something a little queer about the party that he had not expected, and could not quite understand. It may have come from the un-homely feeling of the room: it was cool, but there was something stagnant in its coolness—it was new, and yet a strange mustiness hung in the air—of stale cigars, and varnish, and scent. The Montgomerys, too, were so different to what he'd expected: he scarcely knew Mr. Montgomery from the occasional sight of him in the office, and he had expected to find such jovial, homely people. He had always heard that important people were very friendly and easy in private life.

It was not that either their host or hostess was in the slightest degree unfriendly. Mr. Montgomery's voice was jovial enough—but it was hollow and loud, as if a cheap amplifier were fixed in his throat. When he laughed there was no humour in his eyes—no wrinkles formed round them—only his mouth opened and curled up at the corners—his little eyes remained the same: fixed and staring.

Mr. Stevens sat well forward on his armchair—his wife opposite, and Ernie on a little cane chair beside her. Dick and Mary sat together on the luxurious settee—Mrs. Montgomery drooped in a chair by the tea table, and their host stood on the hearthrug.

If only Mr. Montgomery would sit down! It might make all the difference. Once he reached forward, picked up the plate containing the sponge sandwich, and flourished it before Ernie.

"This is more in your line—eh, sonny?" He said it kindly enough, but Ernie hated being called sonny: he went very red, smiled, said, "Yes, please," and took a thick slice of the delicacy.

"How's old Wilks?" said Mr. Montgomery. He shot the question out so suddenly that Mr. Stevens was quite at a loss. He stared vaguely for a moment, and then smiled. He supposed that Mr. Montgomery was referring to Mr. Wilkins, the Managing Director of the firm.

"He was very well when I left," said Mr. Stevens.

His host took a resonant sip of tea. "Can't understand how your firm ever keeps going with a fellow like that in charge. He really is the most old-fashioned stick-in-the-mud I ever met!"

It was a strange thing to say: a very difficult thing to answer, and Mr. Stevens could only return a smile. He liked Mr. Wilkins: he had always been so good to him. When Mary, as a baby, had been very ill, Mr. Wilkins used to come out of his room and talk to Mr. Stevens—asking if they had a good doctor, and telling him to go home early. He was a quiet, courtly old gentleman and Mr. Stevens reverenced him. It distressed him to hear him spoken of like this—

"How long's he going to hang on?" asked Mr. Montgomery.

"I don't know. Of course, he's growing an old man now—"

"You've been there a good stretch, I s'pose?"

"Thirty years," said Mr. Stevens with a smile.

"I thought you'd been perched up in that corner of yours a pretty good time."

Silence had fallen over the room: it was broken by Mr. Stevens's nervous little laugh, and Dick, sitting opposite his father, felt a cold anger rising. He looked up at the big fat chuckling man, straddling the hearthrug—then down at his father, sitting on the edge of the armchair, his teacup balanced on his knee, his round grey eyes looking appealingly over at him. He saw how carefully his father had brushed his thin brown hair—the crease in his flannel trousers where he had pressed them under his bed last night—his cheap grey socks, and the old canvas shoes he had carefully pipe-clayed in the garden that morning. His father had done all in his power to look nice for the afternoon, and suddenly Dick's anger turned to a pride that was fiercer and stronger than anything he had ever felt before. It blazed up and filled him with a sudden thankfulness. Through every shred of his father's cheap ready-made clothes he could see a finer man than the fat giant on the hearth-rug with his expensive grey suit and silk shirt. His father was just a clerk, struggling proudly and silently on a few pounds a week: this other man had thousands—even his seaside house was bigger and immensely grander than their own little place in Corunna Road—all round lay signs of careless wealth—thick carpets—great easy chairs—shining ornaments and glittering jewels in that faded woman's clothes—yet what was it all worth? When he looked across at his father's sunburnt face he thought of the sea and the sands; a bounding cricket ball and shouts of laughter—walking sticks and fishing rods and fluttering kites; absorbing games and hobbies—the books he read aloud to them on winter evenings. Salt from the sea lay in his father's skin, under that shiny blue serge coat: he watched his father's hand flutter nervously to his tie and saw the long, sensitive fingers and the narrow delicate nails: his eyes rose to the man above him, to the hand holding the teacup; a puffy red hand with a thumb like an inflamed big toe—a small bitten nail embedded in the flesh—shapeless and nerveless. He would not exchange his father for a thousand fat Montgomeries, or the things his father thought and did for a million jars of Butter Nuts. Mr. Montgomery had not meant to be rude to his father: he had not meant to humiliate him—it was just that he did not know—did not feel—could not understand. . . . Dick rose with a smile, and took the fat man's cup from the mottled hand.

"Can I get you another cup of tea, Mr. Montgomery?"

Again that queer expression came to Mr. Montgomery's face as he looked down at the boy. Mr. Stevens, looking up, noticed the expression: his eyes wandered to the faded, wilting lady by the tea tray, and he wondered whether Mr. and Mrs. Montgomery had any children of their own. . . .

Dick's movement to refill Mr. Montgomery's teacup gave Mr. Stevens a grateful opportunity to break the unpleasant conversation about his office. He turned towards his hostess, who was carrying on an insipid conversation about Bognor with Mrs. Stevens. He had heard Mrs. Montgomery say that she was afraid the place was rather relaxing and Mrs. Stevens had said she hadn't noticed it—adding hastily that perhaps it was because she had got used to it. The talk about Bognor now grew general, but it required a great deal of careful handling on the Stevenses' part. The Stevenses, who knew every nook and cranny of the friendly old town, soon discovered that the Montgomerys knew nothing about it at all. They had wanted a seaside house, they explained, and while motoring along the coast, staying at the big hotels, they had discovered Bognor. Deciding that it was the place they were looking for, they had gone to an Estate Agent and requested the best piece of land in the place. They had got it—and here they were. They wanted to be away from the coast because the sound of the sea got on Mrs. Montgomery's nerves.

In gentle, delicate ways the Stevenses sought to reveal to the Montgomerys the splendid things that lay ahead of them—and one by one the splendid things seemed to recoil and fall dead before the dull eyes of their listeners. Dick was telling of the fun on the pier with the automatic machines: the exciting games of chance that sometimes brought your penny jingling cheerfully back to you—the game of football, where you skillfully worked eleven little pairs of legs against the team of your opponent: the haunted house, which for a penny produced grisly spectres from secret, unexpected panels—and slowly his voice died away—Mrs. Montgomery's eyes were on him—faded, expressionless eyes. She nodded her head, and said, "Yes. That must be very amusing."

"Come along!" cried Mr. Montgomery. "Make a good tea! Help yourselves! There's plenty of everything—and plenty more outside!"

The food was good, and the Stevenses did their best, but it was rather like ashes in their mouths. Ernie had enjoyed it until Mr. Montgomery had told him to make a good tea, but the others could not really have been said to have enjoyed it even from the start; there was something strange, and forced about it, and the sea and the sands had grown so incredibly far away—

At last their host stepped forward from the hearthrug and put his teacup on the tray. He crossed to a corner by the window and returned with a large silver casket of cigarettes and a box of cigars.

Mr. Stevens enjoyed a good cigar, and he dearly wished he could pocket the one he took, and smoke it quietly in the evening. He did not enjoy them in the afternoons. Dick and Mary took cigarettes, and the stiffness of the party faded a little under the influence of tobacco smoke.

"I expect you'd like to see over the place?" suggested their host.

"We should, very much," said Mr. Stevens, and Mrs. Stevens joined in to say it would be very nice to see over such a grand house.

They rose and went into the hall, where Mr. Montgomery, with several mysterious and secret gestures indicated a small door which Mr. Stevens assumed to be the lavatory.

"D'you want to—er—you know—?" he whispered.

"It's all right, thanks," Mr. Stevens assured him.

"Are you sure? You're welcome—"

"Quite sure. Thanks."

"D'you think the little boy—?"

"No. I think he's all right, too."

"Very well, then!" cried Mr. Montgomery, loudly and briskly once more. "Where shall we start? Upstairs?"

Mrs. Stevens said she thought it would be very nice to start upstairs.

"You *will* excuse me, won't you?" murmured Mrs. Montgomery. "It's so hot, and I feel the heat so."

"It's been a lovely tea," said Mrs. Stevens as their hostess turned back towards the lounge.

"You're welcome," replied Mrs. Montgomery with a listless smile. She passed into the lounge and closed the door.

The stairs were so much wider and more sloping than the steep, narrow stairs at Seaview that the Stevenses found themselves lifting their feet much higher than the steps required. The carpets were soft and luxurious, and a set of comic hunting pictures decorated the walls.

"This is my bedroom," said Mr. Montgomery—pausing at the door of a large, magnificent room. He blocked the way for a moment and looked round, swelling with pride. He seemed to suck the room in and breathe it out again. Then he stood aside and the Stevenses filed reverently in.

"You see how the lighting works. This turns on the light over my dressing table—and then this knob switches it off and puts on the one over my bed. Saves getting out, you see."

"What a lovely basin!" exclaimed Mrs. Stevens. She had read in house advertisements about lavatory basins in all bedrooms, but this was the first she had actually seen: it was as grand as a Soda Fountain—all in white enamel—with a looking-glass, and silver fittings to hold everything you required.

"Have you seen this?" asked Mr. Montgomery with a smile. He switched on another light, and this time it appeared uncannily somewhere inside a shaving mirror on the wall. "Look in," he said to Mr. Stevens.

"Well—I do call that convenient!" exclaimed Mr. Stevens. There was his face in the mirror, magnified to an enormous size, with his chin lit up from below. He thought he had been quite smoothly shaved, but now he saw, protruding from his chin, an assortment of fierce black bristles of various diameter—like a forest clearing where only the stumps of trees remain.

"*That* gives the old razor away!" laughed Mr. Montgomery, and Mr. Stevens smiled, and said it certainly did.

"You can see the sea from here!" exclaimed Mary, who had wandered to the window.

Mr. Montgomery looked at her rather absently. "Yes. You can see it," he said—"but you don't hear it, you know. There's a confounded foghorn somewhere out there that moans now and then—but I s'pose they've got to have them."

They passed from room to room—all got up regardless: thick carpets, deep soft chairs—shining furniture. The bathroom had a weighing machine in it, a huge jar of purple bath crystals, and a shower. The Stevenses followed their host, wide-eyed, speaking to one another in hushed whispers if they happened to be behind, but keeping up a series of enthusiastic "Well, I never's!" and "I say's!" if they happened to be in front of the procession and alongside their host, and Mr. Montgomery grew prouder and more expansive at every step.

Dick caught a glimpse of his father's face once: he caught him unawares, and he saw a look of wistful sadness in it. He knew what his father was thinking of, for he too was thinking of the tiny bathroom at home, with the geyser that sobbed out gobs of warm water in the morning, when they queued up with their jugs.

"Now then," said Mr. Montgomery, "the garden"—and the Stevenses followed their host downstairs.

Mr. Montgomery should never have shown them the garden—or at least he should have shown them it first, and washed its memory away with the magnificence of the house.

Yet for some extraordinary reason he was immensely proud of the garden. He paused impressively at the threshold of the French windows with his hand on the latch, and explained that three months ago the garden had just been a rough meadow. He painted an awful picture of its wildness, and then threw open the windows.

"Now look!" he exclaimed.

A blaze of sunlight fell across the verandah but the green-and-white blind kept the glare from the room. With a sudden feeling of thankful release the Stevenses filed out into the open air.

A gaunt pergola of varnished rustic wood stretched from the windows to the wire fence at the bottom of the garden, and a few thin rose trees clung to it in panic-stricken loneliness. To either side stretched a lawn of different shades of green and brown where some of the squares of turf had flourished more than others. A row of minute sprigs of golden privet lined the wire fence at the bottom and the flowers in the borders looked as if a puff of wind would break them from their frail anchorage.

"It'll be nice and shady in a year or two," said Mr. Montgomery, fondling the thin neck of a small dead beech tree. "I do like trees."

"I think they make all the difference," agreed Mr. Stevens, glancing uneasily round. There was not a square inch of shade, and the sun beat down on the dry dustiness with sullen, tropic anger. He was just going to say how much nicer it would look when the builder cleared away the heap of rubbish in the corner when his host walked up to it and said, "This rockery's going to be a blaze of colour next year." Mr. Stevens blessed the fate that had kept him silent. It so rarely happens that anything occurs to prevent one saying the wrong thing. "By Jove, yes!" he said, "I can just imagine it!"

Their host led them from flower to flower, prodding them with his malacca cane and explaining what colour they would be next year—and as each poor plant was prodded it seemed to lift its head and whisper, "Water! for pity's sake—water!" Mr. Stevens's eyes roved to the meadow beyond the fence—still soft and green—and he felt that some moral lay hidden somewhere near. A message from Nature which said, "You can buy most things with money, Mr. Montgomery—but you can't buy me."

"We're having a summerhouse built for this corner," said Mr. Montgomery—"and we're having electric light put into it so that we can have our coffee out here after supper."

"Won't that be lovely!" exclaimed Mrs. Stevens—and just at the same moment Mr. Stevens caught her eye. He pulled out his watch—gazed at it in astonishment and looked at his host.

"Good gracious," he exclaimed, "d'you know it's half past five!"

Mr. Montgomery laughed. "Time *can* fly sometimes," he replied.

"We really must go," said Mr. Stevens, "we've—we've got a lot of shopping to do in the town."

"Sure?" enquired their host.

"We really must."

"Then I must go and get the chauffeur out to drive you back."

"Oh—we can easily walk," said Mr. Stevens. "It's no trouble—I assure you! We always *do* go for a walk in the afternoon."

"Oh—well—just as you like."

They returned to the hall, and the stagnant coolness closed round them once again. Mr. Montgomery shouted, "Daisy! They're going."

No reply came from the lounge—but after a moment Mrs. Montgomery came languidly downstairs. The Stevenses had an uneasy feeling that she had been round to assure herself that nothing had disappeared.

"What!—Going already?" she asked.

"They've got a lot of shopping to do," explained Mr. Montgomery. "Well—you must come again one day."

"Thank you *so* much," said Mrs. Stevens, "it's been lovely."

"You're welcome," replied their hostess—and once more the Stevenses felt the warm, spongy flabbiness of the faded woman's hand. They backed out of the door, smiling and bowing, and stood again in the sunlight.

Mr. Montgomery saw them down the gravelled drive to the gate and turned round to admire his house before he wished them goodbye. It was obvious to Mr. Stevens that some remark was called for. Some pleasant remark to happily round off their visit.

"It really is a lovely place," he said, "it's a long way the nicest house I've ever seen."

It was then that Mr. Montgomery shot the awful question at him. He looked silently at Mr. Stevens for a moment, and said: "How much d'you think it cost?—Have a guess."

It was terribly cruel of fate to allow such a question at the last moment of Mr. Stevens's ordeal, for as he had walked down the drive beside his host he had been flattering himself how perfectly everybody had behaved. Neither he nor any of the family had said a single unfortunate thing, yet now, with awful unexpectedness he was called upon to give an answer which might bitterly offend his host, and ruin the whole afternoon.

For how ought he to answer? If Mr. Montgomery was proud of the large amount he had spent, it would irritate him if Mr. Stevens suggested a still larger figure. On the other hand, if Mr. Montgomery was patting himself on the back at the cheapness with which he had managed it, it would be offensive to him if a smaller figure were suggested.

It was easy, of course, to give a flattering answer when you knew your friend considered he had got a bargain: all you did then was to suggest a price far greater than the thing could possibly have cost.

But this was different: desperately different, and Mr. Montgomery's face leered down at him—gloating with expectancy. He must play for time—anything to give him time!

"I really haven't the faintest idea," he said, "I've never had any experience of a great big place like this."

But Mr. Montgomery had him on the rack—and gave the screws another turn.

"Well—just make a guess."

It was no good. He must say something: he must say something unless he was to be labelled an errant fool. What was his own house valued at—in Corunna Road? Five hundred fifty pounds—but that was years ago—before prices altered. He'd better double that—no!—he would make it four times.

"Two thousand pounds?" he whispered in a trembling voice.

He saw his host's eyes open: he saw the eyeballs like little polished pebbles—then only the big red double chin as his host's head dropped back in a roar of laughter.

"You're an optimist—you are!" he shouted.

"What was it then?" asked Mr. Stevens: his voice was hoarse, and strained.

The fat man's eyes came back from the sky, and gazed at him with amusement and scorn.

"Double what you said—and then add another thousand—and at that price all the fittings were wholesale."

He waved to them as they went down the road, and they heard him chuckling to himself as he turned and walked up his gravelled drive. None of them spoke for a while: they walked along silently in a little group. A fresh breeze suddenly fanned their faces, and away to the right, across the fields, they heard the murmur of the sea.

CHAPTER TWENTY-EIGHT

The stage door of the Theatre lay through a narrow, old-world opening, beneath a building that looked much older than the Theatre itself.

The Stevenses had often been to see plays during their holidays at Bognor, but the stage door was something quite outside their ken. Mary could not remember any other entrance beyond the one that took them into a vestibule and then through to their seats, and at all costs she felt she must explore and find it first by daylight. It would be awful to go groping for a hidden entrance, blindly in the dark—possibly never finding it at all.

A splendid excuse had turned up to help her that morning, for during breakfast Mrs. Stevens had suggested that they should both go up into the town to get the china toast rack for Mrs. Haykin.

"Then you can go off and do your shopping," said Mary—"and I can go straight down to the sands. I can leave the toast rack at Seaview on my way."

They had not been able to get a rack to match exactly the pieces they had taken back to Mrs. Haykin in other years, but they selected a very pretty one in biscuit-coloured china. "After all," said Mrs. Stevens, "it doesn't matter a toast rack being a little different."

They lingered a moment outside the shop—then Mary turned with a smile. "So long, Mum!" she said. "See you at The Cuddy at eleven!"

She had hurried off, with the parcel in her hand, towards the road at the end of the Arcade, where the Theatre lay.

Even then the stage door had breathed romance; even in the light of the morning sun, with a milk cart standing in the road outside. But now that it was dark, and the pale glimmer of a streetlamp was all that stirred its mystic shadows, Mary could understand how girls could wait by them in London, through cutting winds and drizzling rain, for a fleeting glimpse of a hurrying shadow.

The door was beyond the passage, in a narrow courtyard open to the sky. A crack of light was all that shone in the gaunt flank of the Theatre which rose before her, dark and forbidding. Pat had told her to go inside and wait, but she could not summon up her courage to cross the courtyard and go boldly in. He could not miss her if she waited here, against the archway. She hoped that no one else would come; they would wonder who she was—it was all so strange and eerie in the dark . . . so utterly different to anything she had ever done before.

Now and then she fancied she heard voices faintly echoing inside the building: voices that rose and fell, sometimes bursting out in rage. Once a strange rattling noise came to her, like heavy rain on a corrugated roof, and she thought it must be the applause. Pat would be on the stage now: it had only just gone nine. She thought of him, standing in the glare of the footlights, with hundreds of eyes watching him— crowds of girls looking up at him, romancing and wondering—it was thrilling—frightening, waiting out here alone.

Back in the past: years away in the past it seemed, she had lain in bed, fighting and reasoning with panic fears that told her it had only been a dream: but it had come to her gradually, with trembling pride and burning excitement, that she could never have dreamt what happened out there on the promenade. Its memories were too vivid; its treasured fragments could never have been gathered and pieced together so firmly had it only been a dream. Pat was real: his laugh and his words were real. She could never have dreamt that wonderful, yearning pressure of his hand—

The splendid reality of it had swept her from her bed; had made her dress with such bursting vigour that a long ladder had shot up through her stocking. With another pair in her hand she had lain back on the bed, only partly dressed, with her eyes half-closed, smiling up at the ceiling.

From within the building came a loud crackle of applause, that rose and fell, then rose again, and died away. Feet were clattering down stone steps, and voices came more distinctly: two or three lights flicked up in windows above her head. The act must be over, and Pat would be coming soon.

She had given no thought to what they would do—or what she would say when Pat came out and slipped his arm through hers. It seemed impudent and futile even to think of a puny little programme of her own in the face of this power that had drawn them together in a whirling eddy of fate, far out in midstream—far beyond the banks of reasoning thought. She felt nothing but intense gratitude that fate should have selected her, and thought her worthy of its care.

And yet through all the wonder of it there lingered the feeling that she had known: known ever since they left their home in Dulwich that something tremendous would happen before the holiday came to its close. As they had stood together, waiting for the train at Clapham Junction; as they had sat together, eating their sandwiches when the train drew out of Horsham; as they had walked together to Seaview through the streets of Bognor—again and again she had felt that it was happening for the last time—that she would never again do this with her father and mother, Dick and Ernie. A sad, rather wistful feeling it had been, and only now did she understand its meaning. They had been lovely times, these holidays at Bognor, but they could not have gone on forever: they could never have gone on, year after year, feebly trying to fan the dying sparks of childhood . . . there would always be the memories . . . and the splendour of its wonderful ending. . . .

With a sudden jerk the narrow door flew open: a dazzling shaft of light shot out across the courtyard, a shadow surged across it, and the door slammed. It was dark again, but somewhere in the dark a man was moving.

"That you, Mary?"

"Here I am, Pat!"

"Why didn't you come inside?"

"I simply *couldn't*!"

He laughed, and gently slipped his arm through hers.

"You little silly," he said.

They walked together through the archway: for a moment the shadows closed round them, and then they were out in the bright-lit street.

"Same place?" he whispered.

"That'll do fine."

"I wondered if it wouldn't be cosier up the pier."

"I say—yes!"—the pier!—with the sea round them—and the wind rustling by!—

"Your friend's inside," said Pat, "she's watching the show. Tommy doesn't get off till the end of the play—so she's got to wait."

"Is Tommy the boy who was with you last night?"

"That's him, yes. A nice kid—just a baby, that's all."

They were passing the front of the Theatre, and some of the audience, who had come out to take the air, were just returning for the second act. A boy was crushing a cigarette beneath his foot, and happened to glance up as Pat went by. Mary saw his look of languid interest change to keen excitement: she saw him turn and whisper rapidly to the girl beside him—"Quick!—Look!—There's the detective!—the fellow who was shot!" Over her shoulder she caught the fleeting glimpse of a girl's wide-open, shining eyes.

They had recognised him: they were gazing after him—and she clung to his arm in overwhelming pride. He had only to let the light of a streetlamp flicker across his face to bring recognition and excited whispering, yet he preferred to go with her to some quiet place: to be alone with her. With all her power she had to fight down the throbbing wonder of it—at all costs she must be calm and natural: he wanted her to be like that: he wanted rest, and understanding—something quieter and more satisfying than the glaring admiration of strangers.

"Good house tonight," he said, "considering it's Monday."

"Are Mondays bad, then?" she enquired.

"Generally they're pretty dud. Business usually gets better towards the end of the week—but the weather's the biggest thing at the seaside. A good pouring wet night's what an actor likes to get"—he paused for a moment, and then looked down at her with a smile—"except, of course, under certain circumstances."

He pressed his elbow to his side and squeezed her hand. Only when they reached the pier did he relax his grip to throw four pennies on the turnstile. It was a calm, moonless night: the sea lapped gently below them, catching a ray of light now and then, and spreading out a cluster of black diamonds.

The little dancing hall at the pier end was ablaze with lights, and the soft music of a string band came to them, rising and falling on the breeze.

"There's some cosy little seats right up at the end, the other side of the dance hall," said Pat, "I remember them from last year. Let's go up there."

"I know the place!" said Mary—and suddenly her heart was beating furiously and her mouth was dry.

A couple were sitting together in one little alcove, but there were two or three other places for Pat and Mary to select from. He chose a place that gave them to one side a great stretch of silent, ink-black sea, to the other the majestic sweep of the glittering promenade, with the

Bandstand twinkling out in the distance with its coloured fairy lights. The beauty of it left her breathless . . . he had led her instinctively to the loveliest place in the world. . . .

"What a little silly you are!—coming out in that frock. You'll be frozen!"

"I'm all right," whispered Mary—"I never wear a coat." But even as she said the words she felt a little shiver down her back. It was a pity her brown coat was so old and dowdy. He gently ran his arm round her shoulders and drew her closely to him. She felt the warmth of his rough tweed coat: she could feel his heart beating, strongly and slowly—only about twice to every three of hers . . . a silence fell between them—a silence that sank down and down, till it lay beneath the stream of time.

The string band was playing in the dancing hall behind them, and when it died away she could hear the distant music on the promenade: it came to her mingled with the rustle of voices, the soft whisper of moving people, and the drone of cars, and through it all there surged the silence of the sea. She scarcely breathed lest the quiver of her body should break the loveliness of it, yet she knew that at any moment the words would come from him now. They must come—they belonged to each other already, no words were needed to tell her that—it was only that something had to be spoken—

Her head was resting against his shoulder and she could not see his face: suddenly she felt sorry for him: she could understand how hard it was for him to find those words and speak them in a way that would satisfy him: she wished that she could look up at him and say, "Don't trouble, Pat—I know!" Her own part would be easy . . . just one quiet word.

"Is that fair girl a pal of yours?"

He must have thought that Mary had been dozing: her head came up with such a surprised, incredulous jerk. She began to speak, then stopped, and cleared her throat.

"I met her down here—a day or two ago."

"I didn't think you were real chums," he said—and then he gave a little laugh.

How strange men were!—Was he jealous—of a girl?

"She's all right, of course," he went on—"but not your sort exactly, eh?"

"Don't you think so?" What else could she say? It was so hard to understand.

"You find lots of her kind at seaside places in the summer. Out for a bit of fun, that's all. There's no harm in it, of course. I could spot the difference between you and her directly you went by us last night. You find lots of her kind on the stage."

"My mother used to act," said Mary. It sounded silly and irrelevant after she had said it, but something in his tone seemed to call for a defence: he meant it of course as a compliment, but after all, did she want to be so very different from Billie?

"Oh?" he replied. Her mother did not appear to interest him very much.

"Only amateur of course."

"Amateur Theatricals are quite good fun."

She stirred a little. A cold uneasiness was stealing over her: his voice was different from last night: it was harder, somehow—perhaps he was tired—acting must be a terrific strain—or was it perhaps, that he was covering his feelings—his way of nervousness?

Then suddenly his whole manner changed—so suddenly that it bewildered her and made it hard for her to respond. He lowered his head towards her—his voice was wonderfully soft—softer even than when he had said good night to her at the bottom of St. Matthews Road.

"You've never been out like this before, have you? It's rather wonderful, isn't it?"

She was about to say "Never!" and "Yes, it's wonderful!" when the whisper came again that she must play a part—even with him—even although they understood each other—

There was Sydney Harrison, who paid her attention at the

Thursday Dances at home. Sydney Harrison, the scoutmaster. She could have laughed when she thought of him beside Pat. Sydney with his gold-rimmed pince nez and his pathetic pride in his uniform. She had tried to like him, even in his uniform, with his pale, transparent white knees and their little wandering blue veins. Why shouldn't Sydney be used after all—why should Pat think that no man had ever looked at her before?—he spoke again when he saw that she had no answer—

"It's the first time, isn't it?"

"Well," she said with a little laugh—"there's Sydney—"

She saw him quickly raise his head; his keen eyes were searching her through the dark.

"Who's Sydney?"

"A boy at home."

"D'you like him?"

"Well—I—" she paused with an awkward little laugh. There was something almost frightening about the way he drove the words into her.

"Do you?"

"Not much—"

She had lowered her head. He had killed Sydney. She could almost see him lying there—a shapeless pulp. Miles away in Herne Hill he must be wriggling about on his bedroom floor, wondering what on earth was happening to him. Her eyes, too, were lowered, and she did not see his hand steal forward until it gently held her shoulder: she scarcely felt the strength that carried her into his arms. She heard his quiet, trembling voice above her—"You little darling!"—

She had thought of life as something that just began, before you knew, and went quietly on, until you died: she had never known that it could end—and begin again so wonderfully.

CHAPTER TWENTY-NINE

I f any of the family had suddenly asked Mrs. Stevens what part of the holiday she most enjoyed, she would have said—"Why!—All of it, of course!" What else could she say? A holiday was made to enjoy, and that was the end of it. She knew that the rest of the family treasured every moment of it from the second they woke in the morning till the second they fell asleep at night. No part of it could possibly stand out above the rest to them, and it was her duty to feel the same about it—to revel in it all.

But supposing, for some reason, she had been sworn to tell the truth in a solemn court of law? She would have been frightened, naturally, and would have hated admitting it lest the family should misunderstand—but she would have told the truth, and said:

"I enjoy the quiet hour after supper most of all: when Ernie's in bed, and the others have gone out, and I'm alone in the sitting-room from nine till ten, with my needlework, and the comfortable armchair, and my glass of port."

It would have sounded so terribly ungrateful: it would have stamped her as a soured, unsociable old woman, a secret drinker: a hater of her own family—and goodness knows what else. And all the time she was miles from being any of these things, she enjoyed this quiet evening hour for reasons of which she need never have been ashamed.

Supper was always over by a quarter to nine: the table had been cleared: Mr. Stevens had filled his pipe, had lit it, and strolled off with a slight touch of bravado to the Clarendon Arms. Dick and Mary quickly followed him, and Ernie alone remained with Mrs. Stevens.

But Ernie could scarcely be counted as a human being after twelve hectic hours of ceaseless activity on the sands, and after he had drowsed away ten minutes on the sofa Mrs. Stevens took him up to bed.

It was after she had tucked him up and turned the gas down in his bedroom that her own pleasant hour began. She would go into her own room on her way downstairs, put on her old but very comfortable slippers, gather up her needlework, and return to the sitting-room below.

It was a pity the family did not know her true feelings about this time when they left her by herself, for they all felt rather selfish as they filed out of the sitting-room to enjoy themselves without her: they thought of her sitting there deserted and lonely—and regarded her assertion that she could not see in the dark as merely an excuse to set them at their ease.

The first thing to do when she got back to the sitting-room was to close the window and draw the blinds, for it was quite dark now, by nine o'clock, and the September nights were cold. The next thing was to draw up her favourite chair in such a way as the light would fall over her shoulder when she began her needlework—and then came the last thing of all before she settled down—

With a slight air of mystery, and a touch of guilt, she would go to the small cupboard by the window, open it, and reverently draw out her bottle of port.

It was Dick who always stuck a narrow strip of stamp paper down the side of the bottle: who carefully drew the twelve pencilled lines across it at even distances apart. He did it as a joke originally, calling the port her medicine, and telling her to take a dose each night. But it was much better than a joke: it was a very good idea. There were twelve evenings through which the bottle had to last, and the wineglass supplied by Mrs. Huggett could only be filled to the brim ten times. It was essential to have some kind of check on it to avoid the bottle giving out before the last evening, and in the opposite way it was necessary to avoid stinting herself each night, and finding some left over at the end.

She would hold the bottle to the light and carefully measure out her evening glass: then she would sit down to her work, sometimes leaning back with closed eyes as the sitting-room gathered round itself a pleasant, peaceful warmth.

There was nothing, at home in Corunna Road, to compare with this delicious hour of idleness. In the evenings at home there was the washing up to do—the breakfast to set, and all those unexpected little things that conspire in a home to keep you on your feet.

But what a difference—at Seaview! It took at least a couple of evenings to realise and enjoy it to the full. No washing up! No breakfast to set!—No shoes to clean!—Nothing to do but sit down and rest: nothing even to think about if you didn't want to think. It was a lovely hour: the hour that did her more good than anything else on the holiday. Her thoughts, when they came, could scarcely be termed thoughts in the strictest meaning of the word: they were memories really, mingled with the pleasant happenings of each passing day, flecked sometimes with stray chinks of light that crept in from the future.

It was on the Wednesday evening, when only two more full days of the holiday lay ahead, that something happened to disturb and startle Mrs. Stevens during her hour alone. Suddenly, without warning, a gentle tap came at the door, and Mrs. Huggett stepped quietly into the room.

Rarely, in all their years at Seaview, could Mrs. Stevens remember their landlady coming in at this late hour of the evening. Mrs. Huggett was so rigid in her etiquette. Every night, as regular as clockwork, she met them in the hall as they came in for their supper, had a word with Mrs. Stevens about breakfast, and smilingly bade them "Good night." They never saw her after that, until breakfast time, and they often wondered what became of her. They used to see a light in one of the basement windows, low down behind the laurel in the front garden, and they imagined she had a room down there, where she sat until she went to bed. And now, without warning, softly and quietly, she had come into the sitting-room—at half-past nine. She stood there, smiling wanly in the light, and suddenly an unaccountable sense of fear crept over Mrs. Stevens. Mrs. Huggett had been rather strange this year, and looked so ill—

"All alone, Mrs. Stevens?"

Her hand was sliding nervously up and down the edge of the door. It was a queer thing to say: she must have known the others had gone out, and that Ernie was in bed, and Mrs. Stevens felt a strange dry feeling at the back of her tongue—whatever was it?—whatever did she want?

Then suddenly it dawned upon her: she had raised her head and had caught something very pitiful in Mrs. Huggett's face. It looked so terribly pale and drawn with its bright little patch of scarlet round the lids of her bad eye—was Mrs. Huggett all alone, too?—not happily alone, as she was, but terribly, unbearably alone? She had never thought of Mrs. Huggett being lonely before: she jumped quickly from her chair with a little laugh.

"Yes—they've left me all alone!—Won't you sit down, Mrs. Huggett?"

"Oh—but I'm disturbing you!"

"You aren't!—reely you aren't!" She had caught the glow of gratitude in Mrs. Huggett's eyes, and breezily crossed to the other armchair and pushed it opposite hers.

"Do sit down. It's nice to have somebody to talk to when I'm alone." She watched Mrs. Huggett as she sat stiffly down with her long creased fingers folded in her lap: she did not relax: she sat gauntly erect, and her eyes roved nervously round the room. Mrs. Stevens's anxiety had dispersed when she rose to push the chair up, but now she felt it closing in again: there was something so strange and frightening about Mrs. Huggett's rigid face and toneless, even voice—she felt that something lay behind this visit—something rather terrible, and she longed to hear the cheerful step of one of the family returning. With sinking heart she saw that it was only half-past nine—no one would be in till ten. . . .

She talked to Mrs. Huggett of the weather, in fevered little spasms, but every now and then would come a frightening stretch of silence—if only Mrs. Huggett would talk—would say something!—if only her fingers wouldn't twitch so queerly!—

A good ten minutes passed, and it seemed a dreadful, endless hour—before Mrs. Huggett began to speak. She did not look at Mrs. Stevens—her eyes were fixed on the dark painting in the corner—the painting of the heap of fruit—

"As it's keeping so fine," she said—"I wondered if you'd like to stay another day—and go on the Sunday?"

Mrs. Stevens could not answer at once: her relief at discovering the reason of Mrs. Huggett's visit was shattered by this extraordinary offer. Another day!—it was impossible!—twelve o'clock on Saturday was the end: it always had been the end. The next people were entitled to come in as the clock struck twelve on Saturday—

"But, Mrs. Huggett—your next people come in!" Not a muscle stirred in Mrs. Huggett's face as she replied: her eyes remained fixed on the picture and her words sent a shudder of dismay through Mrs. Stevens—

"My next people aren't coming this year," she said. Her hand was searching in her blouse: she silently drew out a letter and handed it across the fireplace. The flap was torn raggedly across where anxious fingers had wrestled with it, and Mrs. Stevens pulled out the letter and read:

DEAR MRS. HUGGETT,

I am sure you will understand the regret I feel at breaking our long series of holidays at Seaview. I should have written before, but uncertainty has delayed me until now.

My daughter Isabel has just become engaged to a young
man whose people own a small house at Pevensey, and they
have very kindly placed this house at our disposal.

My daughters have urged me to accept their offer, and
I can only say that I shall always look back with pleasure
upon our many happy days at Seaview in the past.

Yours very sincerely,
SEBASTIAN JONES

"The Reverend Sebastian Jones and his five daughters," said Mrs. Huggett. Her eyes had left the picture now—they roved to and fro, resting for a fleeting second on Mrs. Stevens, and passing on. "For fifteen years I've had them, they've always come after you."

Mrs. Stevens could never have explained the queer feeling that came over her as she read the letter. It was as if one wall of Seaview had suddenly crumbled to the ground. Nothing gave more pleasure to the holiday than the thought that people were eagerly and impatiently waiting to take their places: it was the people before them and the people after them that squeezed the most precious and tasty juices from the holiday. It was like The Cuddy—they enjoyed it most of all because there was someone in the huts on either side—someone in every hut—and people who wanted huts, but could not get them . . . and so it was at Seaview—till now—and now one end of their holiday seemed to trail forlornly in the air.

Mrs. Stevens handed the letter back in silence—then suddenly her voice surprised her—it was quivering with anger—she had never spoken so fiercely before in all her life—

"You'll make them pay!—it's a scandal!—you'll make them pay!"

There was no answering anger in Mrs. Huggett's voice. "There wasn't no agreement," she said. "It was just understood, every year. They always wrote a line in June, just saying they were coming. When they didn't write this year I sent them a line, and this . . . this is . . ." Her words trailed away—and when she spoke again her voice was quite unchanged—just hard, and toneless. . . . "It's come hard on top of—of my August people—not coming—"

"But you don't mean—?" began Mrs. Stevens, almost in a whisper.

Mrs. Huggett slowly nodded. "They let me down. It's come hard on me—this year—"

Mrs. Stevens thought the little movement of her landlady was the old familiar habit she had of wiping her bad eye—and then suddenly she went cold to the roots of her hair: she heard a stifled, terrible sound, between a sob and a cry.

It was hard, of course, to see her Thursday glass of port disappear on Wednesday evening, but the little spot of colour that rose in Mrs. Huggett's cheeks was thanks a thousand times.

"It'll come all right next year, Mrs Huggett: it's bound to come all right—and there's always us—we'll always come—and we'll recommend you to people—you see if we don't—"

She told Mr. Stevens that evening, and he stood gravely listening, half undressed, beside the bed. She told him of Mrs. Huggett's misfortune, about her August people letting her down, and about the Reverend Sebastian Jones and his five daughters—she told him everything, except what happened at the end.

He was very silent when she had finished—he did not even reply when she added a last word—

"I think she'd like us to stay the extra day. She wants us to have it as a present—she doesn't want us to pay."

She saw him cross the room, and stand by the windows, deep in thought. "We'll talk to the children in the morning," he said. "It certainly *would* be very nice to have an extra day—"

He was silent again for a long time: one hand held back the faded yellow curtain, and very faintly and peacefully the sea came murmuring up to them. At last he turned, and looked down at his wife as she lay in bed. It seemed almost as if he were appealing to her, as if he were asking her to help him grope for something that lay hidden somewhere.

"You see the real trouble, don't you?" he said.

She did not reply—she understood his meaning, and turned her head a little on the pillow.

"It isn't comfortable here, any longer—for people who don't understand. We've got to look things in the face, Flossie. Those old chairs downstairs—and this bed. We understand, but some people don't—"

She saw him sit down. She watched him as very slowly he unlaced his canvas shoes.

CHAPTER THIRTY

E rnie could scarcely contain himself at the splendid news, and Dick and Mary were surprised and delighted. An extra day!—a reprieve! It was carried unanimously, with acclamation, and Mrs. Stevens was specially detailed to convey the enthusiastic thanks of the whole family to Mrs. Huggett.

Mr. Stevens had not told the family until lunchtime because it was a matter that required the most careful and anxious consideration before making public. It was not for one moment that he had any personal inclination to refuse this pleasant and unexpected opportunity, for the idea of staying until Sunday was magnificent. The trouble was that their plans for returning on Saturday were cut-and-dried, and it was essential to consider whether the necessary alterations could be carried out at such extremely short notice.

He decided, therefore, to form a small and very secret committee, consisting of Mrs. Stevens and himself. Their duty was to thoroughly explore the whole matter and assure themselves that everything could be done in time. Then, but only then, was the news to be announced to the children.

"If we tell them now," he said, "we shall simply be carried away by public opinion—our hands would be forced: they would never see reason—even if we found that we could not possibly alter our plans in time."

"Yes," agreed Mrs. Stevens, "don't let's breathe a word about it—till we know for certain."

"We can't jump at it without thinking: it would ruin the whole holiday if we messed up our journey back."

"We'll have to write to Mrs. Bullevant and tell her to feed Puss on Saturday," burst out Mrs. Stevens as the thought flashed upon her.

But Mr. Stevens impatiently waved her remark aside. "That's simply a trifle: just a detail in a whole heap of things."

They were lying in bed, enjoying their holiday luxury of an extra half hour longer than they had at home. By force of habit they always woke at half-past seven, but neither stirred till the clock at the top of the road struck eight.

This morning, however, after a few minutes of deep thought, Mr. Stevens got out of bed and returned with his writing block and pencil.

"We'll make a full list of things to do," he said. "A great deal depends on our return tickets, so the first thing for you to do is to go up to the station and enquire whether they are available for Sunday instead of Saturday. If they say it's all right, tell them not to send a man for the luggage on Saturday. Don't give any further instructions at present. We'll do that later—if I find everything else can be arranged."

For ten minutes he worked industriously at his writing tablet—alternately jotting down notes and staring reflectively at the ceiling with his pencil between his teeth. At last he sat up, and looked over the dividing bolster at his wife.

"Tell me if you think of anything I've forgotten," he said, and then commenced to read:

"1. Advise Ruislip not to call for luggage at Dulwich Station as arranged.

"2. Advise Mrs. Haykin *re* canary: tell her to get small packet of seed if short.

"3. Write milkman leave usual cat's milk extra morning.

"4. Tell Mrs. Bullevant to go in Saturday—taking Puss bloater.

"5. Write baker leave loaf on kitchen windowsill. N.B. Tell Mrs. Bullevant to take loaf into kitchen.

"6. Consider financial demands of extra day.

"7. Enquire if The Cuddy can be retained until Sunday midday.

"8. Order half dozen bottles ginger beer.

"Anything else?" enquired Mr. Stevens.

"I think it's absolutely everything," said Mrs. Stevens in admiration. "It's wonderful the way you think."

He smiled at her, and got briskly out of bed.

"It may not be so difficult after all. Everything depends on the return tickets, and whether the money will last. I always allow a margin of a pound—but we'll have to give Mrs. Huggett something extra. D'you think—say—five shillings?"

"I think she'll be very pleased indeed," said Mrs. Stevens.

"All right, then," he replied. "While you've gone up to the station, I'll get the letters written, all ready to post directly we know if the tickets are good for Sunday. I'll have to run through the money, too, and see how we stand. I think ten shillings ought to cover it—and don't let the children see anything's happening. I'm simply going to pretend I'm writing home about our return on Saturday—d'you see?" He gave his wife an artful wink and went off to the bathroom.

They both found it difficult to appear normal and unconcerned during breakfast: the change of plans kept bringing new details to Mr. Stevens's mind, and more than once Dick shot an enquiring glance at his father when he answered some question in an absent-minded, preoccupied way. It surprised the children considerably when Mr. Stevens told them to go on down to the sea, as he had some letters to write home about their return, for all he usually did was to drop a line to Mrs. Bullevant on the Thursday evening.

For over an hour he pored over the sitting-room table with his writing block before him. The first letter was addressed to the stationmaster at Dulwich, and was marked "Urgent":

DEAR SIR,

Before leaving for our holiday we instructed Porter Ruislip to meet the five o'clock down train from Clapham Junction on Saturday next in order to convey our luggage back to our house, No. 22 Corunna Road. Having decided to postpone our return until the following day (Sunday) I shall be glad if you will kindly issue instructions to Porter Ruislip to meet the down train arriving from Clapham Junction at _____ p.m.

Yours very truly,
ERNEST STEVENS

He left the time blank until Mrs. Stevens returned, for she was also to ascertain the times of the Sunday trains from Bognor, and only then could he work out the last stage of the journey by the local timetable.

He wrote at length to Mrs. Bullevant, for there were a great many details to arrange with her. A short note was sufficient to Mrs. Haykin and postcards were enough for the tradespeople. He had to leave the address blank on the postcards, for strangely enough he could not precisely call to mind the title of each firm they dealt with: was the milkman Harris & Son, Harris Bros., Harris & Co.—or just Harris? It surprised him to think of the times he had seen the milk cart in the road and never noticed how the firm of Harris was constituted. Still, his wife ought to know. If she didn't they would just have to put Messrs. Harris.

He took the little pile of correspondence upstairs and left it on his dressing table, with stamps all ready to put on directly he knew that the letters could be sent. By eleven o'clock he was on his way down to meet the children at The Cuddy, pondering upon a strange medley of disturbing thoughts.

He was delighted, naturally, at the prospect of an extra day, with all its splendid opportunities for storing up extra health and vigour for the winter: they would have a magnificent feeling on Saturday afternoon, strolling down to the sands once more instead of toiling up to the station: lazing in the sun and breathing crisp sea-laden air when by rights they should be crushed up together in a stuffy railway carriage. Yet the splendour of this prospect was rather blinding him to certain other things: it would mean, of course, that he would lose the Sunday at home: that he would have to return to work with only the darkness of a solitary night between the warehouse and the sea.

The Sunday that lay between the journey home from Bognor and Monday's return to work had always been a treasured interlude that softened the crude contrasts of work and play: he spent the whole time in the garden, putting it in order: he mowed the lawn, and the sweet smell of new-cut grass would rise to comfort him, and give him courage to gather up the threads of cold reality next morning. But good heavens!—he couldn't have everything!—

It was not the difficulties of altering their plans: it was something else that disturbed him most of all: something to do with Seaview and Mrs. Huggett. The news that his wife had told him last night had shocked him far more deeply than he was willing to admit. To a certain extent he had felt as his wife had felt, but whereas she had only seen the need of pity and sympathy for Mrs. Huggett in a cruel and undeserved misfortune, it had brought confirmation to him of something he had long foreseen and feared.

Yet even these slowly gathering forebodings had failed to ease the shock of disillusionment: half the pleasure of the holiday lay in the feeling that their own time at Seaview was tightly squeezed in between a crowd of other times which were being scrambled and clamoured for by other holidaymakers, all eager to come to Seaview as well. He liked to feel the pressure of the people who came before and after him: he liked to feel that when they arrived they were forcing reluctant people out of the house, that when they went, impatient people were waiting to come in.

And now that feeling had suddenly slipped away; no one had been at Seaview before them, during August—no one was coming in their places when they left: they were just an isolated little party in a house that people did not come to any longer. It was very hard to shake off the unhappiness that kept rising in his throat: they had written for their rooms right back in March lest Mrs. Huggett should fall to the temptation of letting them to someone else.

It was as if he and his family had booked seats for a theatre months ahead, then found themselves surrounded by half-empty seats from which people rose, and quietly stole out during the performance. They stole out because the show was poor and stale, and in his heart of hearts he knew also that the show had fallen on bad days and was no longer worth seeing: that he and his family were sitting doggedly on, applauding and trying to encourage the actors because they felt a stubborn duty to back them up.

He tried to fight the mean whisper that came to him—"Get out yourselves!—others are getting out because it isn't good enough—why should you remain!"

He had reached the promenade, and paused a moment looking out to sea. Suddenly he gripped the rail in front of him, squared his shoulders, and clenched his jaw. Let the others go if they wanted to—if they wanted to let Mrs. Huggett down: let them clear out if they hadn't any loyalty—or any memory of happy days gone by: he and his family would stand by Mrs. Huggett—to the end.

Mrs. Stevens arrived at The Cuddy while the others were in the sea, but Mr. Stevens came out, as usual, a little before the others, and she was able to get a quiet word with him alone. He knew before she spoke that her mission had been successful, for as he came up the beach with his towel over his shoulder she nodded and smiled to him, and made mysterious signs.

"It's all right!" she whispered—"the tickets are all right for Sunday!— I asked twice. I asked the booking-office man and I asked the station-master: they both looked carefully at the tickets and said we could use them Sunday. Isn't that splendid!"

Mr. Stevens sat on The Cuddy steps and began to rub his arms and legs, holding them out to the sun.

"Did you take down the times of the trains?" he enquired.

She dived into her purse and produced the memo book she used for shopping notes.

"There's one at 10:45."

"That's too early."

"Yes. I thought it would be: I just put it down in case. Then there's one at 1:30, and one at 3:45."

"What time does the 3:45 get to Clapham Junction?"

"At 6:08," said Mrs. Stevens, promptly and rather proudly.

"Then we'll take that," replied her husband.

"Shall we tell them now!" she whispered.

"No. Let's wait till lunchtime: I just want another hour to think it over. I think it's all right—but it's best to be absolutely sure."

They had a little quiet fun during the morning as they sat round after the bathe, eating macaroons.

"Oh, dear," said Mr. Stevens, with a mournful sigh—"only one more full day"—and he managed to get a wink in at his wife without the others seeing.

It had suddenly clouded over, and a fine drizzle began to drive in from the sea—a kind of sea mist, cold and clammy. Thoughts of the end of the holiday lay heavy on the shoulders of Dick and Mary and Ernie as they walked up St. Matthews Road, back to Seaview for their lunch.

The news could not possibly have come at a more perfect moment, for while they sat round the table, forlornly eating their lunch, a silent, hopeless rain began to fall outside: it seemed to write *End* to the holiday, for even if it cleared up tomorrow it would be too late to arouse their fading spirits. Tomorrow was the last day: the trunk would be standing on the landing with its hungry jaws waiting for their sand shoes, the kite, and everything that had become such emblems of the holiday: it seemed as if the sun had packed up and gone that morning, with the little cloud of hurrying birds which they had seen—heading out to sea, high up in the sky. Through the half-open window, through the relentless rain, they could hear the foghorn, mournfully tolling the knell of another holiday . . . then, as he pushed back his chair and lit his pipe, Mr. Stevens broke the news—

They would not believe it at first: they thought it was one of Mr. Stevens's little jokes—rather a silly joke—rather badly timed. And then he pulled the pile of letters from his pocket, and read aloud the instructions he was sending to the stationmaster at Dulwich.

The effect was magical: it reminded Mr. and Mrs. Stevens of years ago—when the children were all young—and unexpectedly a splendid currant cake had been produced for tea. Ernie got up and danced round the room, almost shouting with joy. Then he dived back to the table and insisted upon another helping of rice pudding. Dick also took another helping: his eyes were alight again—the clouds had risen from the sitting-room, even if they lingered in the open sky outside.

But what did the rain matter now?—let it pour!—let it hail!—another day—two clear days ahead—Friday!—Saturday!—"Isn't it spiffing!" shouted Ernie.

They put on their coats, hurried down to the pier, and began one of those delightful, unrehearsed interludes that somehow manage to stand out in the memory to the exclusion of things which have been carefully arranged.

They dived headlong into the brightly coloured sea of automatic machines: Dick played Mr. Stevens a tremendous game of automatic football with the family straining over their shoulders, calling out encouragement and laughing: quite a crowd collected to see what the merriment was about, and the family had almost to elbow their way from the machine when the match was over.

"What about this!" called Mr. Stevens, pointing to a large, enticing notice board.

SHOVE-EM

ANYBODY CAN WIN AT SHOVE-EM

THE PERFECT GAME OF SKILL

The statement appeared slightly contradictory to Mr. Stevens.

"How can it be a perfect game of skill," he said—"if anybody can win?"—and after a moment's thought, the others saw the point, and laughed.

They had a pennyworth of Haunted House, then Dick bowled out W. G. Grace first ball on the cricket machine. The rain had driven a big crowd into the covered spaces of the pier—a hearty, good-humoured crowd, determined to make the best of a rotten afternoon: the whole place was filled with bursts of laughter, heavy, rhythmic breathing at the games of skill machines, the clatter of heels on the bare, hollow boards, and the warm smell of drying mackintoshes—but what an afternoon it was! Sometimes the Stevenses subsided onto seats and watched other people try their skill—then they would rise, and try their own hands once again—sometimes they succeeded, and got their pennies back—sometimes they didn't—but what did it matter with two full, splendid days ahead!

"Here!—Mum!" shouted Dick—"Come and have your character read." He was standing beside a machine that offered greater mysteries, even, than those surrounding it. A wizard, in a tall, sugar-loaf hat and a long robe decorated with the signs of the zodiac, was gravely pointing his wand towards a narrow slot that took the penny. In return he offered to reward you with a full and relentless revelation of your character.

At the sight of the machine Mrs. Stevens went a little pale, and shrank back.

"No!—not me!" she said, with a nervous laugh.

She laughed to hide the fears that secretly shamed her: it was silly, of course, to be afraid of a machine, but she always felt a shrinking dread of things and people that offered to reveal your character, or your future—or even your past. Supposing it were to tell her that she would be run over?—or that she would fall down a well and be drowned? True or untrue, it would cloud the rest of her life—"No! don't let's have that," she urged.

"Come on!" laughed Dick—"it's only fun!"

But she drew back, very determined, and Dick caught his father by the arm. "Look, Dad!—your character revealed—for a penny. Let's find out all about you, Dad!"

Mr. Stevens felt very much as his wife did: he had all her unreasonable fears—all her shrinking from these little machines that might—who knows?—say something terribly ominous. But he could not allow himself to appear timid and superstitious before the family. With a nervous laugh he drew out a penny and bravely pressed it into the slot.

The drawer beneath came out with a reassuring *chock*—and there lay the fateful little card, closely and mysteriously printed over. He took it out and was searching for his spectacles when Dick reached for it and began to read aloud:

"'You have a peace-loving disposition, quiet in your tastes and reserved in your speech. Fond of open-air spaces and freedom from convention and country life generally. You have good willpower controlled by reason, and are capable of giving good advice to others. You do not make friends readily, but are constant and reliable to those you do make. You are rather sensitive regarding the opinion of others.'"

Several times Dick had to pause for the family to stop laughing: Mr. Stevens joined in, too—yet all the time he had a queer, uncanny feeling of growing wonder. It was absurd, of course: it was only a machine: it was just a strange freak of chance—but how extraordinarily true it was! It really *did* describe him—there was no getting away from it—even to that sly little dig about his sensitiveness—

Could it possibly be that some mystic power really lay concealed within that tawdry little machine? It was ridiculous even to think so, and yet—there really was something uncannily true about it. He was silent as they passed along the pier: he quietly slipped the card into his waistcoat pocket, to read again more carefully when he was alone.

Suddenly Dick's eye fell upon another machine of the same kind. "Game on, Mum!" he called out. "It's your turn now—it can't do any harm!"

But Mrs. Stevens still drew breathlessly away.

"No!—reely not, Dick. I don't want to—you know I don't want to!" But Dick and Ernie almost carried her to the machine: they almost forcibly pressed her hand with its penny over the slot. They did not understand, of course: they would never have done it if they had really known how she felt about it—they simply thought it was her shyness— her reluctance to waste pennies on herself—

Out came the drawer with its businesslike *chock* and there lay Mrs. Stevens's character—

"Shall I read it?" laughed Dick.

"Go on!" said Mr. Stevens, turning to his wife with a reassuring smile. Dick held up the card, and Mrs. Stevens felt a sudden trembling come over her—a sudden weakness at the knees—

"'You have a peace-loving disposition, quiet in your tastes and re- served in your speech—'" began Dick—"'Fond of—'"

Suddenly he stopped—"Why!—it's the same as Dad's!"

The children shouted with laugher. They had rarely come up against quite such a funny coincidence. It had come from a different machine, too! Mrs. Stevens was relieved beyond measure and laughed till her sides ached—only Mr. Stevens found it hard—hard even to force a smile. It was only a catch-penny after all: he was angry at himself, too, for feeling a sudden annoyance at his wife: why should she think it so funny?

But his anger soon disappeared, for he shot all five cats off the wall at "Pussy," and when at last they went out into the open air on their way back to tea they found the rain had stopped, and a big white shining place in the sky where the sun was forcing through.

They went up St. Matthews Road, strung out arm in arm.—"Let's have another go on the pier," said Dick—"on Saturday night!"

Yes: they could do that—on Saturday night: they would still be here on Saturday night!

"All tomorrow—then all the next day, and even then a whole morning," murmured Dick as they filed in to their tea.

CHAPTER THIRTY-ONE

Mary knew that Pat was standing there, at the bottom of the road, watching until she went in the gate. He stood there every evening. She had never allowed him to come right up to the house lest her mother, from her bedroom over the front door, should hear his voice, and wonder.

It was rather terrible to feel that he was still standing there: that although it was all over, although she might never stand beside him and talk to him again, she could still see him for the last time if she were to look round. It would be quite easy to see him in the pool of light at the corner of the promenade, though he would scarcely be able to see her now. He had told her that he would always wait until he heard the gate squeak, and knew that she was safely in the garden before he went away. She had to fight down a wild impulse to run madly up the road, to wrench open the gate, and get it over.

The shock of it had not come so terribly in the end: it had been dulled by the torment of uncertainty that had hung over every hour of the past three days. Something strangely near relief had come in the last moment.

She felt no bitterness or anger against Pat: she was only angry with herself. Never by a single word had he suggested anything to deceive her: he had behaved exactly as any reasonable girl would have expected. It was just a bit of fun. Billie herself had made that clear on the very first evening of the adventure: just a bit of fun to while away a few pleasant hours of a holiday. Billie was probably round at the Theatre now, saying good-bye to the dark boy, Tommy. Billie wouldn't cry about it. Billie understood.

Would it have made any difference if she had known more about the world?—if her tiny reservoir of conversation had not dried up and left her so quiet towards the end of the evening? She had irritated Pat by repeating things she had said before—irritated him because of all the things she did not know, and did not understand. Perhaps she had tried too hard to be entertaining and clever. It might have made a difference if she had not worn her shoddy old brown coat that night. He had made her promise faithfully to wear it—but then she had seen him looking at its tight, shrunk sleeves. . . .

There was Seaview, a little way ahead. Inside was a room on the third floor: a small, shabby room with a squeaking gas jet and a bed. In a little while she would creep in between the thin, tightly stretched sheets, and lie there. In Corunna Road there was another room. It looked out onto the wall of the next house: there was another bed: she would be in that in two days' time. Beyond lay the workroom in King's Road, with its great gaunt window looking out onto the corrugated iron wall of a garage, and the sky that never framed the sun, but gleamed very white, and hurt her eyes. . . .

"I shan't be able to manage tomorrow night, Mary. It's the last night of the show, and we've got to pack up afterwards. It's been awfully nice. Perhaps we'll meet again one day—if ever you're here when I am."

His words were still ringing in her ears. Would it have made any difference if she had had an attractive coat?—if she had been more entertaining?

A few steps now and she would be at Seaview. The family were in there. Ernie asleep in bed; her mother waiting for the gate to squeak before she settled down and closed her eyes; Dick undressing quietly upstairs so as not to wake up Ernie—her father finishing his pipe before following them to bed.

Tomorrow she would join them in the last day of the holiday: she would join them in their conspiracy to keep back the sorrow of it: she would have her part to play like they had. She would try to forget the rest, if she could, even though nothing like it would ever happen again.

There was a cold dew on the latch of the gate: the squeak of the hinges went plaintively down the road. She turned for a moment before she went up the steps. She could see him standing there in the pool of light. He stepped forward a little, she saw him raise his hand, then turn to go.

CHAPTER THIRTY-TWO

"Well—good-bye, Rosie. Good-bye, Joe. Good-bye, Mr. Baker. Don't forget to come next year."

"I'll be here, you bet," called Joe—"unless I win the Calcutta and go round the world instead. Well—good-bye, Stevens, old boy. Be good."

It was one of the hard moments, and Mr. Stevens was glad when it was over. The saloon door of the Clarendon Arms swung to behind him, and he felt the frosty tang of the autumn night.

They had lit the first fire of the season in the saloon bar that evening, and instead of lounging in the alcove seat they had drawn their chairs up round the blaze. No wonder Mr. Stevens buttoned up his sports jacket when he got outside, and wished he had thought to bring his coat. There was a mist in the air, for he saw the ghostly, rainbow-coloured circles round the streetlamps.

He walked down the side lane that flanked the hotel and took a last glance through the saloon bar window as he went by. They had been quite cheery evenings in there this year. He was sorry Mr. Montagu the solicitor had not come, but old Joe had turned up again as breezy as ever. Mr. Baker had been quite a good chap, too—and Rosie, she was always the same . . . a pity it was all over for another year.

There was nothing like the same crowd on the promenade: the frost had driven the light-clothed people into the cafés and amusement places, and most of those who passed were in their overcoats. The end-of-the-holiday feeling did not lie simply in Mr. Stevens's thoughts: it was all round him this evening: it hung in the frosty air. The warm nights had gone for good now, and the autumn had arrived.

It was one of the comforts of a September holiday to feel that everyone else was returning, or would be returning, very soon: it would be much harder to end a holiday in July—to meet eager crowds arriving by the very train that took you home.

The sea was a long way out across the sands tonight; dark, slaty green, silent and rather unfriendly, beyond the dense blackness of the shore. Over to the right lay the smooth stretch of sands where they had played their games of cricket, and sprawled for long drowsy hours in the sun: through the darkness he could just make out the two posts and the high piece of breakwater that had served to stop the ball when their wickets were pitched in front of it. How amazingly the time had flown! They had scarcely done anything, really—just bathed, and lounged about—and yet it had been a splendid holiday. It was fine to know they could still go on enjoying it like they always had in the past. It had rained, of course, but it had not been nearly as wet as August and July: they had never lost a whole day through the rain, for it had always cleared up by the afternoon, or kept off till lunchtime. A little rain was all to the good, really: it made them appreciate far more those wonderful hours when the sun had baked their skins and saturated them to their very bones. The first week had been the best: those three magnificent days, one after the other, to begin with. It wasn't only the sun that made them brown; the wind, and even the driving sea mist played their part. He looked down at his hands as they rested on the rail of the promenade and he could scarcely see them in the darkness: they were so bronzed that only his fingernails gleamed up at him now. A fortnight ago he would have seen two pale sets of fingers shining in the dark. He took a deep breath of the cold night air, and turned away. The holiday had done them all a wonderful lot of good.

It was not a matter of saying good-bye to the sea when he turned from the promenade and went up St. Matthews Road: the whole of tomorrow morning lay ahead; even another bathe, for luckily they had been able to keep The Cuddy right up till the end.

The first evening came back to him very clearly as he sat in the armchair to finish his pipe before going up to bed. He had known on that first night how quickly the holiday would slip away, and had pictured himself as he would be sitting on the last evening, looking back with mingled pleasure and sadness. How alike their holidays were! Only the tea party at the Montgomerys' stood out as something different from past years, something unexpected. He had thought a lot about the tea party and was still a little undecided as to whether it had been all right. He felt on the whole that it had not done him any harm. Even his bad guess at the price of Mr. Montgomery's house had apparently erred on the right side, and flattered Mr. Montgomery. It would be interesting and rather exciting to see what happened when Mr. Montgomery made his next call at the office: he was certain to come over and have a word with him about the holiday: it ought to be rather an impressive moment, with the other clerks looking on, straining to hear what was said—with possibly one of the Directors standing near, waiting for Mr. Montgomery to finish. . . .

The clock struck eleven, but he still sat quietly thinking in his chair. Would it have been better, after all, to have gone back that morning as they had always done before? He was irritated at himself for worrying about it: it was so pointless, really, and yet it was extraordinary how home had begun to call that evening, just about the time when normally they would have been unlocking the kitchen door and walking in.

He would be sitting in the front room now, before the fire they always lit to celebrate their return: the fatigue of the journey and the wrench of leaving the sea would have been over by now: his thoughts would have been on the long day's work that lay ahead in the garden. . . .

He rose, knocked out his pipe, and laid it on the mantelpiece. It was good to have a home that called you: a home that made you feel a little unhappy when you went up to sleep in a strange bed on the first night away—that lay restfully in the background of your holiday, then called you again when it was time to return.

The trunk stood open on the landing: everything was packed except a few things they would require tomorrow morning, for they stubbornly refused to stow away their comfortable holiday clothes and canvas shoes until the last hour came. They had taken out the kite that afternoon, and the strong northwester had carried it high up over the sea. They had taken it for a last fly because it had to go flat on the bottom of the trunk, and nothing else could go in till the kite was there.

He tiptoed into the bedroom and undressed quietly in the dark.

CHAPTER THIRTY-THREE

It was just on one o'clock when Mr. Stevens took a last glance round The Cuddy, closed the door, and turned the key. He saw in that final glance the wet little patches on the floor where they had brought in seawater from their bathe, and something suddenly tightened in his throat. The Cuddy had been a splendid little friend: it had made a wonderful difference to the holiday.

"Better get back to lunch now," he said.

They went along the front with their bathing dresses and towels: Mrs. Stevens with the rug that they had always left in the hut, Ernie with his yacht tucked under his arm.

It was nearly over now. They left the key with the man at the bathing hut office and gave him a cheery good-bye.

"I expect we shall want a hut next year," said Mr. Stevens. "I'll write and book next time," he added with a smile. "I hope we can get The Cuddy again."

The umbrellas and walking sticks were standing against the coatrack in the hall, strapped together in readiness for the porter's truck. Mr. Stevens's haversack hung from a peg, and Ernie put his yacht down beneath it. They rolled their wet towels and bathing dresses in some stout brown paper to keep the dampness from the clothes in the trunk, and went into their bedrooms to change into the things they would wear on the homeward journey. Tight collars again; waistcoats and hard leather shoes; stockings over Ernie's scarlet legs.

It was a pity there was no train due to leave directly after lunch so that they could have risen straight from the table, gathered their luggage, and gone. The holiday was over now: it would be pathetic to try to pretend for another hour by going back to the sands: it would only mean getting their leather shoes wet and making themselves hot and sticky for the journey. They sat as long as possible over the meal, but it became very silent and forlorn towards the end. The gramophone was playing at The Sycamores on the other side of the road, and they saw two of the girls come out and walk off towards the sea with magazines and rugs. What a long holiday they were having over there! They were at The Sycamores when the Stevenses had arrived, and here they were, off to the sea again, just when the Stevenses were going home.

It had gone two o'clock before the family rose. They went upstairs and packed their cricket shirts, flannels, and canvas shoes. They closed the trunk and strapped it up, and then, as he was taking a last look round his room, Mr. Stevens saw one of his thick grey walking socks right up in a corner under his bed. It was funny how something like that happened almost every year. He felt his collar tighten and his face grow hot as he reached under to get it: it was covered in dusty fluff and he had to hit it smartly on the back of a chair before it was clean enough to stuff into his mackintosh pocket.

The others were gathered in the sitting-room when he returned, and as he glanced at them, silently sitting round, fidgeting with old magazines, he thought they looked more sunburnt than ever in their going-away clothes.

"Well, we *are* a lot!" he cried, "just look at our faces! Like a lot of red Indians!"

Even now it was only half-past two: it would take the edge off the whole holiday if they just sat forlornly round, watching the clock till it struck three, and Mr. Stevens suggested a short stroll—just down to the front for a final blow of sea air.

Mrs. Stevens wanted to reserve her strength for the journey, but the others rose eagerly and went down with Mr. Stevens for a last look at the sea.

They knew that it was very easy to get depressed and sentimental on a stroll like this, and there was a forced casualness about the way they stood there, looking round. It was a gusty, overcast day, and the sea looked very sullen as it came creeping up towards the wall; in an hour the tide would be at full and spouts of spray would go shooting up here and there along the promenade. It was not so hard to go, on an afternoon like this, when the sea was right up over the sands: it was difficult when the sands gleamed up and called to them.

"We never went right along the shore to Felpham, after all," laughed Dick, "we always *say* we will!"

"Next year we'll walk all the way to Littlehampton and come back by bus," said Mr. Stevens.

"And let's go out in the speedboat next year," put in Ernie, who was a little sore that his repeated request had been ignored.

Mr. Stevens took his hat off and let the breeze play through his hair: he had packed his brush and comb but the brilliantine would prevent his hair blowing about and looking untidy in the train. He saw the old pierhead, rather dark and forbidding this afternoon—the line of white bathing huts and the long sweep of coast to Selsey Bill. A year wasn't a long time, really. They would soon be here again. Only the time till Christmas was really hard, for after then the evenings began to draw out and the holidays grew nearer every day. Only October, November, and December were hard—only half of December, really, because Christmas began to call in the middle of the month, and after Christmas the evenings began to get longer until, one evening towards the end of March he would find half an hour of treasured daylight waiting for him on his return from the office. It heartened him to think of the spring evenings when he would find time to work in the garden. Then came Easter—and then, good heavens, the holiday was almost on them! At Easter they wrote to Mrs. Huggett for their rooms. From then onwards they looked forward to it—all through the summer. . . .

He groped for his watch: it was strange to wear a waistcoat again after all these days in a sweater: he could scarcely get his fingers into the tiny pocket.

"Just on three," he said—"we'd better be getting along now." A last glance up the windswept promenade, a last gaze out to sea, and they turned away.

The porter had arrived when they returned, and they were just in time to help him with the trunk downstairs.

"Label it for Clapham Junction," said Mr. Stevens. "We'll take the sticks and umbrellas into the carriage with us."

He saw Molly as he returned to the house, standing in the passage at the top of the basement stairs, and when the others had gone into the sitting-room he lingered behind and beckoned to her. She came up to him and he slipped five shillings into her hand.

"There you are, Molly. Thanks for everything you've done."

"Thank you very much, Mr. Stevens. Are you going now? Shall I tell Mrs. Huggett?"

"Yes. I think we'd better be going along now."

Molly ran down the basement stairs and Mrs. Huggett appeared so quickly that she must have been waiting at the bottom, listening for the moment to arrive. She looked quite smart in her black silk Sunday dress, with its lace collar and cuffs, and she came up the passage with a cheerful smile.

"You're off then?" she said.

"Yes, I'm afraid so," replied Mr. Stevens with a rueful laugh. He heard the clock in the sitting-room begin to whirr, then the thin solitary *ting* that meant a quarter-past three, and time to go.

"I do hope you've found everything satisfactory," said Mrs. Huggett.

"Fine, thanks," said Mr. Stevens. "It's always all right at Seaview."

Mrs. Huggett turned her head a little, and when she looked at him again he saw two spots of colour in her cheeks. "It's good of you to say that, Mr. Stevens. I always do my best, of course. It's nice to know it's appreciated."

"We've been lucky with the weather, too—considering what it was like in July and August." He held out his hand, and Mrs. Huggett had to jerk back her white lace cuff to take it.

"Well, good-bye, Mrs. Huggett."

One by one the family shook hands and squeezed by each other in the narrow passage.

"Well, good-bye!"

"Good-bye, Mrs. Huggett."

"Good-bye, Mrs. Stevens."

"Good-bye!"

"Good-bye!"

From the distance Mrs. Huggett's white lace cuff looked like a handkerchief being waved. They could not see her bad eye any longer, and she looked quite tall and dignified standing there by the gate in her black silk dress.

THE END

FROM THE AUTHOR'S AUTOBIOGRAPHY

NO LEADING LADY (1968)

One day an idea for a novel came out of the blue.

It happened on a seaside holiday at Bognor, when we used to go down and sit on the front and watch the crowds go by.

I watched that endless stream of people and began to pick out families at random and imagine what their lives were like at home; what hopes and ambitions the fathers had; whether the mothers were proud of their children or disappointed in them; which of the children would succeed and which would go with the tide and come to nothing. An endless drift of faces streamed by that you'd never seen before and would never see again, but for a moment, as they passed your seat, you saw them vividly as individuals, and now and then there would be one who struck a spark of interest that smouldered in your memory after they had gone.

I began to feel the itch to take one of those families at random and build up an imaginary story of their annual holiday by the sea.

It couldn't be a play. It wasn't the sort of story for the theatre, and in any case plays were done with.

It would have to be a novel, but all my previous attempts at novel-writing had finished up in the waste paper basket. My vocabulary hadn't been up to it. I'd floundered about, hunting up unfamiliar words that I'd never written down before, getting baffled and entangled and frustrated. But I shouldn't be writing now with an eye to publication.

Even if it got finished I'd never offer it to a publisher and risk another fiasco.

I wanted to write for the sake of writing, and got started one evening in my hotel bedroom. I was soon up against the same old trouble that had bedevilled me before when I'd tried my hand at novel-writing. I began to rack my brain for words, and the ones I found didn't fit together. I was worse off now because I hadn't got my dictionary and book of synonyms to help.

After some fruitless efforts I began to wonder whether I hadn't been right off the track in all my previous attempts. I wanted to write about simple, uncomplicated people doing normal things, and I was groping around for flowery stuff and highfalutin words to do it with. Clearly the best way was to write about these people in the simple, uncomplicated words that they would use themselves to describe their feelings and adventures. I decided to try it that way, to confine myself to the modest supply of words at my command and see whether they would last the distance. It might not produce a book that anybody would want to read, but it would keep my pencil busy and fill the empty evenings.

The story was a simple one, so simple that I shouldn't have had the face to use it if I'd been writing for anybody but myself. A small suburban family on their annual fortnight's holiday at Bognor: man and wife, a grown-up daughter working for a dressmaker, a son just started in a London office, and a younger boy still at school. It was a day-by-day account of their holiday, from their last evening at home until the day they packed their bags for their return; how they came out of their shabby boarding house every morning and went down to the sea; how the father found hope for the future in his brief freedom from his humdrum work; how the children found romance and adventure; how the mother, scared of the sea, tried to make the others think she was enjoying it.

The down-to-earth style of writing didn't come any easier at first than the old elaborate one. It was hard to shake off the habit of looking for impressive words and clever ways of saying things. But sooner or later a few penny-plain words would break their way through a dead end, and as time went on the thing began to run so smoothly that I wrote more each night than I'd ever done before.

Writing in this style had pitfalls of its own. If you got too simple you slipped into bathos, and the writing took on a sort of inverted pretentiousness. If you overdid the business of making your characters simple they got too small and you began to patronise them. It took time to get the story on a level keel. I began by looking down on the people I was writing about: then I went too far in the other direction and found myself looking up at them. It wasn't until I'd really got to know them that I could walk with them easily, side by side.

The attraction of the story was that I didn't lay out any plan and never knew what was going to happen in the next chapter until I came to it. It kept me in sympathy with the characters, because when they went to bed each night they knew no more about what was going to happen next day than I did when I turned out the light on my desk and went to bed myself. When it was finished I called it *The Fortnight in September.*

I'd told myself all along that I was writing for my eyes alone, without the least intention of showing it to a publisher. If I'd had any thoughts of that I shouldn't have enjoyed writing it so much. But when it was finished I couldn't help wanting to show it to somebody to find out what they thought of it. When I read it through it seemed as if it was written in children's language, but off the beam for children. It was no good offering it as a children's book, but I couldn't think what sort of grown-up people would swallow it.

Victor Gollancz had published [my play] *Journey's End* and was the only publisher I knew personally. But Gollancz was an intellectual and a perfectionist. The novels he was publishing were winning acclaim from the critics for their fine literary quality, and to give him *The*

Fortnight in September seemed like offering a fruit drop to a lion. But I hadn't anything to lose. My stock as a writer stood at zero, and my recent failures with plays had innoculated me against disappointment. The novel stuck to the same formula that I had used in those plays: the same ordinary sort of people, the same everyday kind of story. To send it to Gollancz was taking a good deal of licence from our friendship, but I knew that he would read it himself, and whatever he thought about it would go no further than our own two selves. I knew him well enough to be certain that I was in safe hands.

I waited philosophically to get the novel back with a friendly letter of regret, but the letter he sent me was the biggest surprise I'd ever had. "This is delightful," were his first three words, and they were like a ray of sunlight after months in a dark room. It was a wonderful letter. You are ready for publishers and theatre managers to be careful and restrained, but there was nothing of that in Victor's letter. His enthusiasm was absolute. "I will gladly publish it," he said. "I wouldn't alter a word."

And publish it he did, exactly as it was written, and the notices were magnificent. "A lovely novel," said the *Daily Telegraph.* "A little masterpiece," said the *Sunday Express.* "Enchanting," said another. It was *Journey's End* all over again.

And the public, which had turned its back on the same sort of story written as a play, went for it like hot cakes. The first edition was sold out in a week: 10,000 copies as quick as they were printed; 20,000 in a month. An American publisher had it out in record time. It got the same fulsome notices over there, and sold as it did at home. It was taken for Germany, France and Scandinavia, Italy and Spain; finally in nearly as many European countries as had taken *Journey's End.*

Why it took on was anybody's guess. Mainly, perhaps, because the story was easy to read, with nothing grand or pretentious about it, and because it was a story that hadn't been written before. A girl wrote to me from New York that she read it every morning on the ferry boat that took her across the Hudson River to her work in the city, and it made her feel so warm and free and happy.

For my own part it seemed as if I could only hit the bull's-eye if I didn't try. I hadn't tried with *Journey's End*. I'd worked on it to pass the winter evenings without any thought of getting it produced. I'd tried for all I was worth with the two plays that followed it, and both went down the drain. I gave up trying because it wasn't worthwhile any longer, wrote a novel to pass the time, and found myself on top of the world again.

Taking a sober view of it I couldn't see that the novel had done anything to set me on my feet as a professional writer. You couldn't live on the occasional flukes that only came, apparently, when you had accumulated sufficient failures to make you give up trying. I had got my fingers badly burnt by trying to follow up a freak success in the theatre with other plays, and I didn't want to risk it happening again. If I tried to cash in on the success of my first novel by cooking up a second one the critics would probably say it wasn't another *Fortnight in September*, and would no doubt be right—so the thing to do was to leave it alone and let sleeping dogs lie.